Soul
Shift

Soul Shift

Written by
Candace Beck Moesta

authorHOUSE®

AuthorHouse™ LLC
1663 Liberty Drive
Bloomington, IN 47403
www.authorhouse.com
Phone: 1-800-839-8640

Published by AuthorHouse   04/25/2014

ISBN: 978-1-4969-0602-1 (sc)
ISBN: 978-1-4969-0601-4 (e)

For Michael
For Aaron
For Brandon
And P.T. Ratajczyk
Thanks for always being an inspiration in my life

Soul Shift: The Black Thorn Society

The torrential rain fell down hard against the black Chevrolet Suburban as ten year old Claire sat staring out of the glass blankly. Today had been her beloved older brother Austin's funeral. She was still attempting to wrap her mind around his untimely and accidental death. Seventeen year old Austin had been celebrating with friends after a high school football game when he was struck down by a speeding car that left the scene immediately, a "hit and run accident" Claire had been told. He had been their parent's only son and their joy.

The funeral procession was following a giant, dark hearse to the family's country property in upstate New York. They had their very own cemetery there where others had been laid to rest. Also, on the eight hundred acre estate stood a majestic colonial house. "The country house" is what Claire called it. On this day, it's beautiful, Corinthian columns and inviting warmth could be of no consolation to her broken heart. This sprawling manor with surrounding forest and hills was where they had shared so many wonderful times together. Weekends, birthdays, holidays, and summer vacations had all been spent here, playing in the woods, fishing in the lake, and dancing together in the moonlight. Austin had loved his sister who was an unparalleled beauty of a girl.

Claire was feeling unexplainable coldness inside. She was thinking to herself, *"What will I do without him; how will they treat me now that he is gone?"*

Austin had spent so many hours playing with her and watching her practice her ballet for recital. He had never failed to lavish her with the love and attention that her parents had withheld from her. Now that he had left her here alone with them she was afraid of their cold and punitive looks. Without her protector to stand up for her and comfort her she must now be very careful not to upset her parents or stir their wrath towards her. If she could just go unnoticed . . .

1

Austin was meant to be the only child born to Peter and Sandra Campbell. The elite couple wanted an only son to pour out their affections on and they had gotten just what they wanted, at first. As socialites and pillars of the community, they were used to getting exactly what they wanted. Claire was told she had been an accident. She knew that she was not received into the family with great enthusiasm, nevertheless, she had the best of everything that money could buy; she never had the one thing from them that she truly wanted: love and attention. Claire hurt terribly that she did not meet the same requirements for love in their eyes that Austin had.

Warm tears fell upon Claire's adorable, little face. She was thinking of her brother's body in that wretched coffin being taken to his final resting place by that beastly death machine who seemed all but too happy to receive the horrible, enclosing box into it's giant mouth in the rear of it. Her breath caught in her throat. It was becoming difficult to breathe now as she was considering this. Even though it was only a door it seemed more like a toothless monster ready to consume anything that was placed inside. She shuddered at the thought and tried to put that part out of her troubled mind.

Finally, the line of black cars were slowing down, headlights peering through what was now a misty rain. They were zigzagging in different directions as they tried to find ground to park their fancy cars on. Heaven forbid they got a little bit of mud on those representations of status.

Claire's parents had not said a single word all the way here from the funeral home. It had only been a fifteen minute drive, but it was an agonizing eternity for her. The silence was worse than some other things Claire had experienced.

The people who had come to say their final goodbyes to the football star, friend, boyfriend, and beloved family member were beginning to ease out of their cars in finest apparel. Claire stepped out from the backseat of the hulking vehicle her father had driven today only to find the grass was soaked to the ground and becoming a muddy mess. She carefully began walking up the subtle incline toward the looming tent that stood over the grave that had been dug for her brother's coffin. The hollow, six feet deep grave looked more like a gaping hole that was waiting to swallow him up once placed inside and anyone else that may have gotten too close to it. She was pushed along by her father Peter toward the crimson covered chairs that awaited the family under the tent at graveside. Men in their most expensive black suits carried the coffin where Austin lay in eternal sleep to the open rectangle in the ground and placed it on the metal bars that would hold it until all was completed with Austin's service. The parish priest was already standing there. Father John had always been a favorite of Claire's with his gentle and fatherly way with her. She only knew him from his time spent at the family home with them. They did not attend mass but they did entertain the priest on a regular basis so as not to be out of favor with the Catholic Church. Why did they not participate in a perfectly normal thing like church? It seemed that all was well with that decision as far as Father John was concerned. They received communion in their house strangely enough.

When Claire laid eyes on him today it was with joy and sorrow that she surveyed his garments and demeanor. The Father appeared somber and dressed all in black with his priest's white collar standing out from the darkness around it. He did not look at all himself on this occasion. He barely looked at the impish child that he dearly loved along with the rest of his flock. Father John opened the final part of her brother's service with a prayer. All heads bowed as tears were flowing and soft crying could be heard. Claire glanced up to peek at her mother who was staring wide-eyed at absolutely nothing, her expression mostly blank. Looking at her father was almost too much to bear. Peter's head was bowed as it shook slowly side to side as a single tear fell onto his clean shaven cheek. She could feel the despair coming from him as she quickly bowed her head again.

With the prayer concluded, Father John began to talk about Austin's life and how we are not promised tomorrow and how his babble went on and on and Claire began to hate him for saying these things. It was not fair to take someone so young! How could this man of God that she trusted for so long allow them to put her beloved brother in the cold, wet earth? It was unthinkable to do this to him who had so loved her and held her when she was in pain. Who would do that now? "Who am I to have even deserved his affection she had wondered. I was so lucky to have him and that killer took him away from me!" she thought angrily as she glared at the priest and his hollow words of comfort.

Claire suddenly felt a chill run through her small body as the emptiness in her grew. She was realizing that adults were so full of themselves and so self-centered. Did any of them ever tell the truth or was what they spewed out of their mouths simply to placate the weak minded? Even though she was a child she was not stupid. She was, in fact, quite the opposite much to the chagrin of her parents who took her to be some kind of smart mouth. The truth was that she saw through the fake smiles and caught the looks they gave each other when she was in the room.

The service was now concluding as those in attendance were casting rose buds onto the casket as it was going to be slowly lowered soon into that awful dirt cage. These individuals, some she knew and some she did not, were giving their deepest and most sincere condolences to Peter and Sandra. No one so much as even gave Claire a sideways glance.

Claire managed to weave and wind her way through the fly-like gathering of the crowd that swooped in to descend upon the grieving family. The country house was to her left and up the long and twisting drive. It sat atop a gently sloping hill and the sky was ominous behind it. What was usually a warm and inviting place to her seemed like an abode of ghosts at the moment. The dark forest was all around and it was there in front of her across the drive. The sudden urge to run came over her as she entered the dark wood. She ran as though it would make all the blackness behind her disappear and just maybe it would all go away. Austin would not be dead and her hopelessness would disintegrate as quickly as it had come. As she ran, she was being slapped in her beautiful face with wet leaves and small hanging branches. She did not care at all about that as she cried with everything in her. Deeper and deeper she pushed into the forest with wild abandon. Something was different about this part of the forest. She had never entered into this part of the woods before; she began to notice a narrow path that she had somehow come to be on. Claire stopped running and began to walk as she looked cautiously around her into the dimly lit wood. She looked down at her black satin dress. She hated it because it was dull and lifeless. It was tied with a gaudy, pink sash around the waist. Mary Jane shoes were on her feet with little ruffled socks to accompany them. In defiance of this ghastly outfit Claire had put her practice tights on underneath it. "Austin would've approved." she thought to herself as she continued walking not knowing her destination. Austin had been very interested to see his sister dance. She was so graceful and unlike any of the other children at his school who participated in dance. He had always told Claire that he wished she could go to school with him. He had not understood why she was home schooled, but he knew there was something very special about her and he seemed to be the only one in the family who noticed it.

Claire found herself at the entrance into a splendid little glen in the forest. It was a place that she had never been before. There were many parts of the woods that she had not gotten to explore and this was definitely one of them. Over on the farthest side of it, she could see some deer standing all together as they ate the tender grass that was growing in with the Spring. There were Junipers, Chrysanthemums, Tulips, and rose bushes everywhere. So many different things grew here that it was not possible for her to know them all. A tall oak stood here and there as if to greet her. "What a wonderful, secret place I have found," she thought happily to herself. It was the perfect place to give one last performance for Austin without anyone spying on her.

Claire slipped the funeral garb over her head and tossed it onto the soggy ground. She then began to smooth out the little skirt that ran around her waist accompanying the tights light pink in color. With gusto, she bowed to the deer and then to the oaks and began the routine that would be performed at her next recital. So lovely was this performance and graceful beyond measure that birds hushed their singing to watch. All the while, as she danced, the clouds above appeared as giant, gray boulders that would fall and crush the cotton topped dancer where she was.

Claire concluded her dance at its crescendo and allowed herself to fall into position on the wetness of the soft green grass. The rain had long since stopped falling on the unnaturally pale girl. Laying there was reminding her of how her brother would lay in the ground forever. Warm tears began to fall against her lovely face again. She hid beneath her long blond hair and cried aloud once more. She was not concerned that anyone would be looking for her anytime soon so she closed her doe brown eyes with the flecks of gold in them to rest for a moment.

Meanwhile, she was and had been being watched most curiously by Agreus, the Pan that protected these woods and all that dwell there in. He had many abilities and powers because of who he was. He was son of the god Hermes and the nymph Sose, also a prophetess. He had chosen to retire to this area of the world after the great wars in India led by Bacchus.

He was watching Claire earnestly wondering how a human child had been able to penetrate this most sacred place as it was surrounded by a magical barrier meant to keep humans out. In watching her he was able to discern the reason: *an elf's pure soul trapped in a human body*. He was intrigued by this discovery. This troubled him due to his friendship with the elves, but decided to wait until he knew more before ever consulting them on it. He had found her to be the most graceful dancer he had ever encountered but she needed further instruction. He could help her with this. Her elven elegance was remarkable since she was caged in that human covering. The truth was that she appeared more as an elf than a human and her strange looks had made it hard for her to make friends. No doubt, she was a beauty but one that a human could hardly appreciate properly.

"I must find a way to help this girl," Agreus said to himself enamored with the innocent child. He began to walk over to Claire as she lay there sorrowfully. He was so tall, six feet and seven inches. He had the greenest eyes of spring with yellow flecks in them, auburn hair like the color of leaves in the fall hung thickly over his shoulders and down his back. Tan skin covered his beautiful firm upper body as each muscle rippled with his movements. Two little black horns were growing from his head. Unlike other pans, satyrs and fauns, he had human form just like his brother Nomios. His smell was earthy and sweet like the rain and blooming flowers.

Claire realized that someone was standing over her. She sat up with a start. What stood before her was the most beautiful and terrifying creature she had ever laid eyes upon. She was trembling with fear from what he might do to her. Had she trespassed?

Agreus spoke softly to her as she sat looking up at him with wide teary eyes, "Little one, what is troubling you?"

She spoke with a trembling voice, "My brother has died sir."

"Please do not fear me my child, I am the protector of these woods and all who live within. I would never hurt someone like you my dear," he smiled at her with his big eyes so full of care and thoughtfulness.

"What are you?" she asked curiously.

"Why, I am a pan, love," he replied in a rich Mediterranean accent.

"Like from the kitchen?" she asked innocently.

He laughed, "No silly girl, not like from the kitchen. One day I shall tell you but not now."

Claire realized that he could not be from around here. Was he even real at all?

"Why are you laying on this frigid ground my dear?" He asked soothingly.

"I am very upset over my brother's death. He was the only one who loved me. I don't know what to do without Austin. He always protected me from them. Now he isn't here to watch over me and love me anymore!" she cried helplessly. "My parents don't love me and now without him things will definitely get worse."

He was reading her mind and seeing the images of her brother playing games with her, protecting her, and paying attention to her. He did love her tremendously. The girl's parents, on the other hand, were callous beasts with no true affections for this child. Why? It made no sense but he would get to the bottom of this for her sake and protect her as much as he could from their neglect and lack of love. "Look how sweet she is; how could anyone not love her?" he was thinking to himself.

"What is your name child?" he asked already knowing the answer.

"Claire Campbell," she replied meekly. "and what shall I call you sir?"

"You may call me "A." He answered slyly.

"Your name is just a letter?" this tickled her.

"No silly. It's complicated and just easier if you call me this, ok?" he said with a firm look.

"Ok," she said compliantly.

"Now let's clean you up," he snapped his fingers and all of the mud and wetness was gone. "Picture perfect my love."

"Wow!" she said stunned, "How did you do that?"

"Magic and it must be our secret. No one must know anything of this or of me. Will you keep my secret, Claire?" he looked at her questioningly.

"Yes of course sir," she answered hastily. "Will you be friends with me?" I have no friends because everyone seems to think that I am too weird to be friends with.

"I will be your friend always," he said with conviction, "and further more I am going to be taking over your brother's duty of protecting you. I won't let them get away with hurting you anymore." Agreus already felt a strong connection to her and wanted to take her under his care as much as possible. He had to see that her elven soul was still intact on her eighteenth birthday so that the rites could be performed to free her from their blinded human world for good. She was smiling at him now. He liked it. He knew she was a very special girl. Opening his hand, she saw something shining in it.

"What is that?" she asked with curiosity.

"That is an amulet that you will wear around your neck so that no harm will befall you my child." he said smiling back at her. "I am going to help you learn more about dancing as well. I am an excellent teacher in that art!" he said with pride. "You must come to me often. Even when you are not here I can use magic to bring you to me for your lessons, and if you need me to come to you for any reason you only need to think it and I shall know." he said with a protective tone.

Agreus knew that he must guide her through the next few years if she were to reclaim her true nature. Something told him that it must be done and so it would be.

Claire took the amulet which was a sparkling ruby on a chain of gold and put it around her neck. "oh thank you so much!" She threw her arms around him as he was kneeling in front of her. "I don't have to be alone anymore." She was so happy that someone had taken an interest in her.

Claire realized rather suddenly that she was daydreaming again. It was the seventh anniversary of her brother's death. She gazed sorrowfully at his senior picture as she gripped it tightly in her hand. It had made him look so full of promise and hope for the future, a future that he never knew. She believed that this had been the root cause of her parents growing apart all these years. They barely spoke anymore and even slept in separate bedrooms. They did however manage to keep up the image of a perfect couple in public for the sake of appearance. Sandra Campbell was known as a leading psychiatrist in the state of

New York. "What a laugh," Claire mused. "she can't even help herself, much less anyone else!" Claire smiled bitterly.

Sandra had long ago lost herself in a bottle and prescription medication that was supposed to be for patients. It was the same every evening when she arrived home from the office. She would come into the house complaining about her day and her patients, fix a drink, pop a couple of pills, and then disappear into her study to think about how much she hated her life and everyone in it. At least this was Claire's view of her mother. It was never just one drink; it always had to be most of the bottle for her to come out from time to time to remind Claire that she was part of the reason her life was so horrible. This used to hurt her feelings but now she was extremely apathetic towards the good doctor's antics.

Peter Campbell, on the other hand, was a hedge fund manager as well as a stock broker. He was hardly ever present at the house anymore. He usually came in long after everyone was asleep because he was "working late again." He figured himself to be a big shot and maybe he was with his high profile clients. Claire shook her head in disgust. The only thing he was doing that late was Sara. She was his "all too eager to please" office assistant. It was so obvious they were having an affair. At this point, Claire could not care less what her unfit parents were doing with their ridiculous lives. She wondered what her beloved brother would have thought about how they had turned out. They had always given Claire the best money could buy, but they had never shown her true affection or love. It was quite the opposite.

"Why?" she asked herself aloud.

Claire had always felt like a tremendous burden on them for some reason. Parents were supposed to love their children even if they were "accidents." They had placated her with material things and ballet or anything else she wanted to do, but it all felt so hollow. Maybe they were biding their time until she was out of the house so they could finally divorce. She didn't really know. How could she? They never talked to her unless absolutely necessary.

Well, now the letter that her mother had wanted Claire to receive all of these years was there on the antique dining table in front of her. She had not opened it yet for fear that her mother would fly into a rage if she was not there for the initial reading of it. So Claire waited, wondering what the envelope held inside. It was of course from the Julliard School of Dance. Even though she wanted this badly she was sure her mother wanted it more. She could then brag to all of her friends and God forbid if she was passed over! How embarrassed Sandra would be and angry to boot. Claire laid her head down on the cool surface of the table and closed her eyes. She soon was dozing off . . .

"I knew you would come," twelve year old Claire said to "A" with tears stinging her eyes.

"Of course I came my sweet darling; don't I always come when you call to me?" he stared angrily at the hand print on Claire's lovely face. It was beginning to swell and as he softly touched it she grimaced. Agreus did not like it when her parents treated her like this.

"What has happened to your face, my love?" he asked even though he had read her thoughts and knew what that horrid woman called a mother had done.

"Mother was drunk again and she said I wasn't worth anything!" Claire repeated what was screamed at her while being slapped hard on the face for dropping a cup.

Agreus sat Claire in his lap and blew onto her cheek; the pain was instantly gone. She threw her little arms around her protector and cried herself to sleep on his shoulder while he gently held her. Once he had covered her up in her bed he went into Sandra's study to find her still drinking and muttering to herself. She was unable to see him so he watched her for a few moments while reading her thoughts. They were dark and troubled thoughts. She was very hard to read at the moment due to her intoxication, everything was so jumbled. He discovered that Claire was the result of an affair that Peter never let her live down. She was also a very self centered person to whom appearance was everything. She did not like to look at Claire because it reminded her of the mistake that she had made all of those years ago in a moment of weakness. Now, Sandra was a drunk and she was lashing out at Claire who knew nothing of this. Agreus would not stand for it. He waited as Sandra got up to get into the bath she had let for herself. She stepped into the hot bubbles as she let her satin robe fall to the floor. She closed her eyes as she sat the glass of bourbon down on the tub next to lit candles. He approached silently with anger in his eyes at the offense that had occurred. Looking at Sandra he noticed the ruby amulet that he had given to Claire for protection. It was around this whelp of a woman's neck! "How dare she take what has not been given her!" He pulled it off of her and then held her tightly around the neck. She was struggling to breathe and flailing about. Slowly he drove her underneath the water as she struggled. He allowed her to see only his angry eyes that glowed bright green now. Agreus held her under until she nearly drown. The only thing that caused him let go of his death grip was Claire. She had woken up and he could feel her opening the door to her bedroom. Not wanting her to see this he released his intended victim from her fate, but he knew that sooner or later he would see her dead.

Agreus returned to little Claire leaving her mother sputtering and wondering what had just happened. Claire was rubbing sleepy, puffy eyes when he entered her room to check on her. She looked up at him with large, sad eyes and asked, "Why does mommy hate me so much?"

He instantly picked her up as though she were still a babe and answered, "All that matters is that I love you and that you are special no matter what anyone says, love."

She smiled at her gentle protector, "I love you too, always!"

He was her only friend and the only friend that she wanted. She knew he would always be there to watch over her like a strange guardian angel. He gave her back the ruby amulet that her mother had taken away from her.

"Now my dear Claire, I am taking you for a little while but I will have you home before anyone will ever notice." We have a dance lesson today." This happened with much regularity.

Through his magic they entered into the glen. She was not dressed for dancing, though. Agreus took a long look at her as he slowly stroked his chin and furrowed his brow.

"I have just the thing you shall be needing, child." he said with a sly grin.

He closed his eyes and said something that Claire did not understand. She looked down at herself and realized she was wearing a beautiful dance outfit. It was made of all the colors of the forest and was as light as a feather.

"Oh, "A"! It's so beautiful!" she cried thanking him.

Agreus smiled and said, "Let the lesson begin . . . ."

He taught her how to be the best at what she did. He spent many hours just playing with her. Showing her all of the things that grew in the glen and having her recite them to him was a favorite hobby of theirs'. Claire told him that when she grew up it would be just the two of them without any parents to push her around.

"I want to come and live with you here where it's safe," she told him, "I don't want to go home!"

"You must for now my sweet girl, but perhaps one day you shan't have to return to them," he answered as his heart broke for her.

"Oh I can't wait, I promise I'll do whatever you say if you make that come true!" she said earnestly.

"Anything?" he teased her.

"Anything, I promise! I'll even do the dishes!" she said proudly.

"Ok," he laughed. I am going to hold you to that . . ."

Claire woke suddenly as she heard the all too familiar sound of her mother's clicking heels coming down the great hall that led to the overly modern kitchen. It had no life, only cold steel and black and white tiles with giant industrial appliances for the cook to use. Where was the cook today anyway?

"Well Claire," Sandra said looking at her. "do you have the letter?"

She was standing in front of Claire in a casual pant suit, navy blue with button up top, hair and makeup beginning to come undone after her day at work. She was tapping one toe back and forth on the tiled floor waiting for an answer from her daughter.

"It's right here on the table mother," she answered flatly.

"Well let's have it then," Sandra reached for the envelope.

She had it open in just a moment and was reading to herself. Her face began to twist into an angry form with her lips drawn tightly as she continued to read. She looked up at Claire with daggers in her eyes.

"Well, I hope you're happy. You did not get in this year. What is it that you failed to do?," Sandra spat the words out through clinched teeth, throwing the letter to the floor and storming off to no doubt pour a drink to sooth her nerves.

"I did everything I was supposed to do," Claire whispered to herself as she picked up the letter. Tears were streaming down her beautiful face at the awful news. She ran down the hall to the marble staircase that led up to her room. Up the stairs she ran thinking of how she would be made to suffer for this failure. She pulled off her jeans and cotton t-shirt and put on a pair of satin pajamas, light green in color before flinging herself across the bed. She dropped the crumpled letter on the carpet and lay there trying to figure out what she could have done wrong. All the deadlines were met, entry essay perfect, physical performance flawless, why? "A!"

"I am here Claire," he had been watching through his scrying pool hoping she would call out to him.

She locked the door so no one would just burst in on her. "I got awful news just now," she handed him the letter. She was pacing back and forth looking so beautiful with her pale skin, and doe eyes. Her long blond hair hung carelessly over her shoulders while she was going over everything in her head.

"What did I do wrong, my friend?" she asked. "You watched me give the performance for the review board. It was absolutely perfect."

He looked at the young woman that she had become with such care in his eyes, "these things just happen, my love." It is no reflection on you as a dancer. Most people cannot appreciate true talent like yours." He could never have allowed her to go off to this school. He believed that it would have driven them apart and he was not going to take that chance. He had to interfere in her acceptance to the school. Deep down he knew that she would not be truly happy there and going would be to mostly please her parents. Soon she would not need this any way.

"Please just lay here with me and hold me," she implored. "I'm so tired and upset, please . . ."

She lay down and motioned for him to join her. Claire was always so comforted by his embrace. Since the day they had met his embrace could melt away any sadness that she had. She snuggled down in the thick quilt with him as they lay side by side, her back to his chest. She loved the way he smelled. So much like a man and yet so sweet like all the trees and flowers in the forest. He had his face in her hair as he held her. It smelled like fresh apples. She was seventeen now; it would not be too much longer before he could truly help her. While he was holding her he began to notice that he was pulling her very close to him and something was stirring inside of him that he had never felt before. Was he beginning to have romantic feelings for her? She slept while he held her and he did not depart until very late. He needed to search himself further for the nature of his feelings for his precious Claire.

Peter sat in his office awaiting a call. It was no ordinary phone call, it was very important. "*No one can overhear this conversation,*" he was thinking to himself as he waited with a very paranoid demeanor. He looked out of the glass windows into the reception area of the office. Sara sat at her desk taking calls and doing her usual paperwork. He watched her lustfully as she sat there gently twisting the black office chair back and forth. Her dark skirt was climbing up her slender thigh as she did this. Even though Peter was in his fifties and married, he saw no problem carrying on this illicit affair with a younger beauty. Sara was in her late thirties. She had the most unusual color of red in her hair and a bedroom look in her sparkling blue eyes. She reminded him of his wife when they had met and the first taste of love seemed magical. He was glad Sandra had cut him off after Claire was born. She had clammed up like a cold fish as she delved deeper into her work and her own troubled thoughts. He felt justified finding comfort in this lovely little wild cat that worked for him. Lord Ayyn was very good to him and he would show his appreciation when he asked him to. He was touched to be of such importance to his master to have received such a wonderful gift for his role in things. Sara was not only a gift to him but she was also involved with everything that was about to happen very soon. He could trust her with all of his secrets. Sara knew all about his part in their dark plans and still loved him. He was planning to start over with her as soon as it was made possible by upcoming events.

The cell phone in his gray suit coat pocket was vibrating against his side. He reached for it quickly and with a hushed tone said, "Hello. Yes everything has been done according to your wishes. Yes, I will make sure that nothing happens between now and then, my lord." The phone hung up. He looked at it and then put it back into his pocket. Pulling out a white cloth embroidered with his initials he wiped the beading sweat from his forehead as he thought of the plans he had to ensure went properly or there would be hell to pay otherwise.

Claire woke up sometime late in the night and felt like practicing her ballet. She had been mostly kept from the world by home schooling and even a dance studio built in the lower regions of the enormous house that she grew up in. All of her instructors had been hired privately to tutor her in dance, even modern things that she did not care for at all but she did what her teachers said regardless. Even her recitals had always been private. Only friends of the family and tutors were allowed the pleasure of viewing her skills. They all talked of how she would surely get into the best dance school in the country. Some of these friends were of course from Julliard. Her parents were quite influential, after all. None of it made any sense. If she was going to attend the prestigious school then why was she being kept away from others she might participate with? Why could she not attend school like a normal girl or have friends? She was certainly not allowed to talk to or even come close to a boy. Dancing was something that she had been doing her entire life so when stress came this was her outlet. Claire donned a practice uniform and pink ballet slippers. She slowly tied the ribbons around her ankles. The house was darker than night. Without turning on any lights she felt her way along the hall until she reached the door that would lead down a flight of stairs to the studio. Feeling for the light switch around the inside of the wooden door. She flipped it on and watched as the stairs were illuminated. She descended into the depths of the house to her studio equipped with all that a dancer could need.

Claire stood in the middle of the room and looked around at all of the mirrors and surveyed herself. She looked like a little pixie of a girl rather than a human one. No wonder they did not want her around others for most of her life. She wondered why she had been born so different that her despicable parents had hidden her from the world outside. Was it because of her or did they just view a young girl's role differently from that of a young man? She began to stretch with her leg up and across the cold metal bar on the backside of the room. Upon her completion of warmup she began to dance with a wild freedom that she had learned from "A," her best and most trusted companion. She wondered if he was watching her now as he sometimes did when he felt that she was practicing.

Meanwhile, Agreus was watching through his watery mirror to see his beautiful Claire. In watching her wild and seductive dancing, he was coming to realize that he was falling for her as he had no other in his entire existence. He was unsure as to how to proceed from this point, fearful that she would reject him and it would ruin everything he had been working towards for her sake for so long.

He heard her say aloud to herself, "Am I at all beautiful?," He wanted to grab her and say, "*Look into the mirror and see the most lovely creature in creation!*" Agreus continued to watch until she had exhausted herself enough to return upstairs to shower and dress for bed in a white cotton gown. He was contemplating what to do . . .

Claire dressed herself quickly. She could hear her father coming in very late and he most likely had a few too many to drink. She shuddered at the memory of what he had tried to do to her when she was fourteen years old. She had just bathed and was getting dressed for bed that night too. It was just like any other mundane evening in the Campbell household. Her mother was drunk again and passed out in her study. Peter had come in late after his supposed late work schedule that evening. She had payed it no mind until she heard a knock at her bedroom door.

"Claire, are you still awake?" she was hiding under the covers. "Claire daddy wants a good night kiss before he goes to bed. Claire?" Peter walked over to her beautiful day bed and pulled the covers back slowly. She appeared to be sleeping even though she was scared to death. Peter began to touch her. He ran his fingers through her hair, "such a shame to have to come to an end." He knelt down as he attempted to lift her gown. In her mind she screamed for her protector. He instinctively knew from their bond that she was in trouble. Agreus went through his doorway and saw what was happening. He flew into a rage that this filthy pervert would try to do this to a girl he was supposed to be raising as his daughter even though she was not. Claire did not know the truth so she was even more horrified that her "father" would try to do grotesque things to her. Suddenly, Peter was tossed across the room to land against the dresser on the other side of it. Claire sat up and watched as Agreus was beating her father senseless. Peter had been knocked out so Agreus dragged him from the room and through him down the marble stair case. He lay there unconscious but alive and not mortally injured. Everyone would just assume he came in drunk and fell down the stairs.

Agreus returned to his beloved child to see if she was going to be alright. She was sitting on her bed in a huddle crying softly at what had nearly been done to her. He picked her up and she threw her arms around him in thanks for the swift rescue from the monster that had tried to desecrate her body with his filthy hands. He decided she was not safe there that night and had taken her to his home to sleep. He had returned her to her own room before anyone could know that she had been gone at all. The next morning she heard a commotion downstairs. Claire threw open her bedroom door and stood on the landing to see the maid trying to help Peter up in his confused and disoriented condition. "Did you have an accident daddy?" she gave a quick half smirk that only Peter caught. After that, they had called an ambulance to come attend to his wounds and take him to a nearby hospital. She had laughed to herself as all of this was going on because she was the only one that knew the truth of the deeds of the night before. Never again had Peter even attempted to enter her room or tried to touch her in an inappropriate way. He was unsure as to what actually happened but he knew that he was not merely drunk, at least he did not think it to be the case. He never spoke of it to anyone. He would then have to admit why he had been in her room to begin with and that could carry a death sentence for him, particularly.

What Claire was unaware of was why Peter had attempted this molestation in the first place. She had just tried to push it out her mind because it was the most repulsive thing he had ever done to her. The truth was he had probably been watching her for a while and was just intoxicated enough to do something about it.

The now grown up Claire lay down in her bed thinking of troubling things and tried to fall asleep. She soon felt as though someone was watching her as she lay there. She rolled over in the much larger bed that she had acquired last year with its wooden posts at each corner. Standing in her room staring at her was "A". He was a comfort to her in so many ways. He always had on the colors of the forest and yet she did not know the source of the fabric but it was soft. She motioned for him to approach the bed and lay with her. Maybe he needed comfort from her for a change. Why else would he be here? He lay down in the bed beside Claire with dawn not far off, only a couple of hours now. His body was hard and warm. His auburn locks were so beautiful as they hung like a lions mane over his broad shoulders and he had such a look in his eyes. They never moved from her face as he settled into bed with her. They would be safe because no one could see him but her. She looked at him with questioning eyes. He knew he must give a reason for his return this night.

Agreus looked back at her and asked, "Tell me my love, what do you see when you look at me?"

She did not understand why he was asking such things, "I see everything when I look at you my love. Your eyes hold the truth of your soul and I see everything."

"Do you Claire, do you really see everything?" he leaned towards her as he pulled her closer slowly giving her a passionate kiss.

Her head was swimming. She felt a stirring inside that no one had ever made her feel before. For a long time they lay there looking at one another and running trembling fingers through each other's hair, softly. Slowly he began to trace a finger along her collar bone while she continued to tremble at his advances. They were sweet not awful like what had befallen her at Peter's hands.

She looked him in the eye with all seriousness and said, "Do you love me?"

"Yes, you know that I have always loved you," avoiding the true meaning behind her question.

"No, do you really love me, you know how I mean,." she said with determination to ascertain the truth.

Agreus looked at her and decided that he could no longer hide what he had discovered about himself; he did love her more than anything in the entire world.

He gazed into her gold flecked eyes and kissed her again, "Yes, I have found myself in love with you. I did not know that I could even feel this way. Now I must leave you to attend to my duties in the forest, but I must ask you to consider your true feelings for me. When you know how you feel call to me, please tell me, but do not keep me waiting long because I think of you every moment and cannot bear not to know for much longer, my love." he slowly disappeared.

She lay in bed thinking of him. How did she feel about her handsome protector? Had their relationship changed as she had grown into a young woman? What were these feelings that had boiled up inside of her when he kissed her? She had never been kissed before. She liked it. She knew that she must soon figure this out so as not to keep him waiting for her answer.

"Black Thorns, the time is nearly upon us! Have we not waited in patience? Even though I am your master I will not leave you without your fair share!" Lord Black Thorn as he called himself now, shouted as he slammed down his fist upon the oaken table. "What we will do is for the good of all and not just for the good of one, which brings me to my first question. Will each and everyone of you do what has to be done?" Sometimes it is not an easy task to do the right thing but we all must find within ourselves the courage to make the change even if the task that leads us there seems ominous and daunting. The reward far out weighs the sacrifice!"

In accordance, everyone began knocking on the table simultaneously to symbolize agreement which was customary for them. Each member sat there with a look of anticipation awaiting the day that soon was to come when they believed their lives would be changed forever.

Lord Thomas Malfy of Black Thorn was known only to his followers by his true name: Ayyn Kelfinaar. He was a charismatic leader and had the ability to get what he wanted without having to ask very much. Lord Black Thorn was indeed handsome with his long, very light blonde hair. It nearly appeared white with the black ribbon that always tied it back. His skin was a smooth caramel color and he was quite tall at six feet and five inches. One thing not to be forgotten were his eyes, the color of the blue green sea on it's clearest day. They sparkled as bright as any star in the heavens. Yes, he was something majestic to look at. There was never a shortage of devoted followers who wanted not only to follow his every command in his Black Thorn Society, but also to give themselves physically to their master. He was indeed choosy about his intimate partners but it did not matter whether they were male or female. Practiced in the art of lovemaking, he made it an experience for his partner and it was always a truly remarkable one for him in all of his perverse depravity.

The truth is for all of his pomp and circumstance he came from nothing. No one knew this of course; it would ruin his status and his reputation. Being left on the steps of an orphanage in France was not something he wanted others to know about for some obvious reasons and others not so obvious. He amassed his wealth over the last two hundred plus years with slight of hand and charm. Now he was a very wealthy "business" man who preferred discretion. Honestly, Ayyn never actually told them what it was that he did to be so wealthy. It was none of their business. He would not tolerate anyone of his followers leaking anything that occurred in their meetings. It was entirely too important that everyone of the upper class members kept their mouths shut. If they did what they were told then the rewards would be good as they had always been. He knew that it really did not matter what he was involved in when it came to their simple and unimaginative minds because he had greatly benefited them; why should they bother with trivialities? They were given higher positions in their companies and received monetary gains and there was one more thing they were waiting to achieve, but would they receive it? His followers were consumed by greed and status. This gave him power over them and they were too stupid to see what the truth was and was not.

Lord Black Thorn smirked at his thoughts. He was remembering how the other children at the orphanage were frightened of him because of his looks. They didn't understand why he had pointed ears and they did not. His other features had been so striking as well. Most of the sisters thought he was the devil's child. The only one that had never judged him was sister Mary Francis. She was always looking out for him and reassuring him that God loved him. He had wondered back in those days about God. If he was so loved by God then why was he made to suffer and feel unwanted and unloved. The good sister was the closest thing to a mother he had ever known. She had read him stories at night and chided the other children for physically abusing and taunting him. There had been many a bloody nose she had cleaned up and many a blackened eye she had soothed. He felt sorry when she had passed on and a bit resentful. If God had loved him so much then why was the only person that ever cared for him taken away? While she lived he would visit her on occasion after having grown up and left the orphanage. She was dead now of course with it having been so long ago. When the sister died he attended her funeral in disguise so as not to have anyone recognize him for who he was. This failed miserably and the Mother Superior had given him an awful look and whispered for only him to hear, "demon child" They were afraid of him still. They all eventually died as he continued to live. From time to time he visited the orphanage and was not looked at strangely anymore. No one there even knew he had been the orphan, Thomas.

Thomas, as he was called then, wanted to understand why he barely aged at all while others around him grew old and died so he began his quest to uncover the truth. For all of his searching and looking it was not easy to find things out in the mid seventeen hundreds. As Thomas grew, he discovered that he would get feelings about things and he could charm others into doing what he wanted. Soon enough he was able to peer into the past by concentrating on something or touching an object. He still carried the medallion of St Michael the Archangel in his pocket that someone had placed in the basket with him before leaving him on those cold steps at the orphanage. Many times he had held it as the years passed, but one day he felt a tingling in his hand as he held it. He had already been alive nearly seventy years when this happened. It's possible that he was not ready to see the truth it held until then.

Thomas had concentrated on the medal very hard and it proved to hold the answers he had been looking for. He saw a darkly colored man, or at least he had thought him a man at first. He had strange features that resembled his own. Thomas was lighter in color but the resemblance was uncanny. As he watched this memory unfold he became uneasy. The person he was watching was not of a good nature. He could feel the darkness inside of him and his intentions. This evil "person" was following a beautiful woman with dark hair all dressed in her finest as she was escorted by a young suitor into a carriage. They were going to the annual ball given by a duke and duchess there. This young woman was of noble birth. Thomas continued to see all of the memories that the medallion had to offer. This man that was following was in love with her but she did not love him back and he had decided to carry out a despicable plan to force her to love him. Thomas had discerned that the man's true name was Esan Kelfinaar. He was not a man at all! He was some type of elf!

"What in the hell?" he had exclaimed, "This cannot be real!"

As he continued to watch the events unfold he was in disbelief. After the young lady's social gathering of the evening, the young man escorted the Lady Madeleine to the gates of her enormous home. The young fellow left as she turned to enter the abode. It was very late and no one was present to escort her inside which was most uncommon.

This young suitor was Madeleine's fiance. Thomas had understood from the thing in his hand. She was still smiling to herself as she was grabbed very quickly. The next memory it provided was the evil elf standing over her in a room somewhere dimly lit. She was shuddering in fear at his anger.

"Esan," she pleaded, "I cannot help the way that things are, you know that! Please do not do anything that will ruin us both. We are from two different walks of life and you know that my father will never allow us to marry."

The Lady Madeleine looked up at her attacker with teary eyes hoping he would understand as she had tried to make him so many times before. He gave her one last chance to change her mind.

"Madeleine, I grow tired of the same excuses you offer. Now, I am going to allow you to think for a moment, I know nothing of what class system humans use. I myself am not human." he sneered. He pulled back his cloak to reveal his white hair. She watched as he pushed it behind his pointed ears.

She was confused and astonished, "What are you if not human?"

Smiling slyly he said, "I am an elf and not one from your story books. Elves are as different as humans. Some are royalty and others are not. Some are light in color while others are not. We have dignity as well. This class issue is not the problem is it? I am, in my family, a member more noble than you!"

She was trying to wrap her mind around fairy tails come to life in front of her, "Then why are you in my world and not your own?"

This angered him further, "That, my dear, is not for you to know. It is my own business why I am here. All that you need to consider is that I love you and if you do not give into me I will make you."

Esan was indeed here for a reason that he did not want to reveal. He had been banished to the human world for unforgivable crimes in his own realm. What was it that he had done?

"What is to be darling? I await your answer." he smirked.

"If you truly love me then let me go. I beg you," she was in a panic.

"That is something I cannot do," Esan replied callously.

He approached her slowly as she leaned away from him on some kind of bed. He stared at her intently with wickedness in his heart. She became very still as his gaze met hers. She became obedient with just a stare! Esan proceeded to remove her clothing and admire her small, firm body. She had the milkiest skin, so smooth and soft. He then did the unthinkable to her to this noble woman.

Esan redressed himself and returned Madeleine to her home, but left her shabbily covered with her clothing on the stairs that led up to the door. He looked upon her with disdain now. No one would reject him or they would suffer the consequences. She became pregnant from the encounter, so she was sent to the country until after the birth to avoid scandal. When the child was born he was placed in a basket on the steps of an orphanage.

Thomas had sat in shock as he came to realize that he was the child and the people in the memory were his parents. He was not wanted by either of them! This hurt him so badly he had cried. When he had finished he began to want to know more about who he was and what he could do. He had wondered where this realm was and if he could get to it. Was he immortal? He wanted to know so he concentrated and listened to his blood to see if he could locate the one that should still be living: his father.

On a cold, rainy day while in London on some knew business prospect he felt that same tingle from a man passing by him in the cobblestone street. Thomas had followed him to a townhouse there and waited.

"I know you are there," Esan said. "Come in out of the rain."

Thomas walked in to face his father. "Why?" he asked.

Esan read his thoughts, "I see, Madeleine had my child and now you are confused and want to know about yourself. Your mother should have accepted me. I loved her and she refused me just as she did you."

"You took her by force," Thomas answered dryly, "Why would anyone accept that?"

"Even though you are half human you are still half Dulerian elf. You will have many powers as you probably have come to realize by now." Esan replied avoiding the accusation.

"Am I immortal?" Thomas asked hopefully.

"You will age very slowly, but only being a halfbreed you will not be immortal as I am," Esan smirked. He saw her in the young half elf's eyes.

"You denied me my right to nobility here in this world and you have done it to me in yours as well. You will tell me if there is a way to change this!" Thomas said as he angrily moved closer to his father. "What is it that you did to be sent to this awful place? I fit in nowhere even though I am able to charm and out perform humans on every scale. I still do not belong! I am alone."

Esan was amused but understood the poor boy's plight. He was annoyed at how winy he was, though. As dark as Esan may have been he still divulged the secret to immortality that would work on him and how to open the door to the realm he so desperately desired to leave this world for. Why did he even care to tell him? Who can know the answer to why Dulerian elves do anything? He explained to Thomas that he must first know his real name, the name given to his half breed soul. Esan placed his hand on Thomas's chest and began to say something in his elven tongue. Soon he was telling him the answer "Ayyn." Esan had given him a leather bound book that contained dark magic. He had no use for it any longer. Everything in it was memorized in his own head.

"If you really want to see the realm of our people then you must perform the ceremony I have shown you my son." Esan turned to pour himself a cup of tea from the stove. He had become accustomed to living as a man in this world. Unlike Ayyn, he enjoyed being better than all of the other beings he was accustomed to engaging on a daily basis. To him it had become rather like a sport of some kind. Other women had accepted Esan's advances but he never loved any of them the way he had Madeleine, if you could even call what he had felt for her love. He was a very handsome Dulerian elf but in this world Esan would never be accepted by the aristocracy for marriage requests. Humans would consider him a devil of some sort in that day and age. Esan suddenly decided to tell Ayyn the truth of his exile.

"If you must know boy, I killed my father, Essian, who was the king of the Dulerian elves in our realm. Fortunately for me they could not ever prove that I was the one who had it done so I was banished to never be able to rule the throne instead of being sentenced to torture and death. Law dictated that this was the punishment I must endure. My father's brother was placed on the throne and he most happily handed down the sentence without proof. He had always wanted to rule our kingdom so he was much obliged to rid himself of me."

"Why did you do it?" Ayyn asked.

"I wanted to rule the kingdom and the bastard killed my mother when he believed he had caught her in an affair with his chief adviser, which I must say was entirely untrue and a perpetrated lie by my uncle."

"What is this uncle's name?" Ayyn asked from curiosity.

"Cassen is his name and I do not like repeating it as it has become a word of cursing to me," Esan sneered.

Ayyn held the book and asked his father, "Why are you helping me?"

"I do not really know except that maybe it is because no matter what I do they will never allow me to return, but maybe I will gain some vengeance by having my son return in pure elven form after the ceremony. They will not harm you. After all, what have you done to them?" Esan laughed to himself. "Cup of tea, perhaps?" He believed deep down they would never let the boy remain if they found out Esan's line had returned. Maybe Ayyn would overthrow the current king and reclaim it for them. Esan could then return, perhaps and regain the kingdom for himself. The boy would have to pave the way for him. What a wonderfully wicked idea this was! He only wished he had known about Ayyn sooner.

Over tea, Esan explained what needed to be done so that Ayyn would not be discovered until the deathly deed had been done to his uncle. He coaxed the boy, he thought, into believing that this was all for him to return some honor and dignity to the throne by ruling in his stead. Ayyn was not an imbecile and figured on what the mad elf was up to. Ayyn would not be a scapegoat for his father to reclaim the throne. He wanted it for himself if he could just make it there.

There was something else Ayyn's father was hiding. He could feel it's power in the next room as it lay hidden in a wardrobe. It was some sort of powerful item.

After the visit to his father's house he had returned that very night under the cloak of an invisibility spell and burned it down while his evil creator was asleep to avenge the wrongs that had befallen him. Ayyn did not care what Esan had done or why. All he knew was that he would not get away with the dishonor he had caused to him. Immortal or not, burning up in a fire would kill anyone. Ayyn made sure that he retrieved the magical item he had sensed before the barrage of flames incinerated everything else.

"If I am a prince then I will be a king! It is my right and I have done nothing to have it stolen from me by anyone!" Ayyn was angry.

25

Ayyn had also paid a visit to his dead mother's estate. He saw his half brother from a human man being let out of a carriage and walking up to the house to enter it. When the door opened he saw a young woman, most likely his wife, waiting for him happily to hug and kiss him. Ayyn had never personally known these things but he would not be denied his inheritance or love any longer. He was now practiced in the art of enamoring and had decided that his half brother was going to share their mother's wealth left behind in death. The man's father had passed away fifteen years before Madeleine and all wealth and estate had been left to "Lady Madeleine" so half was Ayyn's.

Dressed in his finest attire and black great coat he approached the house with it's beautiful columns and buttresses. Statues and fountains were along the walk. The estate itself sat upon sprawling and immaculately kept grounds and was lavished with a most beautiful garden in the rear of the well kept home that should have been his. Ayyn used the heavy knocker on the door to announce his arrival. A butler opened the door to ask his business and then showed him into the parlor to await the master of the house.

"Lord Thomas Malfy is here to see you concerning some property, sir," the butler reported the visitor to his own Lord Michael Westingham at once.

"Property you say? hmmm, Well I cannot say I know the man but I will see him right away." Escort him to my study at once, Jeffrey." Lord Westingham insisted.

Lord Michael Westingham was in his late sixties with streaks of gray running throughout his hair but still a very attractive and refined gentleman. He was dressed as one would suppose, in a fine dark tailored suit and black leather boots of the finest quality. He was reclining in a big leather chair behind a very large desk made of the most expensive cherry wood. Books lined the wall in the study as well as maps and other such things to be found in an English gentleman's private rooms. On the desk were cigars and some brandy to offer his guest. As he waited for the man to enter he stared at his trophies on the walls in this room. He loved to go on safari in Africa. He had taken many an exotic animal there and had the heads mounted to remind him of these good times. Michael was still musing over his last trip when his guest was announced. He turned to greet the stranger.

26

"Ah Lord Westingham, it is good to finally make your aquaintance. Please, forgive my intrusion," Ayyn gave him a firm handshake, "I am here about a piece of property that I would like to purchase from you."

"Pleasure first," Michael said, "Brandy and a cigar Lord Malfy?"

"Please call me Thomas," Ayyn said in a friendly tone, "Yes, that would be lovely, thank you."

"Well I suppose if first names are in order then please call me Michael." It is an honor to make your aquaintance though I cannot say I have ever heard of you before."

"That is of no surprise to me at all sir. I have been in South Africa for so long now," Ayyn said slyly, "It is only now as a grown man that I wish to return to England which is part of the reason I am here. Your property known as "Black Thorn" is what I wish to discuss."

"Oh yes I see, Thomas, well in that case let us get to the business part of our visit. I am sure we can work something out as well as become good friends," Michael was happy to have someone new around. He had really tired of most of his companions. They were all too content to sit around a gentleman's club complaining about political issues and women. Michael really thought a few women allowed to entertain the men who were interested would be a fine change to the rules of "no women allowed." In the case of Thomas he was happy to be of some service to this gentleman; after all, it was a lovely estate that he wanted to purchase and at a hefty price, too.

As Michael looked up at Ayyn he caught his gaze. Michael instantly handed over his mind to Thomas. It was so easy for him now. "You will sign over half of everything you own as well as give to me half of all monies gained from our mother's death; it is my right as eldest son!" Ayyn said in a commanding tone.

"Yes, I will do what you ask. It is your right," Michael replied rather monotone in nature.

After business was concluded in the study they were off to the bank for business to be done there. Michael took out half of everything as was commanded and handed deeds as well as money over to Ayyn that day. This is the main reason he had become so rich and had become richer still over the years through investments and other more devious actions. He never saw his brother again from that day forward nor did he care to. He was the elder brother shunned by his mother while the younger had inherited everything. Ayyn left him alone with his family.

He wanted to cause him harm but why risk getting caught when he had gotten all he came for? Besides, this man had not been responsible for the wrong done to him. He was sure that he had eventually died and any children that he had were in possession of the estate and anything of monetary value that was left in the family back in England.

The years went by and Ayyn had come to the New World, the United States of America as it was now called. He set himself up in New York as a business man and he flourished in society. A rich, handsome man such as himself was readily accepted in the high social groups. Ayyn was charming and very good company when he chose to be, but to get on the wrong side of him was a death wish. Although his business was just a front and the offices fake no one ever noticed. He formed the Black Thorn Society to ready himself for the time when he would need help to do what was called for to become more than a half breed elf. He would need them and more precisely their sacrifice of souls for the ceremony, but nothing could be done until the full moon peaked on the summer solstice of a certain year. There would be one more thing needed for this ceremony and he had to choose carefully for this part for the ritual to work.

Sandra Campbell sat in her office with the heavy door shut awaiting the arrival of her next patient. It was about ten o'clock in the morning. Her work in psychiatry had become tedious at best. Summer was just around the corner and it was getting to be quite warm. She stood up out of the black rolling office chair to adjust the thermostat. She sat and looked out of the window at the cars and buildings. Her mind began to wander into the past, back to that night. Shortly after a fight with Peter she found herself in an upscale club they had been to a few times before. Sandra was intent on drinking her troubles away in a martini glass that night. She wasn't even sure why they had fought in the first place.

"Bastard," she said angrily whispered to herself.

Sandra and Peter Campbell had been married for nearly twelve years. They had a nine year old son, Austin whom Sandra loved dearly. Everything had been fine until recently. Peter had begun to act strangely and was starting arguments for no reason at all. She wondered if he was cheating on her. Sandra had been a very attractive woman in her thirties. Her red hair and blue eyes were both eye-catching. She was slender and of medium height. Sandra's career was taking off in the field of psychiatry. Just when everything seemed like it should be going right everything was all wrong.

"Mind if I join you," Ayyn had said smiling at her, "I couldn't help but notice you seem a bit down. Why not talk to a complete stranger about it?" He met her gaze and as much as she wanted to tell him to go away and leave her alone she couldn't.

"Yes, please sit down. What's your name?" she asked as she stared at this striking man with all of his lovely features.

"Thomas," he said, "and may I have yours madam?"

"Sandra," she told him of her troubles and soon he was escorting her to one of the finest hotel rooms in the city. She had no idea why she would even agree to go back with him to his hotel room.

Her head was swimming from the alcohol and something else, but what it was she did not know.

Ayyn slowly began to undress in front of her, and she had watched with an ache for him that she could not explain. He approached her and began undressing her one piece of clothing at a time as he continued to look at her with that penetrating gaze. They went into the bathroom and had showered together as he kissed her. They made love for hours it seemed. Afterward, they lay in each other's arms for a long time talking and laughing until they fell asleep.

She had woken up to find herself alone in the room the next morning. She looked for him or a note; anything that would suggest why he was not there. Nothing. She sat down on the bed and as she slowly dressed herself thoughts of *why?* and *what happened?* were running through her mind. Sandra was not a cheater so why had she allowed this to take place? A few weeks later she discovered her pregnancy. Horror set in. What was she going to tell Peter? After all, they had not slept together in at least six months. She told him with teary eyes exactly what happened and he had never let her live it down that he was raising another man's child, Claire.

The worst was yet to come for her, though. She confronted Peter several times with the belief that he had been cheating also and he had vehemently denied it. One evening she left work and instead of going straight home she drove to his office. It was supposed to be closed by now but a light was still on in his office. She had crept up to it and peered inside only to find Peter having a very good time with Sara the assistant. She could see them as she peered from a crouched position through the rectangular window. Instead of busting them she decided to follow when they left to see where they would go from here. Sandra waited in her car where they would not see her. Soon enough they exited the building and got into Sara's car. Sandra followed them to what appeared to be an old abandoned warehouse. They got out of the car and went inside. Sandra got out of her car and looked around cautiously. No one was outside to notice her. She sneaked up to a window close to where they were in the building and saw them donning black robes. That was really strange to Sandra, but she figured it was some sort of club or something for people who were bored with their lives. She continued to listen and watch. Her worst nightmare was about to come true when out stepped Thomas! The father of the child she was carrying. He knew Peter! Things were getting stranger and stranger, but still she listened on. What she learned that night shook her to the core of her soul. How could they even talk like that? Why had she been chosen to bear the child for him? This was madness and it was depraved! Thomas was not Thomas at all. His name was Ayyn, he was not human, and she was having his child!

She had thought to confront Peter about all she had seen and heard but figured it was best not to say anything yet for fear of what they might do to her. Nine months later she had given birth to a daughter, Claire. She resembled him somewhat but she did not have pointed ears and all of her tests when she was born were normal. She appeared to be completely human. Maybe she had gotten lucky on that part.

"Mrs Campbell, your next appointment is here," Linda buzzed in.

"Alright, send her in, thanks," Sandra immediately went into professional mode.

It had been a couple of days since "A" had been here. Claire was laying across her bed thinking of everything that had gone on over the years with "A" and remembering his protectiveness of her as well as his comfort. She always found comfort in his arms. Now that she was seventeen, almost eighteen had she begun to feel more for him? Deep down inside of her she knew that she loved him but she wondered how on earth they could be together. He had once told her that a day would come when she would not have to come back here if she did not want to but what did that even mean? She was confused about things now. She needed to know what it meant to not have to come back and if it was even possible for them to share a life together seeing as how his was immortal and hers was not.

Agreus was watching her and reading her thoughts. If that was all that was holding her back then it would soon not be a problem for him. The time was almost here when he could change her existence forever and he would never have to be without her again. He was dying on the inside thinking of holding her in his arms. He needed her answer.

It was about a quarter of nine now. Claire had begun to doze off when she instinctively knew that he was there. She called out to him to come and climb in bed with her like always when he came in the night. He noticed she was wearing a white cotton gown. It had very thin straps over the shoulder and little ruffles around the bottom that just barely covered her slender thighs. Looking at her was unbearable for him without wanting to touch her. He knew that he should not do this knowing what he knew but he must do it. This time she turned to face him rather quickly and before she could say a word he grabbed her tightly and kissed her with hot passion. His face was flushed as was hers. Claire did not stop him. He looked up into her eyes and their was an understanding of love between them. Kissing her on the mouth gently he said, "I will make everything possible." Agreus held her to him for a long time as he whispered wonderful secrets to her. She was smiling as she slowly nestled herself down into him for the comfort he always brought to her. For once in his life, he was happy and in love. She loved him back with the same ferocity. He would make it possible for them to share a life together and no one was going to stand in the way of his plans for them. As she was falling into a gentle contented sleep at his side he whispered next to her ear, "I love you my darling," with that same rich Mediterranean accent that he always had. It was comforting to her, "I love you too, forever." Claire fell fast asleep in his arms.

Agreus lay there holding her for a while as he imagined how eternity with her would be. She was his destiny and he knew that now. He never would have believed that one day she would grow up and capture his demigod heart. The time had come for him to soon reveal to the Allerian elves what he had understood could have happened with Claire's soul and how it may concern them. He was hoping they would just be happy that he had found her and not dwell on the fact that he had not brought it to their attention until now. They were, after all, of a higher born nature than their elven cousins called the Dulerian elves. They had a merry disposition and respect for everything and everyone. He was pondering these things when he heard Peter coming in late to the house as usual. Agreus saw an opportunity to read his thoughts and find out why he had always treated Claire so badly. He waited for Peter to get into his study which was separate from Sandra's, before easing out of Claire's bed and stalking him down the hall. Peter could not perceive his footsteps or his presence because he was just another blind worthless human being. While he was pouring a drink for himself Agreus walked up behind him and watched as he sat in his leather chair sipping the brandy he just poured for himself as he attempted to light a cigar. He began combing through the spider webs of Peter's mind. What he discovered there was shocking beyond anything he could have imagined.

"Ayyn? The son of the dark elf will not get his hands on Claire for that sickening purpose!" Agreus was angry. "So that is how she came to be stuck in a human body. I will solve that problem and then deal with these "Black Thorns" myself. I must not let Claire find out what is going on here. It would destroy her to know what they have planned. I will protect her from these fiends and their so-called master!" Agreus was fuming with rage.

He knew what he had to do. It must be done on her eighteenth birthday which was going to fall on the summer solstice this year. "His plan will never work now; she is mine and no longer untouched. How could this half breed elf, steal a pure Allerian soul and father a physical body for it with a mortal woman and then plan to use her for his own gain like this? I must find him and expose him for what he is: the illegitimate son of a dark elf!" The question is why was his father hear in the first place? I must consult with the elves on this matter. Perhaps they may know something that can help."

Agreus froze time in this room of the house. He looked at Peter, "You are truly a wretch of a human. You sold out your wife for something you can never have. You treated Claire like nothing all of these years, and for what, a whore called Sara and the possibility of living forever? I will not allow you to live. In fact, I will make you suffer worse than you could ever imagine." He unfroze time and watched as Peter resumed what he was doing.

He returned to Claire to be sure that she was alright before he could, in good conscience, leave to speak with the elven historians. She was still sleeping deeply. He kissed her on her forehead as she rolled over onto her back. Momentarily, he rested his head on her belly just thinking of their love. He made a sudden and surprising discovery. She was pregnant with twins! As a demigod, he would instantly be able to tell such things, especially when it was his own offspring. Agreus was overjoyed at the thought of having his very own family after so much time alone. He had not been like his brother. Agreus was never content to frolic with nymphs and have no sense of responsibility. How could the elves refuse to give her to him now that she would bear his children? He knew they would not do that to him. The summer solstice was still a little while away so he believed she was safe for now. He looked at her one last time and then disappeared through the veil that separated worlds to seek the truth about the monster in hers.

"So, Peter is our little daughter still pure for our ritual?" Ayyn asked of the caretaker, "She is quite beautiful, such a shame to have to waste such a specimen. I would have her myself if she was not necessary for this ritual to work. She is after all only my daughter in flesh, not soul and that it what matters to my people."

"She is pure my lord, I have let no man come near her as you know." Peter said earnestly.

"I have provided for her all that money can buy so that her short life has been pleasurable, have I not," Ayyn asked.

"Yes you have and very generously, master," Peter was unsure why he was even being questioned.

"I want you to bring her before me so that I may assess her soul for myself," Ayyn commanded him.

"Yes of course, when would you like this to be done?" Peter asked with anticipation.

"Plan a trip to your country estate. It is away from everyone is it not? Once there, I will come on the day of the solstice. You can make up whatever reason for going there that you would like. Bring the entire family so it is more believable. When the time is upon us the others shall all arrive and the ceremony will commence," Ayyn was sure of himself now.

He wanted to see for himself this child's shell that he fathered to be the vessel for the elven soul that would make him pure and make it possible for his entrance into the realm of his ancestors. Until now he had stayed away. He had only seen pictures of the girl. On occasion, he saw her from a distance. Part of him had wished there was another way. He would have taken her with him instead of having to kill her to get what he wanted. "Oh well," Ayyn muttered to himself, "better her than me." He was satisfied for now with the answer from Peter and said goodbye to him as he hung up the phone.

Before he had impregnated Sandra, he had performed the rite that would capture an elven soul waiting to be born to another elven couple and placed it in the human child he and Sandra created. He had kept her away from everything and everyone, placating her with things. He did not know the abuses she had suffered, otherwise he may have slapped the caretaker around a bit as Ayyn intended for her not to endure pain and displeasure while she lived. Ayyn knew what it was to suffer at the hands of humans. Even though he planned to kill her he felt her life should be free of torment. The most important thing was that she not be tainted. She must be a pure girl untouched by anyone. This was the secret for his transformation. Otherwise the rite would not work and she would die for nothing. He had entrusted the task of her care taking to Peter Campbell who had been in his inner circle for years. Peter helped him move Sandra into position to be used in this manner and had not thought twice about it. He would start arguments for nothing and then blame her so that she would be desperate enough to seek comfort elsewhere. For his cooperation, Peter was given Sara who was a younger woman from the order that he was enamored with. All seemed to be falling into place for Ayyn. He smiled his dark and sinister smile at himself in the mirror on his desk. He was now quite arrogant and narcissistic, after all. The old "Thomas" was far away from his nature now.

Agreus had consulted with the elves and what they may know of a Dulerian elf in the human world. They had told him that a particularly dark elven prince by the name of Esan Kelfinaar was banished for killing his father, the king of the Dulerians, and he was never to return.

Agreus told them of the child that Esan had fathered, the half breed elf called Ayyn. They had become very disturbed by the unsettling news of the ceremony the mad younger elf had in mind. If he was ever able to get back to this world he could usurp the throne and wreak havoc on them all if so inclined. The tribes had lived in relative peace for far too long for this to happen. They also had an inclination that the soul he had stolen belonged to the still born daughter of their Allerian Lord and Lady who had been devastated. All of the times matched up perfectly for it to be so. Still, they would need to examine Claire before that could be determined and there was only one way for that to occur. The ritual that Agreus had planned for her from the day he met her was the way it must be done. He told them of how things had unfolded over the years and they were glad he had been there to guide her and help keep her safe. He also confessed that they were in love and she was very early on in pregnancy with his children. Once it was confirmed that she was the daughter of Lord Kefna and the Lady Ashana, he would seek her hand in marriage. The Lord and Lady were the leaders of the Allerian elves in this world and they would be ecstatic to find out that their daughter had lived on unbeknownst to them as well as anxious to have her joined with her family after all of this time. They would be very angry at the one responsible for the current situation of her soul. As a demigod and father of her children he doubted they would refuse his offer of marriage once all of this had been resolved considering past and current relations between the elves and himself. They had been friends for a very long time and they had sought his council and assistance on more than one occasion.

Agreus and his elven friends rushed to get things in order and prepared for the rite he would be performing on the summer solstice with the full moon peaking in the sky. The elven clerics would be assisting so that her elven body could reunite it's essence with the soul that it had lacked. This information had not yet been presented to the leaders of the elves just yet. They needed to hurry with the preparations before it was too late. He was now more determined than ever to save his love and his children from the dark one. Agreus knew that the Black Thorn Society would be anxious to try and get hold of Claire at the same time. They were about to commit a pointless and heinous act that would result in nothing gained but much lost. He would never allow this to happen.

Several days had passed and Peter found himself in another meeting with his deranged peer group. This was the one meeting that they were all waiting for. Peter and the other members of the Black Thorn Society were in their robes waiting for their courageous leader to appear. He did not wish to ever encounter the bad side of him. He felt like he was sweating bullets. What if he had not done something right or what if he had done something that Ayyn felt was not good enough? Peter did not know what he should think. Maybe he was just being paranoid but he felt like something was different with Claire lately. It could be that she was just growing up, but what if she had been secretly seeing a boy or something? No, that could not be possible. Where would she have even met one? Ayyn was sure to find out as soon as he saw her in the country if something was wrong with her. Then he would never have what he wanted. None of them would have anything they had been promised if she was not still pure. He believed she was but something just felt out of place.

"Ah my fellow Black Thorns," Ayyn walked in and bowed to his audience of about twenty. "I hope everyone is well and ready for our upcoming event? We only have about a week to prepare so until then you will not see much of me for there are things I must make ready for that night. You have all been given personal instructions and the proper elements to conduct these instructions upon your selves before arriving for the ritual. If anyone needs any information on where and when then you must speak with my good friend Peter Campbell. He will know anything you may ask," Ayyn gave his usual striking smile to everyone there, "Also, I will be needing two female volunteers for a . . . . project this evening," He gave a sly grin.

Two of the younger females in the society offered themselves for the service, Jaina and Carlina. They were twenty somethings and the daughters of a prominent wall street investment manager who was present at the meeting.

"Yes, the two of you will do very well with this project I believe," the dark leader smiled. Ayyn continued to posture and prep his followers for about thirty minutes concerning what they believed they were going to soon achieve.

"If there is no further business then we shall conclude the meeting. Ladies I will need you to report to my home on the upper east side. You know where it is," Ayyn dismissed the meeting.

He looked at the women once again with a devilish smile. There father would not deny his use of them. He was far too involved with what he wanted for himself and this was a small price to pay to get what he wanted in life. Besides, he believed it would benefit the two of them as well.

Ayyn's previous reminder of the "instructions" was actually a spell they would put on themselves prior to the evil ritual. Unknowingly, they would be giving their souls over as a sort of battery to fuel the rite. They would die of course. This was no concern of his. Ayyn laughed to himself quietly.

Claire was washing some things that she did not feel comfortable allowing the maid to handle when Peter got home rather early for a change. He walked over and kissed her forehead and said, "Pack your things my dear, this weekend we will be going to the country house!"

Claire looked at the calendar, it was only Tuesday, "Ok dad what's going on?" He never acted this way. Something was very off.

"Oh I just think we need a little weekend vacation; we need to visit Austin's grave, and maybe your mother and I can spend some time together while you get to enjoy your precious countryside dear," he lied with a smile.

Even though she seriously doubted his honesty she, nevertheless, agreed to pack and be ready to roll come Saturday morning. He hurried out of the room to his study and shut the door. She wondered if he had informed her mother of this absurd reasoning for the visit to the country, but she did want to visit her brother's grave. Claire figured that they had not realized that her birthday was this weekend but what did it matter? She would be where she was happiest and she would surely see her lover and get to visit the glen.

Sandra was walking into the kitchen where Claire was settling into a chair to eat a sandwich.

"Mom, has dad told you where he plans to take us this weekend?" Claire asked curiously.

"No, when did he mention it dear?" Sandra was curious too.

"Just now, when he came flying through here and up to his study. Sounds a little weird but maybe you should just talk to him yourself," Claire figured that would be happening anyway.

"Yes, I believe I will go and find out right now," Sandra marched up to the study to ask Peter a few questions.

Agreus was sure that now Claire was pregnant she did not need to be under any unnecessary stress. He did not want her to lose their twins. He did not want her life to be put at any risk either. After all, she was still mortal right now. Hopefully, she would know nothing of the troubles happening until her transformation when she would truly be safe from Ayyn. That evil monster may have genetically fathered her current form, but her soul is eternal and that was taken, so he was not her father at all. He was just an evil half breed that would soon taste the wrath of the king for what had been done to his child as they suspected she was their royal princess.

Agreus was planning to visit Claire this night to see how she was doing and how their children were doing. He needed to go ahead and tell her what he knew of the babies sleeping in her womb. Even though she was still early in the pregnancy he could communicate with their eternal souls; that was one of the perks of being a demigod. He would be able to tell many things about them. He just knew how excited she would be to know because he had read her thoughts and he knew that she wanted to bear his children.

"Your wish is my command," he laughed to himself overjoyed, "I was definitely not thinking that would happen the first time we made love!"

Agreus went out of his home in the glen to perform his duties in the forest. The vines were under his command as well. When he came and went they rolled back to let him out of the entrance to the cave and rolled back over the entrance tightly to hide it and keep others from entering. He admired all of the green things that were growing and all of the little animals tending to their own duties. Why can people not be like the animals of the forest? The squirrels worked diligently to save food for the winter while it was still warm and there was plenty to be gathered. It was a matter of priorities. The humans used to be this way so many ages ago. What had happened? They had become greedy and lusted after things that were of no consequence in the grand scheme of their short lives. When they had been simple in their living and their habits, the gods and spirits had enjoyed helping them when they needed it, but now they worshiped themselves and riches, so no help for those who did these things would be coming. As a demigod who cared for the growing things and the animals as was his duty it saddened him to see things this way. With the skills of the prophet that he inherited from his mother, he saw how they would become if they did not change and it was unthinkable. He would never have abandoned Claire to this world even if they had remained only friends.

Meanwhile, the elves that Agreus had consulted thought it best if they informed their lord and lady of the possibility that lay before them. They only hoped that it would be true for the sake of Lady Ashana. She had been so devastated when her child was stillborn. That just did not happen to their people. They knew it had meant something but no matter how their scholars had poured over the matter, there had been no answer. The entire ordeal had been shrouded in darkness.

"My Lord Kefna, I have some most interesting news for you and our gracious Lady Ashana!" cried Tannas as he entered the royal throne room and flung himself at their feet. He was one of the historians that had been with Agreus during the consultation.

"For goodness sake, Tannas get up and tell us what it is!" the king said with anticipation.

"My lord, the demigod Agreus has come to the historians to consult our history about a Dulerian elf that was banished from this realm long ago," he continued to explain all that had been revealed to him by Agreus, the demigod.

"Can it be possible?" the king turned to his lovely wife and smiled at the thought of regaining what had been denied them.

"If this is true, we shall know upon the completion of the rite of soul shift," and if I find out that this Claire as she is known for the moment is truly our daughter there will be an eternity of suffering for the one who caused this atrocity! Lord Kefna turned to Lady Ashana as she sat there crying for her lost daughter and said, "Do not worry my darling wife, I will determine if this girl is our daughter."

The Lady Ashana replied quietly through tears, "I know she is mine, she has to be." The little queen then left the throne room to be alone with her thoughts.

"Tannas, I need to speak to our clerics at once to see that they are in line to help Agreus with what must be done to bring her back to this realm," the king said with purpose.

"It has already been put in place your majesty," Tannas bowed low before his master.

"Good, now we wait for the summer solstice, when the moon is at it's fullest peak the process must begin!" the king said with authority.

"Everything has been put into action my lord! I swear it shall be done!," with that Tannas left the chambers to return to his duties.

"Agreus come to me please, I must speak with you," Lord Kefna said with wet eyes as he looked into his own watery reflecting pool.

"I am here Lord Kefna," Agreus announced himself, "I assume you have been informed of what is happening?"

"Yes and I must tell you we are at your service in any way that we can be, we must have her back," the king said humbly to the demigod.

"I will need your clerics and the body of the infant that was wrapped and anointed from the tomb it was placed in." We must rejoin her soul to what should have been her true body. "She will reclaim her true self if indeed she is your daughter. She will still remain eighteen once the ritual is complete. She will then become the royal daughter that was taken from you. You will perform the memory rite to bring her into the tribe with all memories that she should have of your ways and who her people are," Agreus was instructing the king on all things that must be done for her when the king asked him a question or two.

"Is it true my lord that the two of you are in love?" the king asked him with a sly grin.

"It is true and a very happy love it is!" Agreus replied.

"Is it also true that she is carrying twins, your children?" he asked still grinning.

"She is indeed carrying my twins, she is not aware of it yet. Tonight is when I plan to tell her of these blessings. I know she will be happy, she wants to bear my children, your highness," Agreus said with dignity.

"Then, my old friend, if she is indeed my child, she shall be your wife!" the king knelt before the demigod.

"Thank you for your blessing of our unity. Once this atrocious matter is attended to we shall be married and celebrate both the wedding and the children," Agreus was so happy to have the blessing of the king ahead of time. One less thing to worry about.

"Yes the children, once you have spoken with their spirits this evening will you come tomorrow and tell me all you know of them, my lord?" The king asked of his age old companion.

"I will indeed come to you and tell you of your grandchildren," Agreus smiled, "Now remember my friend, we are hoping she is indeed your daughter, but even if she is not she is still going to be my wife and she is carrying my twins so whether or not they are your kin by blood they are still your kin in my mind," They tenderly shook hands and Agreus parted from his teary eyed friend.

The king went to check on his queen and tell her all of the story that he knew to cheer her up. She would be so happy to have grandchildren, as would the king. They needed to go ahead and have the dress makers prepare the royal garb that their daughter would be needing. Several outfits and slippers. She would also need a proper circlet to be worn on her head to signify she was the daughter of royalty. The last thing to be made would be her lovely wedding gown. Although elves traditionally married their own kind, this was a special circumstance for many reasons. The elven builders were going to be instructed on having a special home built for Agreus and their daughter combining their customs. The king knew he was getting ahead of himself with these thoughts but he could not wait to know her true name and whether or not she was his. He already believed in his heart that she was indeed his daughter.

Sandra came out of the study with a pale look on her face. Peter had told her the same thing he had said to Claire. Normally, she would not have thought quite so much about his strange behavior but she could not forget what they had been discussing in that meeting when she eavesdropped on Peter and his twisted friends. She had managed to half way convince herself that they would not do anything like what they had mentioned to anyone, especially her daughter.

Sure, she wanted to visit Austin's grave. It had been a year since she had been out there to "visit" him. She knew Peter had to be lying about wanting to spend time with her and Claire, though. While he had been explaining she remembered what Ayyn said about the summer solstice falling on Claire's eighteenth birthday and the moon being full. She remembered how he said to gain immortality for all of the members and himself that he must plunge an iron dagger into Claire's heart to take her soul. Only the soul of a pure blood elf could make this happen he had told them as she had listened while five months pregnant with their intended victim. That kind of stuff could not be real could it? Well, whether it was or not, they believed it and she had a feeling that they were all pawns in Ayyn's game. She glanced at the wall calendar in the study as Peter talked and saw that this weekend was Claire's eighteenth birthday and the summer solstice.

"Ok Peter, she said, "We'll pack and head up there if you want."

"Good, good," he had stammered as though he were nervous.

She had pretended not to notice and smiled as she left the study. What was she going to do? She couldn't let them kill her. Claire had always scared her whether she was what they said or not and she had neglected to be a present mother most of the time, but she knew Peter was only trying to get them out of town to perform their sick ritual. Sandra knew she had to do something about it before that day got there. The next few days went by quickly. It was Friday before she knew it. They would be leaving in the morning.

Claire returned up to her room from her dance studio about eight thirty. After dinner, she had decided to dance for awhile to clear her mind and focus. It had always been her outlet. Agreus watched from his mirror as always. He waited for her to have a bath and a cup of tea on the little reading table in her room to come to her. "A!" I'm so glad to see you my love. I was missing you so much." She kissed him knowing that he could not always be with her due to his duties.

"Claire, I need for you to sit down and listen to what I have to tell you, my love," he began to tell her what he knew, "My darling, you are pregnant with my children. We are going to have twins!" Her face grew into the most excited expression, "Further more, I must tell you the truth about who you are," He explained everything that he knew about her and who her true parents most likely were. Agreus told her how she came to be here instead of there. He also explained the rite that must take place at the proper time in a few days to change everything into all that she had ever dreamed of. She sat there and listened awestruck. Claire's head was spinning from all of this wonderful news. She was also a bit upset that there had been someone messing around with her soul. The sheer joy she felt at this moment could not be undone by any of the bad.

"I'm going to be immortal like you and we are having two babies?" she cried with joy.

"Claire, you are in danger, those beasts including Peter have it in their minds to kill you to gain immortality. What they do not understand is that the dark one, Ayyn has brainwashed them into believing it. Only he could become immortal by doing his dark ritual because his father came from the realm that humans can not see. He killed his father after he found out a few unfortunate details of his life, but not before gaining the knowledge to do these things. Claire, he seduced your human mother with his enamoring gaze and impregnated her but had already performed a ritual on himself to plant within her an elven soul for the human body to hold until he could use it. Peter knew and went along with it all of this time. I did not want to tell you of the danger you are in, but it is now necessary I believe even if it does cause some heartache," Agreus related this things with much concern.

"Well that explains a lot about him," Claire said bitterly, "What shall we do my love? I am ready to be with you and my real family."

"I have spoken with them and they are ready for the same thing but first I must talk to our little ones. I promised Lord Kefna that I would bring him tale of all that I knew of the children tomorrow when I return to him." Agreus asked her to sit quietly for a moment. He was so happy about the things that would take place within the next few days and now he was going to speak with his children!

Claire sat back in the chair she was seated in and was very quiet. She was thinking to herself how wild it was that he could talk to the babies and know what their spirits were saying back to him. There was more to him than met the eye but she had always known that to be true. Certainly, these things would be revealed to her soon enough. She wanted so badly to return to her real family. She had always known that she did not belong in this world. Claire finally knew why everyone she had been around had treated her in a strange way. She was to be their tool or so they thought. He would not let that happen to her. All of the distractions that had been provided were just that, distractions to keep her unaware of what was going on around her. She had been placed in dance which she had come to love so much because they thought it would just keep her busy! Well, they screwed up with that one! Without it she may never have met "A".

"Alright my love, I am finished talking with our children now."

Claire got up from the little white chair and sat down with him on the rug. She wanted to be close to him for this moment.

"So, tell me all about our babies, my love!" She smiled excitedly.

"They are both male. One is an elf and the other is like me. The child that is an elf will be the ruler of your people one day, an heir for the kingdom. The one like me will learn to do what I do and eventually take over doing the same thing when I retire from it. They want you to know that they can feel your spirit and your warmth. They love you and know that you love them already, too." He was smiling at her. She had teary eyes of happiness as she got to her knees and threw her arms around his neck to hug him; he hugged her back tightly. They looked at each other with intensity and he kissed her gently on the lips.

"I love you Claire, soon I will be calling you by your true name," He whispered to her.

"I love you too, and soon I shall call you by yours," she whispered back.

"Do you know that Lord Kefna is already having everything planned for our wedding? Even all of the royal clothing and circlet for you is being made. They are constructing a private dwelling for us of such magnitude so that we will raise our family in comfort. It is to be very near to the castle that already stands so that we will have all privacy but remain close to them. Of course I still have duties but it works out just fine. All this is being done before we even know for sure you are his daughter! They are so sure that you are. The Lady Ashana was in tears from the knowledge of what these "people" are planning. Your parents want you home my darling!" he exclaimed knowing this would make her happy.

"My parents . . . those are my parents names?" She was crying now, it was a foreign concept to her to be loved and wanted by parents. Agreus comforted her as he was thinking of how best to torture the mortal "parents." She now understood why Sandra and Peter never cared about her. Hell, Peter had nothing to do with making her at all; it was that half breed elf, Ayyn, the dark one. This would have been extremely upsetting to think he was her father but in the elven world the parents of the soul were the true parents and this was relieving.

"When can I know your real name and the secrets that I know you keep from me?" she looked at him curiously.

"Soon my love. After your soul-shift is completed you will instinctively know who and what I really am. I believe you may be a little surprised to know. I will tell you all you wish to know and if you like I can show you the truth with my mind as well," he wanted her to know all about him now.

"I trust you. I am just anxious is all," she said smiling at him.

"Our little ones are a bit anxious as well but I have assured them that I will make everything alright for us all. I will not let anyone harm you. I want to see your belly big and round with my little darlings growing inside!" he grinned at her lovingly.

"Tell me what an elven wedding is like, please," she was so looking forward to it.

"Well normally it has a elven bride and and an elven groom but an exception has been made happily for this special circumstance. You are royalty my dear, the princess of the Allerian elves. They are preparing a beautiful gown for you to wear to it and do not concern yourself with traditions. After the rites are completed and the memories are gained from your parents you will know all of the customs required. I have been very close with your father for many an age now and the tribe your tribe also. I am already aware of what to do and there are reasons I would know anyway. It is in many ways like a human wedding except more beautiful. Their are a couple of main differences like the fact that no one divorces because it is a crime. No one has ever wanted to divorce either, and they have no word for something such as that. It is an unfathomable thing to be without the one you love in that realm. Elves mate for life so to speak. Our love is true and pure so I know that you and I shall never part. You will see soon. Everything you want to know lies behind the full moon this weekend on the night of your eighteenth birthday. After that, you will have no more questions about yourself or your people," he looked as his future bride, "I have something for you my love," Agreus passed his left hand over hers and a large, beautiful emerald was now on her ring finger, "I just realized, I had not asked you properly. Will you please be my wife for all of eternity?" he asked her sincerely, looking deep into her soul.

"Yes you know I will!" she exclaimed through happy tears. They hugged and kissed happily over the occasion.

"Now how shall we celebrate my dear?" he asked her, "Would you like to become invisible for a little while and spy on everyone in the house?" He knew she would find this very amusing.

"Really? You can make me invisible?" she implored.

"Of course I can," he said proudly.

"Alright, let's go to it then!" she wanted to see what Peter was doing.

He placed his arms around her and whispered an incantation into her ear. She became invisible to other humans. They began to explore the house together. They came into Peter's study and found him on the phone with someone. They were talking heatedly. They decided to listen to both sides of this conversation. Even though it was really loud enough to be heard already with the harsh tones Agreus elevated the other voice only for them so it seemed the conversation was taking place in that very room.

"Peter, I noticed how strangely you were acting in the meeting today. What are you hiding?" it was Ayyn, "If anything goes wrong with our rites I will personally kill you! You do understand me do you not?"

"Yes, Lord Ayyn, I know that but I must tell you that Claire has been acting rather strangely herself as of late. I can not honestly claim to know why; she just seems different," Peter said nervously.

"She will be looked over by me on her birthday and perhaps I can discover if anything is wrong that would put a damper on our festivities. You say she is still untouched my friend? That is the key to the entire ceremony! She must be a virgin," Ayyn reminded him.

Claire was giggling to herself. It's not as if Peter could hear or see either one of them. She was definitely not pure, she was pregnant! She instinctively knew that fact would not save her. If Ayyn discovered this he would kill her and probably everyone of his co-conspirators out of rage. The thing for her to do was to act like nothing was going on and then disappear just before Ayyn arrived and there would be nothing he could do to her.

Agreus wanted to push Peter's eyes through his skull at the moment and have him laying dead as he stood over him but that would come soon enough. The moment for retribution had not yet arrived. The prophet in him told him to bide his time and all would be handled properly. He had been searching for this dark one and now through his voice on the phone he knew just where to locate him. His spells of protection had just failed. He would pay him a visit later tonight, but for now they were spying.

"Just remember Peter, you and Sandra have been her caretakers all of this time. I could not in good conscience kill someone that I had raised myself," he lied knowing he just did not want the responsibility, "I need you to come through for the Society and for yourself. Remember, Sara will be waiting for you as well. You will be free of your wife and you can start anew," Ayyn lied so well.

"What will become of Sandra? I don't want her to be harmed. She was the mother of my dead son, I don't love her anymore but after everything that has been done to her I would like her to live," Peter said with a shaky voice. He was not accustomed to making any demands of his master for fear of some harm coming to him.

"Of course Peter, I will only make her forget everything so she will not have bad memories," Ayyn soothed him with more lies.

Ayyn intended fully to kill Sandra. He had not enjoyed that night as much as Sandra had but he managed to make her believe it well enough. She meant nothing to him anymore than did Claire. He was disgusted by having to pretend to be friends with any of these humans. They were his path to the life he wanted and that was all.

"Peter, you know that you are one of my most treasured friends so if you need anything at all you must always come to me with it, alright?" Ayyn said smirking on the other end of the phone. "Never fear me my good man. I am here to not only lead but to serve," Ayyn thought that last bit was a good addition to the other things he had not meant either. He was laughing a little to himself at how blind Peter was to the fact that Ayyn could not stand him. Humans!

Next, they went into Sandra's bedroom to see what she was doing. She was sitting at a little reading table smoking and drinking a whiskey sour. She kept muttering about how she had to help Claire. She must have found out somehow what the Black Thorns were up to. Sandra's thoughts had been so jumbled when he first read them years ago that he had missed this. She had found out by accident and had been out of her mind ever since. This would have been overwhelming to a human with no knowledge of the hidden realms, especially finding out she had been used like this. Agreus wanted to feel bad for her but he wanted her to pay for her crimes against the innocent Claire who had nothing to do with this sick society. Claire's real parents would want justice on them all, as well. They left the mentally unstable woman to her troubled thoughts. Claire and Agreus returned to her bedroom. She was made visible again.

"Well that was rather enlightening. How can Peter believe such lies. He is more of an idiot than I thought he was. How he sold out Sandra is just crazy," Claire felt sorry for her.

"Please do not worry my dear, everything will work out right. I promise I have the power to make that happen. Besides, our little ones do not need to worry either," he told her with confidence, "Ah, I have just the thing," he knelt down and kissed her belly where the babes lay asleep. Rubbing a hand over them he whispered an incantation. They would be unaware of any stress now. Claire loved to listen to his incantations in that lovely accent of his. It was beautiful to her, as was he.

"Now my dear, they will not be affected by anything going on out here. It is time for me to pay a visit to this half breed dark elf. Do not worry love. He cannot harm me," he reassured her.

"Please come back to me soon my love," she missed him already, "What if he wants to harm me after he sees you?" she said worried.

"I will come and immediately take you away to be hidden until time for your change, darling," He felt protectiveness for his family. With a kiss to the forehead he disappeared to go to this beast to confront him on this wretchedness.

How did "A" know how to do all of these things and how was he so sure that harm would come to none of them? She believed him and marveled at it all the same. Soon he would tell her everything and then she would understand how and why.

Ayyn was sitting in a leather armchair staring out of the big picture window that his penthouse offered. He was imagining how much better things would be when he was with his own kind and could take a wife from his own people. He was sick of these humans and his human side. He wanted nothing more to do with humanity. It made him feel too much. Just as he had felt sorry that he must kill the girl and other things over the years. Soon enough he would no longer care.

"Yes you will," Agreus said out loud appearing before Ayyn.

48

"Who are you and how did you get into my apartment?" Ayyn growled.

"Oh wait, that is right, you are dark and have no conscience," Agreus said to him, "I am afraid I cannot allow you to harm Claire."

Ayyn was looking Agreus over to see if he could read his thoughts. His mind was like a wall of steel. He could not penetrate it at all. This had never happened to him before. This creature must be very powerful so he had to tread carefully.

"What concern is it of yours, creature?" Ayyn sneered, "I have no quarrel with you."

"Yes, I am afraid you have made quarrel with me by doing this." Agreus retorted, "I can freely pass back and forth from this world to any of the unseen realms. I can even go to the one that you wish to go to at anytime I choose and I know everything about you and where you come from, Ayyn. I will not allow such evil to happen and have you come to the elven realm. I know of the dark magic you want to perform and when you wish to do it so I am giving you one last chance to back down and stop this."

"Why should I and why do you even care? Unless . . . have you befriended the girl somehow?" Ayyn asked remembering what Peter had told him.

"Have you any idea whose soul you have stolen for this purpose? She is royalty, the daughter of the Allerian elves of the realm. They are not at all very happy with you as it is. If you back down now you can remain in this world of humans unharmed and in exile like your father had been, but if you do not then severe punishment will be what you obtain," Agreus smirked at him.

"There is no way for you to know that! Who are you?" Ayyn was angry now.

"All that you need to know is that I am a demigod who is not pleased with you and I could destroy you now but that would deny her parents the choice of your punishment," Agreus smiled callously.

"I see, so you are aligned with the true parents of the little elf inside of her and have ideas of changing her back," Ayyn charged. "I am afraid that I cannot allow it," Ayyn said dryly. "What must I do to obtain your favor and have you let me be to perform the ceremony?"

"Nothing in existence could make me allow this to happen. She is my intended wife and she carries my twins. I will not allow you to take them from me and if you try you will feel the fullness of my wrath!" Agreus shouted at him.

"What? You have defiled her? She is no longer pure! Do you know what this means for me?Everything that I have waited centuries for is in vain!" Ayyn was furious beyond compare.

"What YOU have waited for? I am as old as the ages, boy! I have waited forever for the love we share and the family it has brought to me!" Agreus' eyes were glowing bright green now with rage.

"If you are a demigod then take pity on me and help me out of this dying form. I was denied my rights in this world and in the world of my father," Ayyn pleaded, "Please do not deny it to me as they have."

"I owe you nothing and as far as I am concerned you are not worthy to look upon me or my future bride. You have done everything the wrong way! Had you but called out, perhaps a god or spirit would have answered you in your plight but instead you make others pay for what you seek," Agreus refused him, "No one will help you now. I shall surely see to that!

"Then as vengeance I will take everything from you!" the angered half breed answered.

Agreus laughed, "That is not possible. I am more powerful than you shall ever be," Still laughing Agreus disappeared.

Ayyn was so angry with Peter. He knew there was no way Peter could have known this but he was going to have someone pay dearly and it would take so long to restart this entire process! He would find a way to make that demigod suffer and take Claire away from him out of spite. He could not think straight now. He needed to get to the Campbell household quickly. If vengeance was what he could have from this then he would have it.

Agreus appeared to Claire and said, "Let us leave now!" He grabbed onto her and through the portal they went. In a moment they were in his home in the glen. She was alarmed, "What has happened my love?"

"The terrible creature would not listen to reason! He was going to come for you and kill you to hurt me. You are no longer safe in the human world. Your birthday is the day after tomorrow so not much longer to wait now," he held her closely, "I am sorry that this is happening love."

"I must return to your father to tell him of the nature of things and of the children. Stay here and you will be safe. No one can enter here unless I want them to, I will be back very soon," Agreus left soon after. Claire was tired so she lay down on the bed to sleep until he returned home. She had been here so many times before that she felt right at home in this place.

Agreus came to the giant hollow tree in the forest that led to the world of the elves. It looked like an ordinary tree but it was a portal to those who knew how to use it. He wasted no time in getting to the king.

"Your highness," Agreus said as he appeared in the giant throne room full of color and life, "I must tell you of the way things have become. The parasitic half elf would not deter from his path and now he hunts Claire to take her and the babes from me out of vengeance for his lost efforts."

Agreus also told the king everything he knew of the twins. The king was overjoyed at the uniqueness of the twins. Their would be a male heir for the throne! The other would be heir to Agreus' magic and responsibilities. How wonderful for everyone. Now they must protect Claire with full force until the time of the soul shift.

"Call the guard!" the king shouted with authority, "Have them surround the glen until the changing time is done!" the half elf would not be able to see any of them as elves have the ability to be invisible whenever they choose. They would stand guard until their princess was in form and in the kingdom where she belonged. Out through the portal they went into the magical glen to follow orders with pride for this moment. They each nodded with respect towards Agreus as they went.

Peter and Sandra had gone out for dinner that evening. Peter was trying to make things look especially good to her so that she would suspect nothing, and he knew that soon he would be with Sara forever so why not one last dinner out with his wife? Sandra was not fooled by all of this show Peter was putting on to make her believe they could reconcile. She felt more like a prisoner of circumstance and was sorry that she had ever met him. The only good that had come from their union was Austin. Getting to be his mother was the only thing that had made it worth it. Ayyn arrived at their house to take out his wrath upon them all but no one was home. He stewed with anger and decided to wait for their return. He looked around the house at all of the things he had furnished and spent money on for the girl to enjoy only to have the entire purpose of that ruined. The demigod had obviously taken Claire so he could not get to her yet but he would think of a way, he mused. He still had other methods that were unknown to the demigod or his elves. Now he would have to kill the entire order to maintain his secret. It would look like a mass cult suicide and in time people would forget it.

Agreus and the king were watching through the pool in the throne room. They first checked on Claire who was sleeping and safe. Now they were looking at Ayyn as he plotted to kill everyone that he had duped into believing him. Agreus would not allow him to deal anything out on them. He was going to do that himself. Ayyn was another matter. Lord Kefna wanted the honor of punishing the wicked half breed elf for being the cause of so much grief to his family. They devised a plan to stop Ayyn and separate Sandra from Peter, as well as take the other members of the Black Thorn Society. The members would be lured into a false meeting with Ayyn and gathered through Agreus' magical abilities. Sandra would be put to sleep and so would the devil's advocate, Peter. They would then be placed into separate magical chambers for questioning meant to bring out every strumpet of the truth. As for whatever the lord of the Allerians had planned for Ayyn, Agreus had not yet been told. He figured that his dear friend was devising something most appropriate for the evil pestilence that he had created.

Agreus appeared in the living room of the Campbell residence still invisible. He watched Ayyn for a moment as he brooded. With the words of an incantation spoken with authority, time stopped for Ayyn and he stood in the same position unable to do anything or know that anything was happening. Agreus whispered in his ear and he was transported into the magical chamber that would hold him until the time of sentencing. Through time and space his form was carried into this place of holding. He would wait there until his time had come. Next, he made a call from the Campbell household to every member of the Black Thorn Society. He caused his voice to sound like that of Peter's so no one questioned the emergency meeting being called in the old warehouse downtown. It was to be immediate. All should arrive as soon as they could possibly get there. In the meantime, Peter and Sandra arrived home from enjoying a nice steak dinner at their old favorite restaurant. It had been ages since they had been out. They came into the house and retired to the den for night caps and smoking. Agreus watched unseen as Sandra uncomfortably joined her husband. She was quite unsure of all of his intentions. The demigod whispered incantations into both of their ears and they were transported immediately to the magical questioning cells where worthiness of life would be determined through the truth. Agreus was satisfied with his efforts here. It was now time to herd the sheep.

The members were hurrying into the meeting place of their master. They awaited his arrival anxious to know what the fuss was all about. Each one had been told that Lord Ayyn must speak with them at once. They placed their dark robes on and hooded themselves to appear ready to do his will. Agreus appeared and took stock of all of the members. They had arrived and obeyed his command to wear the robes, *"sheep"* he though to himself of these pitiful creatures so blinded by the corruption they had chosen to follow. They were not necessarily under a spell to follow. They needed to obtain status and power; they were greedy and selfish. The worst part was they were going to sacrifice their own souls for their evil intentions and they did not even realize it. Unseen in their presence, he used an herbal blend that had been pounded into a powder. Pouring it into his hand he blew the substance onto them and said aloud the incantation to move them into the holding cell to await fate.

With all of this done, Agreus returned to the king to tell him it was accomplished as planned. He also expressed his need to go and see Claire. He expressed he would return very soon. The king agreed that he must go to her and then return to make sure the elven clerics were prepared for the summer solstice. Agreus departed from the realm of the elves to his own glen to check on his beloved. It was the now the day before her birthday.

He entered the cave as the vines closed behind him tightly and unbreakable. "My love?" Agreus called out for Claire.

"I am here," she said weakly, "I feel very ill, my dear."

He could tell she was suffering from the pregnancy. In her human form she was entirely more vulnerable to this sort of thing. When she was turned this would no longer bother her at all. He made a concoction of special roots and herbs and mixed it with water from the magical spring that billowed up from the ground in the glen then he bade her drink the potion he had made for her. Agreus helped her with the wooden bowl as she was very shaky now. Claire collapsed into his strong arms to rest. He felt her forehead. She was clammy and paler than usual. He lay there with her in his arms and held her as she slept it off. While she was still in her feverish sleep, he whispered to the babes and caused them to sleep as he surrounded her womb with magical protection.

Claire woke after a couple of hours to find that her handsome lover was still holding her to him as though he would lose her. She smiled up at him feeling much better from his intervention.

"Tomorrow is the day my dear," he whispered to her. "The day that I will make everything better forever," Agreus was ready to get it done.

"Yes, tomorrow is my birthday isn't it?" Claire could hardly wait for all of this to begin.

"You must eat for our little ones and yourself my darling," he instructed, "You slept for quite some time." He passed a hand over an empty plate and there upon it was fresh fruit and cheese for her to eat. She was always amazed at the things he could do.

"You are so wonderful, my love," she said to him smiling.

"No, it is you who are wonderful. You have saved me from an eternity alone without love and family," He kissed her cheek as she continued to eat.

"I must soon return to the king, but his guards surround the glen invisible to those who remain blind," he told her assuredly, "I must be sure the elven clerics are prepared properly for the ritual. They will be attending me during the rites and I promise you everyone there is ready to regain their stolen princess!" He smiled at her lovingly.

"The others in the kingdom besides my parents already love me?" She was amazed at this. No one had ever been so caring with her besides her fiance. "They are excited to have me return to them?"

"My dear, not everyone is like the evil people you have been exposed to," he reminded her. "The elves are the most honorable friends I have," Agreus said praising her people.

She was contented to know that soon she would have a family to love her and accept her just as she was and nothing needed proving when this rite was complete. Claire was indeed ready for the ceremony to be finished so that she would have everything and even more than she could have ever hoped for. Happiness did not come close to explaining what she was experiencing just thinking about meeting her parents for the first time and finally getting to marry the one whom she loved more than life. She rubbed her small hand over her belly where their children lay sleeping and smiled.

Agreus suddenly pulled her to him and gave her a long and passionate kiss that conveyed everything he felt for her within it. She kissed him back with such love that he thought he could die in her arms. He took her by the hand and led her to the opening of the cave to walk in the glen for a while. They walked along taking in the beauty of each flower and growing thing. He laughed lovingly as she marveled innocently at the magical pool of water that lay below the hidden waterfall there in the inmost part of the glen. She laughed at little fish trying to jump over one another for her attention at the water's edge. Unbeknownst to her, the elven guard was watching them. They knew once they saw her beauty and the aura that surrounded her, she was their princess and they were indeed happy that she was coming home to them all. The captain shed a tear at the thought of how happy his Lord and Lady would be at the sight of her. Claire could feel them; she gave a little smile at the unseen persons who were silently following orders. They each looked at one another nodding and smiling. Agreus and Claire spent many hours just laying in the grass and watching the cotton like clouds overhead in the bluest of skies. Today she tried to make little animals out of them and Agreus of course found himself amused at this and joined her. Sometimes they were silent as they lay there and just held each other. He was running fingers through her soft hair as she lay there with her little fingers resting on his bare, muscular chest. Nothing, it would seem could ruin their happiness he thought. They returned to the cave and he told her stories from the ages until they fell asleep.

The next day was spent enjoying each other's company until the sun began to lower in the skies with streaks of purple and pink as it went. Agreus knew that now he must leave Claire back in the safety of the cave and retrieve the clerics as well as everything needed for tonight. They walked slowly back to his home from roaming in their precious glen and once again the vines obeyed their master. With her safely tucked inside he left for the big hollow tree and entered the realm of the elves.

"Your majesty," Agreus greeted the king, "Where is our Lady this evening?"

"My Lord, she is retrieving the infant body from the tomb with her maids and a couple of sentries. She'll be along very soon, and how is our child?" Lord Kefna asked in earnest.

"She is very safe and can hardly stand another moment of being human!" Agreus smiled.

"Well, I can say I hardly blame her at all for that. They are such an dishonorable bunch these days. I am quite disappointed with the lot of them!" the king said with authority, "I just do not understand what has happened to them," He shook his head with eyes closed.

"Agreus, I have retrieved the little body for the ritual," Lady Ashana entered the throne room. "My maids are watching over her form until you are ready."

"Thank you My Lady," Agreus replied, "It shall be very soon. Just as soon as the clerics have brought everything I requested of them and are ready to follow me out through the great tree we can begin the preparations. Will you be in attendance tonight?" Agreus asked with a respectful tone. He knew this had been a very trying time for them.

"Yes, we would not miss this for anything, my lord," She gently bowed and exited to alert the clerics that it was time.

Shortly, she returned with the elven clerics all dressed in their green robes. They had with them all of the required spell material and the little wrapped body that should have been Claire's eighteen years ago.

"Agreus, my old friend, we shall follow very shortly. Please go on ahead and prepare everything," the king said insistently.

"Of course your majesty," Agreus ushered the clerics out of the throne room and into the hollow tree that would lead them to the other side where Claire waited.

The company of elves and the demigod entered the glen and headed for the cave where she was waiting for them. The moon was beginning to rise now.

"While I am getting her ready, begin the processes necessary for the rite. Make the circle and prepare the center stone" Agreus said as he approached the entrance to his home. Something was noticeably wrong upon first glance. His alarm was immediately raised as he noticed the vines were hanging loosely instead of tightly wound. He ran in and yelled, "Claire!"

Agreus entered the room to find that she was being held captive in the arms of the evil, dark half breed. She had tears streaming down her face as the monster held a dagger to her belly. He was entirely too big and strong for her to struggle free from.

"Move wrongly and I shall dispatch your entire family right here, demigod!" the dark one insisted, "I told you I would have my revenge on you for what you have chosen to deny me. Now I am thinking that once I have my immortality I shall have your bride for my own," Ayyn laughed as he licked her neck. Claire cringed at his touch.

"That will not happen you beast!" Agreus shouted as his eyes glowed bright green in anger.

The elven guard realizing something was not right ran into the cave to and stumbled upon the situation. They were in shock at what they saw.

"My lord," the captain was horrified, "I am so sorry! How could this "thing" have gotten past our defenses?" Indeed, this was most unusual for someone to escape the magical cells the elves had in the dungeon of the castle, and how had he managed to get into Agreus' house?

Expecting that someone may try some magic on him Ayyn had cast his own spell that would dispell their magic and transport him to the dwelling place of the one who had done it so that he may take vengeance. How convenient for him that it was the demigod who had made that mistake.

"I am sure this creature has been underestimated in some way," Agreus answered with concern showing on his face, "Alright you devil of a half breed! What shall it be then? If you hurt her or my children I shall personally oversee your torture for eternity!"

Ayyn laughed, "That may be true but right now I have what you most desire in all of the realms. You will help me gain my immortality and I will give you back what you want before I get too attached if you know what I mean," He ran a hand over her body as she cried out to be released.

She was feeling extremely violated by this thing that had helped to create her human shell. Once the ritual of soul shift was complete she would no longer bear any of him in her. The tie would be broken, *"I have to live first,"* she thought fearfully.

"That is right my dear," Ayyn said callously. "You have to live first if you want all of me out of you! The only one who can make that happen is your lover so look to him for mercy because I have none,"

He continued to hold her tightly as he was beginning to hurt her with his grip.

"Claire, just hold on my love, this shall be over soon," Agreus was fuming at Ayyn.

"Yes, Claire it shall all be over soon as your lover bows to my will," Ayyn smiled heartlessly.

"Your father was a Dulerian elf. It will be much easier to gain immortality for you. You must release her before anything can be done," Agreus hated him so much for making him do this.

"I do not think I will release her until it has been done. Do you really expect me to fall for that trick of yours?" Ayyn said slyly.

"As I said before, if only you had called out to a god or spirit instead of doing this . . . ," Agreus waved his hand in a circle above his head and said a strange incantation as he directed his hand in Ayyn's direction. Ayyn immediately felt warm all over and he knew he was receiving what he craved most: immortality.

As this was happening he let go of Claire who ran over to Agreus and buried her face in his side. She was still crying from the ordeal. As Ayyn was wholly transformed he smiled wickedly.

"Now I shall have my vengeance!" Ayyn cried aloud.

As he was saying this, a magical embrace came down around him. It was very tight and he could not move of his own free will any longer. The king stepped from the shadows.

"My boy, you have gained what you have most desired, but for your wickedness you will not enjoy it," the king said solemnly.

Suddenly, a dampening box formed around Ayyn and he was sent straight into the elven realm and placed 700 feet under the ground, surrounded by guards at all times. The historians took note of all that took place on this occasion.

"That dampening box will conceal him forever," the king said to Agreus, "His magic will not free him from it!"

Everyone rejoiced at the king's timely appearance. The elves, the demigod and Claire all ran out into the glen. The moon was rising high above in the darkened sky while the stars twinkled brightly on this summer solstice.

"Claire, now is the time my dear, lay upon the center stone as we make ready to begin," Agreus instructed her.

Agreus focused on what he was doing now. He was anointing Claire with a potion of special roots and flowers taken from the elven realm. The circle of light had been created already by the elven clerics. Now, one of them was holding the little form wrapped all in white that should have been her real body all of those years ago. They began to chant in a strange language that Claire did not yet understand. The seven clerics made a circle around her with Agreus at her head. She could feel others watching who began to appear to her as the rite was taking place. The king and queen were standing together watching fervently while the guard encircled the entire group in the glen. Claire could not talk at this moment. Agreus, through incantation was calling for the soul shift to happen. He took the form of the infant in white and held it over her. It began to glow as the clerics chanted in harmony. Agreus beckoned the body to join the soul on this night. Claire began to feel light headed as the infant form transformed into a whirling mist and encircled her body. She was changing, she could feel it. She knew her name was not Claire. It was her true name she was sensing . . . Kefshana. Her eyes began to see many things not visible before. Everything had a glow about it. She had mildly luminescent skin herself. The body and soul had now been joined. Agreus was finished with his ritual and the clerics all took a knee as did the guard. Kefshana sat up to look around her. Everyone was bowing to her! Her parents ran over and embraced their daughter for the first time as they cried with joy to be reunited. Her hair was as white as the lilies and her eyes were big dark pools that were encircled with the most lovely shade of lavender. Kefshana was looking at her arms as they were glowing with her pure nature. Agreus watched with loving eye. The guard and the clerics rose and gave a shout. After the Lord and Lady were contented to allow their child to stand up off of the center stone Agreus approached her. "My love . . . ?" He called to her.

She smiled at him, "My love!"

Kefshana or Ana as he began calling her ran over to throw her arms around her demigod. She bowed before him. He caught her up and said, "No, you never have to bow to me," She knew him now, who he was and what he was through and through, "What an honor to have you soon be my husband."

"What an honor to have you as a wife," They embraced for what seemed an eternity before the king was beckoning everyone to return to the palace for the entire tribe of elves to greet their princess. One of the clerics placed a royal robe over her shoulders to cover her until she could be properly attired. The group was all smiles and happily talking as they entered into their kingdom with Princess Ana and Agreus in tow. As they entered and passed in procession to the castle all of the elves in sight stopped and bowed at the announcement, "All hail the Princess Kefshana!" The village was all a flight with the momentous news of her return. They shouted and cheered with joy at the sight of the family that had been reunited.

A formal banquet would be held and the entire kingdom would be in attendance, but only after she had rested. The announcement of her upcoming marriage would be made by the king then. This would be tomorrow evening for her.

Ana was so happy she could hardly contain herself. She wanted to see everything and meet everyone. Agreus stopped her by saying, "My dear Ana it has been a very hard day for you and our little ones must rest."

"All right Agreus, my love I will wait until you say it is safe for me to do these things," She kissed him realizing it was the first time she had ever been able to use his full name.

Her parents kissed her and hugged her so tightly. The king then ordered the royal robes be brought to her chamber and made ready for her use. She would be formally given her circlet at the banquet for all to see.

Agreus accompanied her to her chamber to ensure that she was taken proper care of in her delicate state. Soon she was dressed for bed and he was putting her to sleep with his fingers in her hair. She drifted off into a deep and contented sleep.

Agreus returned to the throne room to speak with Ana's parents.

"So when is the wedding to be, your majesty? I am sure you know that I do not want to wait very long," Agreus said with anticipation.

"Anxious are we?" Lord Kefna asked grinning.

"Why, yes a bit anxious is a way of putting it, your majesty!" Agreus answered with a smile.

"My dear friend, you have given us back that which was wrongfully taken from us. We are forever in your debt, if we were not already. I will not delay the marriage very long at all. In fact, at the banquet tomorrow evening it will be announced along with her coronation. We are overjoyed at our Princess' return. She shall have all of our love and that of our kingdom's, as well," the king was beaming with gratitude.

Suddenly, the Lady Ashana reached out with both of her small hands to Agreus and he took them as she gave a bow to him. With teary eyes and a smile she said, "My lord, thank you so much," I have been a grieving mother for so long and now I have my daughter and soon two grandchildren," she kissed his cheek and excused herself from the throne room. She would finally be able to sleep through the night for the first time in a very long time.

"To business then?" the king asked of Agreus.

"To business!" Agreus knew exactly what his friend had in mind.

The elven holding rooms were in the lower recesses of the majestic castle. The two of them walked slowly down many passages talking of good tidings as they went to torture the wretches in their cages until they were fully satisfied that justice had been done. The dungeon itself was masked by a secret entrance way. Both Agreus and the king had knowledge of where it was, of course. This was not the first time that either of them had doled out a punishment or two in the lower recesses. They were smiling and making plans for the next evening when they entered the area they sought.

There were many guards here and that was a good thing. They may need someone extra to help out with details depending on what was going to occur in a few moments. Now was the time for dealing with the followers of Ayyn. He was dealt with and it was their turn to answer and be judged for the crime they were so willing to commit.

The king turned to the jailor with an intent look upon his face." Folgath, would you be so kind as to bring parchment and you do know the one I mean don't you?

"Yes, my lord," bowing low Folgath reached into a special box and pulled out a seemingly ordinary piece of parchment. It was not so ordinary though. In fact, quite the opposite was true. As the prisoners were questioned and punishment dealt out, the very page would record name, deed, and sentencing. This would then go to the historians for safe keeping.

"Well, into the holding chamber where those ridiculous people are cowering in their black robes," the king was laughing, "What do you have in mind for them my dear, Agreus?"

"You shall soon witness it first hand, your majesty," Agreus approached the cell and with a wave of his right hand it was opened.

Inside, the group of humans looked rather like a dark undulating mass in the back corner of the room. Agreus, being so tall, frightened them with his appearance. Never before had they encountered such a magnificent and terrifying creature. He was glaring at them in anger and they could feel his tangible rage reaching out to touch every single one of them. They all knew in their hearts that escape was not possible.

Two sentries entered at the behest of the demigod. They were instructed to line the sniveling prisoners up so that each may be dealt with individually. Each one would step forward to answer and be sentenced. Upon completion of this ordeal sentence would immediately be carried out. The two elves imposed with this duty could not help but to snicker softly as they entered the cell to assist with the upcoming wrath the nasty human offenders were about to experience. Fully armored with weapons in tow they stood one on each side of the row that led up to the front of the room where the judging would begin.

"Send the first one forward," Agreus said in a low voice.

A trembling man stumbled forward as he was poked sharply with a spear in the back. He was wondering, "Where am I? What are they going to do to me? What are they?" His name was Jonathan Smith. He had met Ayyn through business ties and thought much of him. Ayyn had such a way with words and after all, he had helped Jon climb the corporate latter.

"Your master was a wretch and has been dealt with accordingly. He was a criminal and deceived you all into believing you would receive immortality for helping him. It is not possible for that to happen and yet you believed his lies so readily. You believed him so much that you all were willing to kill an innocent young woman. For this crime against the king's daughter and my future wife I am going to sentence you in accordance with what would be fitting to animals such as yourselves," Agreus spoke with a flat tone.

All of the guilty were looking down at the floor considering what Agreus had just spoken to them. They knew he was right about their willing participation in the horrendous act they had nearly committed. Begging for mercy would not help them and so each one stepped forward and literally were judged for animals! The first man brought forward was scared and had a hard time facing Agreus so he was turned into a fowl. The next was extremely greedy so he was turned into a pig. This went on until they were all turned into a fitting creature. With no human memories or intelligence left they were indeed mere animals at this point so they would be placed in line for the dinner banquet tomorrow night and consumed by those in attendance.

"What a wonderfully fitting punishment you gave!" the king exclaimed, "Couldn't have done a better job myself! Folgath, please notify the head cook that he may send for the beasts to be prepared for tomorrow night's affairs."

"Yes, your majesty," with a low bow Folgath did as he was instructed.

Agreus was proud of the compliment even though he may not have seemed so at the time. He was still angry with the situation and had two more conspirators to handle. He nodded to the king and said, "Lord Kefna, I would like to check in on the princess before I deal with the others. I need to see that she is well."

"Of course, anything you wish," The king smiled as Agreus disappeared from view.

Agreus was concerned for Ana at all times. She had been through the most and he needed to ensure for his peace of mind that she was not dreaming feverishly as he suspected she may. He entered her room without a sound to observe her sleeping. She lay in a very lavish bed made from the finest wood and silken linens. They were royal blue and very soft indeed. He quietly walked around the bed and drew back the sheer curtains that encompassed it and then sat down without so much as an indentation in the down mattress. Ana was covered in a clammy dew that made her appear mildly ill. She was so beautiful in her royal attire but she could have worn leaves from a maple tree and still been just as lovely. He held her head as she continued to sleep peering at the dark dreams inside and they were just that, dark dreams. Agreus whispered soothing incantations into her ear and she immediately began to calm down and sleep well again. When he was satisfied with her well being he listened for the children in her womb. They too were in a perfect state of sleep at the moment and required no intervention, but he had known it would be this way. They had been protected from the evils of the human domain during the trials that had taken place. He must watch Ana carefully until the memory shift had been completed in the morning with her parents and the clerics. She would remember everything about this realm and become stable in it with full knowledge of her people and customs. This would seal any darkness out of her mind for good. She would begin to forget everything from the world of the humans rather quickly now. He took leave after kissing her forehead and returned to the lower area of the immense castle. Work was still awaiting him there.

Peter sat in a cell by himself. Measures had been taken to ensure that he would wake prior to his questioning so that he would be in ultimate fear and in darkness. Peter woke to find he was in some sort of room with stone walls. He was trembling and near tears as he tried to see any pinpoint of light.

"Help!" Peter shouted in terror when he realized there was no light to be found.

Suddenly, two glowing green eyes appeared in the darkness in front of Peter. He was instantly in a state of panic. What hell was this? What had he done to get here? He had the distinct impression that whatever those eyes belonged to meant him serious harm. He was right in that assumption, of course. Those eyes held within in them eighteen years of hatred that would soon be dealt with in this interrogation and sentencing of the wicked Peter Campbell. Slowly, a dim light without a seeming source began to emanate from inside the cell. As this was happening, Peter began to make out the form of what seemed to be a very tall man with black horns curved backwards on his head to whom the glowing green eyes belonged. He was very frightened at the one who stood before him. Peter could feel the malcontent coming from the stranger in the room.

"I see you have awakened," Agreus said in a flatly, "I had rather hoped you would have woke sooner to enjoy the darkness of the cell before I arrived. Luckily for you sleep lasted for much longer than I had supposed it would. How did you enjoy it?"

"I am not sure where I am or how I got here, sir," Peter managed to stammer out.

"You are here for crimes you have committed for the last eighteen years," Agreus grinned wickedly at Peter, "As for where you are and how you arrived it does not really matter now."

"Please sir, tell me what offense I have done and I will make it up, I swear!" Peter was confused and shaking.

"Peter Campbell, lowest filth of the human race, there is nothing that can be done to "make up" for your crimes," Agreus answered.

"Then may I know what it is that I stand accused of?" Peter was becoming mildly arrogant now.

"The king's daughter, everything you have done to her," Agreus reached out his hands and placed them on either side of Peter's head and performed a thought transference of everything that was relevant against him and how things actually were instead of how Peter had thought they were.

When this process was over, Peter slumped to the floor with wide eyes. He could not believe everything that he had just learned and now he realized why this creature was so angry with him. Peter's fear could not be any fuller at this point. He was in shock at the deception that had enveloped him for so long. The thought of how he had treated the girl produced some guilt now.

"Am I in hell?" Peter asked.

Agreus threw back his head and laughed, "No Peter, I am not the devil or anything close. However, I do believe you might be meeting him sooner than you think," A strange ball of glowing light appeared and hovered over Peter's head.

"Shall we begin?" Agreus prepared to interrogate the prisoner.

"What?" Peter barely was able to ask as the ball of light made a semi-circle around his head.

"What's happening?" Peter wet himself.

"I am going to ask you some questions and you are going to give an answer. If it is not truthful then the device around your head will cause severe pain. So, do you understand how this works?" Agreus asked grinning again.

"Yes, I think so," Peter knew he was in a load of trouble.

"Why did you follow Ayyn, the dark elf and his evil plot?" Agreus asked the first question.

"I don't know why I did at first. I was bored with everything, I guess. He offered me something that I believed would make life worth living again. He said I could start over with everything including a new wife. If you knew mine you would understand," Peter shook his head.

"I do know your wife, she discovered long ago what you have been up to all of this time and she knows you sold her out to Ayyn for his usage. I suppose that would be enough to make a wife dislike her filthy husband. As for what you and the others wanted to do she knew that and it drove her a bit mad. Also understandable, as well as your continued infidelities with the woman called Sara. She knew that, too. She saw you and Sara together. Why would you do that to the woman you married?" Agreus was so ready for this to be over.

"Ayyn helped me move up in my company. He was responsible for a lot of the success that I had. He said I owed him and I would become immortal with him. I was bored in my marriage. I figured Sandra would never discover the truth and he promised to make her forget. No harm done. That is what he said," Peter knew nothing he said really mattered as far his punishment went.

"Why did you treat the girl the way you did all of those years?" Agreus' eyes narrowed.

"I really don't have a reasonable answer for that. I suppose it is because she was a pawn and nothing more. If I had cared about her it would have been hard to dispose of her in the way that had been agreed upon. That really is the only thing I can say. It makes me a horrible person but I was going to get what I wanted at any cost," Peter was resigned.

"Well at least you admit it freely," Agreus was disgusted, "It is nearly time for your punishment to begin but if it even matters to you I think you should know that Ayyn was the one who arranged your son's accident. He did it so that you would have no one to hold you back when the time came. Also, he was intent on killing Sandra and never letting you know," Agreus began to turn around and walk towards the door.

"What, what did you say? He killed my son!" Peter became hysterical. "That bastard! I did so much for him!" He was crying now.

Agreus turned and faced Peter. He was trying to decide whether to have him tortured horrendously first or just kill him with his bare hands now. Maybe, torture and then kill him. As he was considering these things he felt Ana wake up.

"Call in the specialists," Agreus spoke to a guard near the cell, "He is to be severely tortured, but not killed. I will handle that after the torture has taken place for a period of three days. For now, I must attend to my future bride."

Momentarily, Peter was being carried off to a "special" room for certain "procedures" to commence. He screamed the entire way but to no avail because no one cared. The specialists were all too eager to get their hands on the wretch for his part in what had been done to their princess all of this time.

It was just after dawn now. Agreus was standing in Ana's room as she was stirring about. He walked over and kissed her forehead as he sat down beside her. She smiled up at him.

"Good morning," Ana said still smiling.

"Good morning to you, my love. After you have had time to wake properly and have breakfast your parents and the clerics will be making ready for the memory shift to take place. While this is happening I will be away attending to my duties, but I will return shortly. Please do not venture out to do anything without your parents until I return to check on you and our little ones, ok?" Agreus looked at her sincerely.

"Of course, my love." Ana said compliantly, "I will be very careful and I will wait for your return before I go frolicking about!" Ana laughed.

Agreus smiled at her and laughed, too. He loved her playful nature and he could barely stand another day without a wedding. Ana was his world and soon the children would come and they would be complete. He placed his head on her belly where the children were. They were hungry and wide awake.

"I will send for your breakfast and maids to attend to you, darling." Agreus left the room and shortly thereafter three young elven maids entered the room all smiles. They were honored to attend to their princess.

Meanwhile, the king and queen were already preparing with the clerics for the rite of memory shift. They would send for Ana when everything was ready to begin.

"Oh, I am so excited my dear, to finally be able to share everything with our daughter!" the Lady Ashana was ecstatic, "This is the most wonderful thing."

"Yes my dear, I too am extremely happy about it!" Lord Kefna was smiling from ear to ear.

Three clerics stood by preparing the proper incantations and listening blissfully to their happy leaders. They were very glad that this day had come. They wanted everything to be just perfect for the princess when she arrived.

Shortly, Princess Ana entered the sacred chamber escorted by her maids. She was dressed in the most beautiful yellow gown and slippers. She sparkled with radiance. The king and queen stood up to greet their lovely daughter while the clerics bowed before her. The maids were excused from the room to attend to Ana's chambers and linens.

"My darling girl! How wonderful to see you looking so well this morning!" the king held her small face in his hands and looked upon her adoringly.

"My child," the queen held out her arms for Ana.

"Mother!" she ran into her mother's arms and held her and was joined by the king.

After the family embraced for a few moments, the clerics announced that all things had been properly prepared for the ceremony.

"Come Ana, it is time for you to know us and your people," The king and queen held her hands as they stood in a circle.

The elven clerics began to rub a potion on their foreheads and the tops of their hands. Then the clerics began to chant in a rhythmic pattern as they recited the incantation. The king and queen joined them. Ana began to see flashes of things that had happened. She began to know the ways of the tribe. She even felt the emotions from her parents. She was receiving the knowledge that she should have had all of this last eighteen years. She felt warm and happy. All was right with her and her family now. As the ceremony concluded her father and mother hugged her once more.

"Shall we walk for a moment or two in the garden?" the king asked smiling.

"That would be lovely," Princess Ana was delighted.

"How are the little ones this morning Ana?" the queen asked.

"They are more than fine. I can feel them growing! They will be wonderful children," Ana beamed with a soon to be mother's pride.

The king bent over and was talking to her stomach. He was cooing over his grandchildren.

"Oh, my dear stop that!" the queen said laughing at him.

"They like it. They will know the sound of my voice when they come into this world!" he was giggling at the idea of having to babies to make a fuss over.

Ana was so pleased at the idea of having such a loving family. She smiled at her father acting so silly. After a walk in the garden and some lunch with her parents she felt the need to lay down. Ana's maids were called to assist her to her room and into bed for a nap. She was soon fast asleep and waiting on Agreus to return. She slept peacefully. All of the darkness was gone from her mind.

Agreus walked in the glen. He was checking on all of the growing things and the situation of the trees as well as what had been his home for so long. He would still use it when he was here, but now he was going to be sharing a new home with his soon to be wife. Agreus smiled to himself about everything. She was not showing yet but the babies were growing. He knew it each time he talked to them. He could sense it. Agreus continued to walk along checking on the animals and the hidden waterfall with it's clear pool and happy little fish. When he was assured that his duties were completed he returned to the realm of the elves. He did not know it but the king had ordered several suits of clothing and slippers for him as well.

"My dear Agreus," the king welcomed him back, "The banquet will be starting in little while. Here are some wonderful outfits for you to choose from for the evening."

"Your majesty?" Agreus was confused, "I have never worn such items, I will look silly."

"My lord, if you do not wear one of them you will look silly considering that everyone including Ana will be dressed formally," the king reminded him, "Don't forget that your wedding will be announced this evening."

Agreus raised an eyebrow at the outfits. He knew it was the right thing to do so he did not argue further. He gave the king a grimace as he went to try them on. The king smiled knowing this had to be extremely odd for the demigod of the forest. He also knew he would do anything for Ana. The king was chuckling to himself.

These outfits were made of the finest materials that were possessed by elf kind. Agreus was honored but felt ridiculous while trying them on. He finally settled on one of the more subtle, neutral colored suits. He looked at himself in the giant mirror in this changing room. It really was not so bad of an outfit at all. Agreus knew he would be just fine in it this evening. The slippers were ridiculous but they were comfortable. He continued to ready himself and then went up to Ana's room to see that she was awake and ready to be escorted down to the great banquet hall.

"Ah, what a handsome devil you are!" Ana exclaimed as he entered into her chambers. She was marveling at him in his "outfit." She walked hurriedly towards him and embraced him lovingly. "I missed you terribly today. I am so glad you are back," Ana kissed his lips gently.

"I missed you just as terribly, my love," Agreus was admiring her in the beautiful lavender gown that so perfectly matched her eyes and made them stand out so well.

"You are a sight to behold," He held her hands and pulled her close to him. She smelled of lavender as well. "My dear, are you ready for your suitor to escort you to the banquet being held in your honor?" he smiled at her.

"Why, thank you for the generous offer," She laughed a little at there pretend formalities. Ana took his hand as he guided her down the stairs to the massive banquet hall. They entered to find others arriving. The king and queen were seated at there proper stations and motioned for Ana and Agreus to join them.

"My word!" the king exclaimed, "You looked very charming Agreus.

"Thank you your Highness," Agreus and the king shared a smile.

"My daughter is the picture of radiance this fine evening!" Agreus, you are so lucky to have such an exquisite future bride," the king bragged.

"Yes, I am the lucky one," he looked lovingly at his fiance.

"Oh, now I should be so honored by your compliments but I am the one who should thank her lucky stars for Agreus!" Ana laughed and blushed at everyone making a fuss over her. She was feeling much better but she was still not used to anyone making a big deal over her, especially in a positive manner. Her memories of the other world were fading and she could no longer recall the faces of the ones who had been there. She was glad of this. Ana did not want to be haunted by terrible memories and at the moment some wonderful ones were being made. She leaned over and kissed both her mother and her father.

The king and queen were happy she had responded so well to all of the changes that had been made in her life. They too were looking forward to her marriage and their grandchildren.

A lovely banquet was laid out before them and everyone had arrived. The king was calling for everyone to rise.

"Everyone arise to greet your princess!" the king shouted happily as a cleric hurried over with a green velvet pillow. Upon it was the most beautiful golden circlet that had been made for Princess Ana. The cleric stood directly behind her awaiting the king's instructions.

"As you all know, we have regained that which was taken from us and gained a future son-in-law. The fact that he is a demigod is just a perk," they all giggled at this. "Now, my daughter, will have her circlet placed upon her head to signify her royalty," The king nodded to the cleric to place it upon her head. As he did so everyone in the room bowed to the royal family.

"Now let us have a shout of joy for the Princess Kefshana's return!" The king was delighted in this moment.

Everyone shouted with happiness at their good fortune. The kingdom was once again whole. The king remembered to announce when the wedding between his daughter and the demigod would take place, "Tomorrow evening vows will be exchanged in our customary way at the wedding of my beautiful daughter and her soon to be husband, Agreus," the king exclaimed with all authority. Another shout of joy was issued forth from the crowd gathered for the feast.

Everyone in the kingdom knew the story of Ana and Agreus and how things had come to be as they were. They were so happy for the both of them. It was a fairy tale come true for the lovers. Everyone knew she would soon begin to show with her darling babies. They were all excited to meet the little ones. The kingdom knew how happy the king and queen were over the entire affair. Even if this was a little outside of how things were usually done there was, after all, very good reason for everything that was now taking place and their subjects looked upon this all as a blessing. It was meant to be this way.

"Without further delay, let the feast begin!" the king commanded.

Everyone began to feast and dance as the elven musicians played. There was an air of pure joy and innocence here. No one had ill will towards anyone. The other elves were truly happy for each other's success when it happened; there was no greediness or jealousy. It was all so amazing.

"My I have this dance?" Agreus reached for Ana's hand and bowed to her as she curtsied to him.

As they danced, they gazed into eachother's eyes like star-struck lovers. They must have danced and feasted for hours with everyone else doing the same before Agreus saw how tired his Ana was becoming.

"Your majesties, Ana has grown tired. May we be excused so that I can see to her needs now?" Agreus asked very politely.

"My lord, of course. We must not wear out the soon to be mother of your children," The king gave permission for them to be excused. As they were leaving the room everyone bowed and then resumed what they were doing.

"Agreus, I feel quite faint, darling. I believe I have over excited myself." Ana said with shallow breath.

"Soon we shall be in your chambers and I will see to it that you are properly taken care of. I must check on the children as well," Agreus held her close to him as they ascended the stairs. He did not want to take a chance of her falling.

Upon entry to her room he asked her maids to bring sleeping attire and everything she would need for her bath. After they had complied he bade them to leave. He was going to take care of her this evening.

"Thank you for staying with me until bedtime, my love." Ana said with a sleepy smile.

"I would not have it any other way, my sweet," Agreus began to bathe the elven beauty that belonged to him.

After she was dressed for bed, he helped her to get comfortable and as she lay there looking at him he became very serious with her. "Ana, I love you so much. If anything were to happen to you."

"Nothing is going to happen to me or the children," she smiled, "I love you with all of my heart and I am here."

He held her to him and kissed her, "You need your rest and I must return to the king, my love." He used his magical fingers in her hair as he had always done to put her to sleep. He laid his head on her belly and listened for the children. They were having a dance of their own! He asked them to sleep so their mother would rest now. They obeyed their father, at once. He smiled as he thought of them.

"Tomorrow is our wedding, and we will never be parted," He delighted in this thought. If anyone tried to come between the two of them they would pay with their life!

Agreus returned to the dungeon after changing into his usual clothing. Now, it was time to wake the woman called Sandra. He was not sure what to do with her quite yet. She had been a victim in all of this, too but also a perpetrator of pain, as well. People had a saying, *"Hurting people hurt other people,"* but he was not a human so this saying was of no consequence to him. Now that Claire was Ana, she was no longer human either. Agreus felt this human belief was of no more consequence to her. He would soon be her husband and she would do anything for him and he knew that. She would have agreed with whatever decision he made regarding the humans. This was his belief on the matter. There was absolutely no need to bother her with these things. It would only remind her of what they had put her through. It angered him to think of it. Agreus had been considering letting Sandra live after some punitive action but he was thinking differently now.

Agreus entered Sandra's cell and woke her with a whisper.

"Where am I?" she asked him.

"You are in a very special prison, Sandra." Agreus answered with no sympathy.

"What have I done?" she implored.

"Hmmm, it is more about what you have not done as opposed to what you have done. See, mothers and fathers are supposed to care for their children. Now, Sandra why do you suppose you are in this special prison?" Agreus waited for an answer.

"Where is Claire?" Sandra was shaking.

"Claire? There is no more Claire. She is now the beautiful elven princess she was always meant to be. She is no longer your concern but mine and her true parents," Agreus was grinning wickedly, "However, while she was in your care you omitted your responsibilities and caused heartache. Your heart was cold to her and so was that devil Peter's. He has been dealt with already so you have no need to worry about him."

"Please, let me go! I never wanted to be a mother to her. It was done to me without my . . . ."

Agreus cut her off, "Sandra I know all about that and I am not moved with compassion for you. Instead of treating her like the innocent child she was you abused and neglected her. Your reasons are immaterial to me. What was I saying about you being heartless?" Oh yes, I remember now," with that he drove his hand into her chest and removed her still beating heart from her body, "You will not be needing this as it has been of no use to you where the mother of my children is concerned."

Sandra slowly slumped to the floor as she died. Agreus was happy with his decision. The heart caught fire and was consumed. He snapped his finger and her body disappeared as her soul was dragged to the underworld. He was so excited for these wicked things to be gone that he entered the special room where Peter was being flayed alive. It was made to be that he could not die from torture so that it could last as long as they wanted it to.

"I have decided to cut short your torture, Peter," He was in a state of shock and did not respond.

The elven "specialists" stepped back to allow room for Agreus to do whatever he had on his mind to do.

"You see Peter, my wedding is tomorrow and I can not go through it happily knowing you still breath," Peter's eyes were trembling back and forth.

Agreus drove his hand into Peter's chest and removed his heart. It too, caught fire and burned in front of him before the light flickered from his eyes.

"Well, my friends, now you have more time to focus on "other" things," Agreus grinned at the two elves that had been torturing Peter. They gave back a wicked grin and bowed as they turned to refocus their work. Agreus, once again, snapped his fingers and the body was gone. He watched as Peter's tortured soul was dragged off to the underworld.

No one was ever punished here that did not deserve it. The punishment was always befitting of the crime. Agreus walked out of the dungeon and sent a mental message to the king of the Allerian elves, Lord Kefna, "It has been done, your majesty."

"Ah, good," the king murmured out loud.

"What dear?" the queen asked looking at her husband.

"Oh yes, the banquet has been quite an event and now off to bed very soon dearest," the king insisted.

Everyone was bowing and making there good evenings. After the last of them had left the castle the king met with Agreus out on the main balcony in the courtyard.

"So, it is over with?" the king was ecstatic.

"Yes, your majesty. It has all been completed and I am satisfied with the outcome.

"Oh, this is happy news!" the king exclaimed, "We can proceed tomorrow evening with the wedding without any of that business still hanging around. Wonderful, my lord," the king was grinning from ear to pointy ear, "I must be off to bed. I need my beauty rest," With all said the king departed happily and Agreus stood looking out over the courtyard that would soon be decorated for him and his bride. No one would know if he slept in her room tonight. He felt the need to be close to Ana right now. He made it appear as though he were not there. Only visible to Ana, he climbed into bed with her. He pulled her to him and they slept peacefully, entwined with one another. He was smiling in the dark at the things he had done to those disgusting humans. It really made him happy to avenge her in this manner. After all, being a Pan, it was in his nature to do such things from time to time.

The sun was just coming over the horizon when Ana woke from a very refreshing sleep. Agreus was still there for only her to see and she was happy that he was there, indeed. She rolled over and grabbed him playfully, "Wake up my dear! Today is our day!"

"Yes it is, I am already awake and have been watching you for some time now. You slept very peacefully," He was glad she could finally rest. "I must get out of your room before I am discovered. I love you. Allow me to fetch your maids for your breakfast," He knew she had to eat more often now. Carrying a demigod's child will take the strength out of you, let alone two at once!

"Alright, I will be waiting to see you this evening. I know they will not want us together until the wedding ceremony is to begin," She looked at him with a wanton expression.

"Tonight my darling," He kissed her forehead and left her quarters. Soon her maids were entering.

"Good morning Princess!" They all bowed as they began attending to her.

After Ana had eaten a wonderful breakfast and was properly dressed she was to be taken to the dressmaker for final fittings and then off to have her beautiful hair dressed for this occasion. All of this would take quite some time to accomplish. She still had to be adorned with the finest jewels and made a fuss over while the courtyard was being prepared in traditional elven decoration.

Agreus went to attend his duties in his forest, but would return before time to be dressed in the traditional garb of a husband of such magnitude as to be marrying the princess. His glen was so beautiful and he knew that it meant just as much to Ana as it did to him. They would still spend plenty of time together here. He was glad that all of the offenders were gone for good. Agreus wanted nothing to be on his mind that was not of a happy nature. He knew once the wedding party was over they would be given several days alone to just be together without interruption. He was daydreaming of what his sons were going to be like as he walked throughout the forest and glen attending to anything that was needed and generally making sure it was still safe from outsiders. His duties did take most of the day but he returned to the elven realm earlier than he usually would have. After all, it was his wedding day.

"Agreus, my old friend," the king said, "I see you are returning from your responsibilities."

"Yes, it has been a very good day in the forest," Agreus responded.

"Good, now let's get you dressed for your wedding!" the king smiled.

Agreus raised an eyebrow at him in fun. He was not accustomed to wearing elven costume but he was not protesting. Soon he was the best dressed of all the men in the kingdom short of the king himself.

"Come. Let us go and walk in the garden while we await the ceremony, my lord," the king asked of Agreus.

"Of course your majesty," Agreus was honored to walk with his friend and his soon to be father in law.

"I know you love my daughter and she loves you. I wish you both all of the happiness in this world," Lord Kefna was tearing up, "I just wish she had grown up here."

"Come now, she is home and all is well. Do not be sad but grateful that she is here and remembers nothing from before. She only knows you and your lovely wife as her parents. Only your customs and memories are with her now," Agreus comforted Ana's father.

"Of course you are right, my dear Agreus. Thank you for everything," the king wiped away his tears.

The two of them walked to the lavishly decorated courtyard. It was stunning. Everything glistened and had an ethereal glow about it. All of the tribe had turned out for this momentous occasion in their history. Elves were taking their seats. Ushers were attending those who were in need of assistance. Those in service of every kind to the castle were setting up and making last minute adjustments. Everything was to be more than perfect for the daughter of the king. At last, the time had come for everyone to take their places as the sun set behind the trees. Agreus walked forward to stand at the front where the chief cleric was awaiting him. He nodded to him and smiled. The king entered the room set up outside where his daughter was awaiting his escort down the sparkling isle.

As he entered his mouth fell open in amazement at her beauty. Her hair was pulled up with a few lose wavy strands with silver intertwined. Small lavender flowers were placed perfectly. Ana's dress was shimmering silver with lavender and emerald embroidery. It billowed out like a soft cloud with each movement she made. Small slippers of the same colors in her dress were on her feet and the jewels around her neck were of the purest emerald to match her wedding ring. There could be no one more angelic in his sight than his child. He began to cry and embraced his daughter. Lady Ashana was also present. They were both crying with tears of joy.

"My dear, you are a sight never seen in all of existence," the king said weeping.

"Father, mother I love you both so much that I know not how to express it to you. I am honored to have you as my parents. I never thought that I could be so happy, but I am," Ana said embracing her parents one last time before she was the wife of Agreus.

Ana's mother left the room to take her place in the front row. All of the elves chosen to attend as bridesmaids and groomsmen were standing in place. A lovely song began to be played by the elven musicians as the curtains drew back to reveal the bride to be. Everyone rose to their feet and made a bow as the proud king and his daughter made their way down the isle.

As Ana was walking, she glanced around at the loveliness of everything and much to her amazement saw tiny fairies flitting here and there. Obviously, she still had many discoveries to make here in her realm. In time, she would discover everything it had to offer. She gazed at Agreus waiting for her at the end of the isle. He was handsome whether he believed it or not. She knew he did not like to put on these types of attire. She smiled at him.

They reached the alter and the king kissed Ana's cheek and gave her hand to Agreus. He took his seat next to his own wife to watch with her. The cleric began the ceremony by placing especially made rings of vines and leaves upon both the heads of Agreus and Ana to represent the purity of their union. Ana no longer spoke anything but the language of the elves now. All of the horrible memories had faded into the distant past. She was truly the elven princess she was meant to be. With joined hands, the happy couple took turns expressing their love for each other. The ceremony was blessed by the cleric and the marriage was complete. The handsome couple kissed gently and turned to face the guests. Everyone gave cries of joy as the wedding party exited down the isle.

A dining area had been set up in the garden for everyone to feast and dance. Agreus escorted his bride. Even though there were many in attendance they saw only each other in this moment. The king and queen looked on with contentedness in their faces. Soon everyone joined in the dancing and revelry. Bacchus himself would have enjoyed this great affair!

For the feast, plenty of pork, fowl, roasted venison and many other items most succulent had been prepared for the guests. Late into the night they made merry until the princess and her husband asked to be excused. Permission was granted by the king and soon everyone else was making their way home.

Agreus and Ana returned to her quarters just for tonight. They were happy to finally be alone. They made the most of their privacy.

When they had contented themselves in each other's arms they fell into a happy sleep. They would belong to each other forever now.

Many months past and the happy couple were now in there dwelling. The children had just been born. Agreus held his sons with pride. He was beaming with a father's love. After he handed them to the nurse maid he kissed his wife's forehead.

"You did very well my dear!" he held her.

"Finally, our babies are here! Mother and father will want to see them soon," Ana was quite sure of this.

"They shall come to visit us all very soon but for now, rest," Agreus had everything he could have ever wanted and so did Ana. They talked about how the children would grow and how their lives would be prosperous and happy.

Meanwhile, something stirred deep within the earth. Seven hundred feet below the ground there was an evil seeping into surrounding land. The dampening box was indeed effective at holding it's prisoner, Ayyn Kelfinaar, but it could not contain his evil essence forever. The pure earth was now becoming tainted and poisoned by the monster it concealed. He was far more powerful and malicious than anyone had given him credit for. He was perfecting his dark magic inside the box and becoming stronger with each passing year. After all, he had memorized the dark book and he did what he could with this knowledge from his confined space. He carried a secret with him that the others were unaware of and it would be the ruination of them all. Time went on and Ayyn continued to grow in his evil and his thirst for vengeance.

"One day I shall have it . . ." Ayyn smiled wickedly in the darkness.

Soul Shift: Rise

Ayyn sat in the dark pondering all of the many devices of destruction he might dole out upon those who had dared to imprison him. What had he ever done to any of those wretches any how? His business was well in order until that demigod and those high and mighty elves had gotten in his way. Ayyn had not forgotten any of this during the many centuries he had been in his would be eternal tomb, but soon that was to change and he would have his revenge on them all. He would gain much from his efforts here in this world. He was very sure of this. After all, had he not had all of the time he needed to scheme and prepare for the day when he was freed from this hellish cage? Continually, his black and shadowy poison had been seeping into the ground and was directed to his kinsmen: the tribe of Dulerian elves on the other side of the vast forest. This evil was already hard at work within the council's ranks in their unstable kingdom.

Ulenn and Athulenne were sitting on the little stone bridge that rose above the stream beneath. Ulenn's twin sister loved to watch the fish as they playfully chased each other in the clear, bubbling water. He liked watching her watch them. She was the most fetching of the dark elven beauties in their tribe. Many of her would be suitors were out of luck. There father sat on the council. It would be absurd for her to marry a commoner.

"Lu, are you nearly done with your fish watching?" Ulenn asked impatiently, "We still have to walk home and we are losing the light dear sister." He had never called her by her entire name. Ulenn preferred the affectionate pet name he had given his sister.

The pair were nearly inseparable and he was of a jealous nature with those who admired her. Many times their father had told him it was not natural for a brother to favor his sister quite so much. It seemed that he was taken with her rather than looking out for her best interests and protecting her honor. Ulenn always denied such accusations but deep down he knew he loved his sister better than anyone could. This meant he would find it extremely difficult to marry and have children with the elven girl his family had chosen for him. He had been growing very angry at being forced to do something that he was not happy doing. Bitterness had risen inside of him against his father for insisting that the arranged marriage should continue to take place. It was supposed to happen in a few months but he was going to find a way out of it. Ulenn knew his sister was unaware of his feelings for her but he could not hide them forever.

Utenn Seyennes was Ulenn and Athulenne's father. When he retired from his council position Ulenn was supposed to take his seat. That would be impossible if he disgraced his people by not going through with his marriage to another council member's daughter. She was delightful enough but he did not feel the way someone should towards a mate.

"Ulenn?" Lu looked at her brother who appeared to be somewhere else entirely. "I am ready now, my brother. Let us go home before we have trouble for being late again."

Agreus and Ana were taking their usual daily walk in the magical glen where they first met. She loved to attend his walks in the forest and help with his duties. She mostly just kept him company. The two of them were inseparable even after all the centuries that passed. To them time was nothing but an idea that could not touch them. Their children were now grown into men and learning the positions in life they would be responsible for holding. Agrieness was the twin who was like his father and Kashenn was the elven twin. He would inherit the responsibilities of his grandfather when the time had come.

"Father!" Agrieness was in the forest with them, "I have done all you have asked of me."

He was beaming with pride at his accomplishments. He wanted nothing more than to become the Pan his father expected him to be.

"Ah, my son you make me very happy," Agreus hugged his grown son as though he were still a boy.

Agreus intended to retire his duties to this young one so he could enjoy his time with Princess Ana. He loved his beautiful, little wife more than anything. The time was fast approaching when this would happen so Agrieness must be ready and capable of the duties a caretaker of nature must know how to appropriate accordingly. Agreus was confident that his son would have no trouble with anything at all. He was clever and intelligent and was the near image of his father. Agrieness was in the process of learning to use the magical powers that resided inside of him already. With a bit more practice he would have it perfected.

Ana was proud of her family as well. Agrieness was a constant reminder of his father and always a source of constant joy. Kashenn was equally a delight. He was a handsome elf who resembled her mother's side of the family and had plenty of powers of his own. His grandfather, Lord Kefna, King of the Allerians, was teaching him to use his elven magic for the good of the kingdom when he would rule in his stead.

All seemed to be going quite well in the beautiful kingdom where they lived and made merry with family and friends. There had been no trouble for centuries and it had quite been given over to the archives to remember alone.

Soon, these three would enter the hollow tree which was not just a tree but a magical portal back home. Ana wanted to stop and speak to the little fish that she had always been amused by in the hidden pool. She began walking the narrow path to the hidden waterfall that emptied into the pool of water with a smile resting on her porcelain face.

"Agreus, I won't be long," Ana called out in her elven tongue.

"Be careful my dear," Agreus was always overprotective of her.

Father and son continued attending the latter's lessons as Ana made her way to the water's edge. She bent over to call the little ones in the water to come to her as they always did. They seemed to be hesitant to heed her voice today. She was dangerously close to getting her emerald colored dress and slippers wet now. She took a step back and wrinkled up her brow to consider the difference in the fish and what could be causing it.

Suddenly, she was grabbed and whisked away. It was as though she was in a whirlwind that could not be escaped.

"Agreus, Agrieness!" The princess called out but no one answered. Everything was so deafeningly loud in this vortex of wind.

The sound of howling winds ceased and died down. She looked around and did not recognize her whereabouts. Ana was suddenly overcome with fear. She was without the one thing that she new she could depend on and that was her family. Had they even seen what had happened to her? She took a few steps and noticed a lit torch ahead on a stone wall. She began to move forward through cobwebs and tried to breath in the dank air of this musty room. It would seem that no one had been here in a very long time. In a moment, a tall figure appeared ahead of her but she could make out no features except that he appeared to have the outline of a tall elf.

"Excuse me my lord, will you help me? I seem to have had something terrible happen," Princess Ana implored of the stranger.

"Ah and who is this lovely creature before me that I may be of service to?" Ayyn called back from the darkness.

"I am Princess Kefshana or Ana if you prefer. I am the princess of the Allerian elves. Where am I? One moment I was walking with my husband and one of my sons and the next thing I knew I was here in this room of some sort. They will be terribly worried about me," Ana said wary of this stranger, "What is your name?"

"Ah my lady, nothing to fear. I will help you to sort out this mishap. I am Ayyn Kelfinaar, soon to be king of the Dulerian elves of this land. You must live on the other side of the forest," Ayyn replied in a cool tone.

He had not become king yet, though he had a seedy plan in place to make that happen. Now that he had escaped that horrid box and gotten his hands on his princess he could take the next steps needed to secure the throne. It would take some time but he did not mind at all because he would need that time to hide Ana away and use his magic to convince her he was her intended and make her forget all about the others. Also, he would need to thoroughly take over this place and people. Their alliance and recognition of him as king would be needed to successfully defeat the Allerian elves if they dared attack the city at some point. They would if they found out where their little princess was being hidden away. Maybe he wanted this. Maybe a final showdown with her demigod and he could sleep again. Ayyn seethed with rage at her family but hid it very well.

Ana had heard of the Dulerian elves but had never met one. She was told they could be quite underhanded at times and helpful at others. It just depended on their moods at the time. The Allerian elves kept mostly to themselves to avoid disputes with their more unstable cousins. How odd that she should be here now.

"My lord, I am at a loss for words. It would seem some magical force or otherwise has sent me unwittingly into your kingdom. For this I apologize. I must return to my kingdom at once or I fear there shall be trouble," Ana was unnerved at this strange unfolding of events. What could it possibly mean?

Finally Ayyn stepped out of the shadows and lit a torch on the wall behind her. He was very tall for an elf. She noticed that he was strikingly handsome with caramel skin and the bluest eyes she had ever seen. His hair was very white and shimmered in the light. He was also very well built in his figure for an elf with muscular tone and a commanding presence that accompanied him. She blushed a little for the fear that he might have noticed her looking at him for too long without saying anything. Ayyn smiled at her and led her from the room through a door that seemed to appear from no where in the stone wall in front of them. There was plenty of light within this room. It was well adorned and a table was set with a feast.

"My lord, where are we? I must return home," Ana protested.

"Yes my dear, home is where you shall be soon enough. For now please enjoy this meal with me. I have no one to dine with. Then I will be happy to have you home," Ayyn said. He was hiding his meaning of course. He intended for home to be in the castle he was taking over and by then she would not remember hers. Ayyn's room was a sort of magic bubble that others would not take notice of. In the foods that he had placed upon the very decorative table was a forgetfulness potion that he had managed to instill into each dish at her end of the table and also in the wine.

"Well, I suppose I must not be rude to my host. I will dine with you and then you will help me to return? I am sure my clerics can figure out what sort of thing could have caused my transportation here. There should be no need to trouble your people with this," Ana said earnestly.

"Thank you for accompanying me to dinner. It is an honor to meet such a lovely princess as yourself. I am sorry you ended up in the lower regions of the castle. It has not been used for such a long time and is not worthy to have such a flower hidden in it's recesses.

"You flatter me, my lord. Thank you for agreeing to help me. I am glad it was a prince and not someone else who found me. They may not have understood at all and thought me a spy!" Ana giggled.

Ayyn laughed at this, "You could not be a very good spy hiding down there!"

Still laughing he poured her some wine and proceeded to make a toast, "To new friends."

She raised her glass and agreed. As she was sipping out of the crystal goblet she noticed that no servants were here. Normally, a royal figure would not be doing the pouring or serving and would certainly have servants standing by for anything he may wish. This was so very odd.

"My lord, where are your servants?" Ana implored swooning a bit.

"I prefer to not have them pestering me and skulking about whilst I dine. It causes me displeasure. You would not want to see this prince in the midst of displeasure would you my dear? I would be dreadful company," Ayyn flashed his most charming smile at her.

"I am so sorry to have asked, my lord. It is none of my concern," she dropped her head with embarrassment.

"Oh no my sweet. There is nothing to feel sorry for. I am just a bit eccentric is all," the phony elf replied with concern in his voice. He noticed how lovely she truly was and he knew she had no recollection of him. He knew that if it were not for him she would not have met her demigod and made it back to this world. Maybe he should have taken a different path than the one he had. There would have been no need to have all the problems with the Allerian elves and the demigod because they never would have known. She could have been raised as a wife for him in the first place and he could have performed the ritual that brought her back to her true form. She would have been loyal and royal which is what he wanted. Why did he not find some other way of doing this. He wondered at it now. Perhaps he had been blinded by rage at all that had been done to him in the past by those who should have loved him. *Am I evil?* This was a question on his mind. Ayyn believed he was owed a "thank you" from that beast. In no way did the prince believe that the demigod pan was worthy of her beauty and grace and now they had two grown sons. She must forget them all! He did not consider that she would have been here all that time with her family if he had not meddled with such dark magic in the first place. It was entirely too late for repentance on the matter now. Ayyn would have to make the situation work. Ana was the one thing that he realized he needed to show the kingdom his new and remarkable ideas. Peace would be his platform in their eyes for marrying a princess outside their own race of elf. She would be the most sweet and submissive queen when he was done with her reprogramming and he would just have to wait to enjoy her as he intended to do quite often once vows had been exchanged. Ayyn had decided that at this point he could not treat her unkindly. He had grown quite fond of the little one he had so many ties to. As an elf she had the ability of glamor, as well. It was easy for someone to become entranced by her because of this. Truly, there could not be a better choice in a mate for him. A prince such as himself would require the most perfect queen by his side when he became ruler here. She could have been trained all along to serve him instead of becoming the sacrifice that he had wanted. That had failed miserably and centuries were wasted in that box. It was all his father's fault!

He thought the women in his tribe were beautiful but not like Ana. She was somehow capturing his blackened heart and that was something no one had ever been able to do. He must have her for his own regardless of the price. This would be revenge as well. Ayyn would love nothing more than to make them all suffer for interfering. Although, it would seem that this was turning out for the best.

Ana was beginning to have trouble retaining her thoughts. What was she doing again? She needed to do something but could not remember what it was at the moment. It would come to her eventually, she hoped.

"My lord, this wine must be very strong. I feel like a must lay down for a moment. My head is positively swimming," Ana began to slide a bit sideways in her chair.

"I have you, my dear. Perhaps you should lay down for a moment and please, call me Ayyn," he was using every bit of charm and glamor he possessed now.

Ana's family was not in her thoughts now. As she slid into a mild slumber Ana saw that beautiful smiling face as he lifted her off of her chair. She mumbled back to him with a smile and heavy eyes, "Ayyn . . ." she trailed off into sleep.

Agreus and Agrieness were searching everywhere for Ana. They had called out and searched every nook and cranny. It was to no avail. They were shaking with emotion. Together they returned to the kingdom of the Allerian elves to begin an immediate search from all magical perspectives. The rest of the family was notified and they were heartbroken. It seems that while all of this had been happening the guards of the underground tomb that held a long forgotten prisoner had become empty.

"How could this have happened? Where is my mother?" Kashenn was angry and hurt at her disappearance.

"My son, we are all in despair at this news because of whom we suspect is behind it," Agreus and the king looked at each other at the demigod's words.

"Who do you believe is responsible father?" Agrieness asked with tears in his eyes.

"That is a long and complicated story but it is necessary for you to know if you are to use your powers to help me find her and get her back," Agreus appeared weary.

"Come my dear Agreus," the king called him into private chambers to discuss the matter. "Boys, come with us. It is time you knew the story of the dark times that we had tried to put behind us so long ago."

The queen was sobbing quietly to herself as her maids attended her. The Lady Ashana had lost her daughter once before and now it was happening again. It was more than she could bear. Without a word she left the throne room to seek the help of the clerics. Perhaps they could bring comfort and some helpful information on how to deal with the this darkened elf of ruination whose sole purpose was to tear apart her loving family.

It took quite some time to tell the entire story to the twins but when it was done they sat with somber faces and understood now the worry their father and grandparents had when it came to this dark abomination. As for the box that had contained him for so long they were still investigating how he managed to escape. There must be some secret to him that no one was able to find before. This was unheard of to escape an elven prison of any kind. The only reason the guards had raised the alarm was the small cracks that had begun to form around the seal. They had kept it all of this time and had never seen such a thing happen. After having reported it to their king it was ripped open to discover that the prisoner called Ayyn had found a way out of his prison. They knew instantly at the report of Ana's disappearance that it was very likely that the monster had taken her for revenge. What he planned to do with her was something they did not know or care to consider. They just needed to find her before he could carry out whatever evil plan he had constructed. They began all using their powers to attempt scrying, picking up magical signatures of a dark nature, a formal letter was being sent to the land of Ayyn's forefathers to inquire of them anything unusual and anything else that might help. Unfortunately, that letter would be intercepted by Ayyn and a formal response would return without helpful information. For the moment, they were not alerting the village in the hope that this could be solved without them ever knowing anything had happened at all.

Meanwhile, in the special quarters that Ayyn had constructed from magic the quiet princess lay sleeping. Ayyn sat beside her and watched her as she lay on the most lavish bed that he had prepared for her. That demigod and his elves had completely underestimated his powers and he knew it. He was pleased with himself. In his possession was an artifact that had been kept a secret and undetected and now Ana would be his, after all. She must be completely convinced that she was here all along and must have bumped her head or something. He would work out all of the details. Now he needed to dispatch his uncle who was the king that wretched, liar that had banished his father and started all of this. Ayyn held him just as responsible for his troubles as he did the others. Tonight he would move unseen throughout the city and listen. He was searching for any malcontent that he could use in his cause. Just in case, he had thought it better to use an invisibility spell that could not be broken by others. For now, he waited and watched. The most splendid of any of the elvish women lay before him. He could not help but feel a connection with her after everything that the past held for them. He was thinking of everything that came before in the realm of the humans. He remembered her lovely form even before her ultimate reconnection of elven soul and body. Then, he was her biological father but in the elven realm all that was changed when she was restored. No longer was he any kin to her so there was no qualm in his mind about loving her now. Everything had been restored to match her true parents. Ayyn leaned forward and kissed her on the cheek as she continued to be effected by the forgetfulness potion coursing through her small body.

Night was falling and he was ready to listen to this world. Ana would not wake up for hours so he used his spell and slipped out of the magic pocket and into the dusty room at the end of a long unused hallway. He slipped into the throne room. He saw his uncle sitting on the throne with harlots making a fuss over him. King Cassen made no secret of his love of women and strong drink. Ayyn would be surprised if he could not find someone to help him overthrow the careless old elf if necessary.

Ayyn scurried past guards and sentries to get out of the castle walls and into the dark city. He could see light flickering in the windows of each house. Some of the houses were simple and others more elaborate. As he was listening to those passing by he noticed a couple of younger elves. They were in a hurry to get home it seemed. The boy and girl were brother and sister. It would seem they were twins. He was reading their minds now. They were both about twenty years old and the brother Ulenn seemed to have some serious secrets and dark thoughts. The girl Athulenne or Lu as her twin called her was as innocent minded as ever. Maybe he could use these two. He followed and continued to listen and read thoughts. It would appear that their father was an important man on the council. Ayyn continued to unravel all of the boy's secrets. He smiled devilishly to himself. These two would work out perfectly. He moved on and listened through open windows and to others passing by and talking. There was certainly unrest in the realm and almost everyone he heard speak of the king was unhappy or disgruntled in some way with his rule. Some wondered if the right thing had been done when his brother was banished. Maybe he would have been a better ruler even though he stood accused of terrible crimes against the kingdom.

Ayyn new he was the rightful heir to the throne in this kingdom now such as it was with all of it's unrest and alliances. This much was true. He could not be held responsible for what happened with his father. He had no part in it and had dispatched the human lover himself. Even with all of this being true he seriously doubted he would be welcomed by his uncle. He would surely be looking for a way to have him either killed or banished to hold on to the throne. After listening and thinking on it for a while Ayyn cooked up a marvelous plan on how to solve that little problem tonight. He made his way back to the castle wall and found his way back inside the grounds. Looking up to the king's balcony outside his chambers Ayyn could see disgusting things through the window. He knew he was not one to judge on that matter but he did not want to see some one else doing such perverted things. That should be him up there and he was about to make that happen. Using a little spell he had been working on, Ayyn walked invisibly up the castle wall to the balcony and misted inside through the barely open door. There was a chamber off the main room. He made his way unseen into what now was obviously the king's personal bathing and ablutions area. He waited and listened in the dimly lit room to the nasty king doing things with those younger elven women. Eventually the older king would have to come into this room even if only for a moment.

Sure enough, the moment came when the king told the girls they would have to excuse him momentarily. They acted displeased and called after him as they giggled. This was it. Ayyn changed his form to match that of his uncle and waited for him to begin relieving himself. He walked silently up to him from behind and broke his neck. After a disappearing potion concocted by the clever elf was poured on the body it vanished. He took the place of the king and joined the harlots in the other room for a night of pleasure. He would return to his fair princess in the morning. The giggling and depravity continued until everyone was asleep in a pile, everyone except for Ayyn. He could not stop thinking of his great fortune and all of his plans coming together as though the fates themselves had woven it just for him.

"Lu, we made it in time. I must tell you that I love you. You know that don't you sister?" Ulenn asked with a look on his face that she could not understand.

"Of course I know that. You love me and I love you dear brother. Come let's go inside," Lu wanted to get out of the night air.

"Wait, not just yet. I am worried for you. Father is making me marry Mariella and I am concerned that when that happens I will not be here to protect you," Ulenn just wanted her to plead with him not to marry that girl. It would be reason enough to forsake all he knew and take his sister away from here.

"Ulenn, I know that you must marry for political reasons and know that it does not change that we are family. Please, do not worry for me. I want you to think of your future. Besides, father will be choosing a suitor for me and I will have to marry too," Lu reminded him.

Ulenn had not given much thought to that but she was right. He could not let that happen so he must try to find out who his father was favoring on the matter. They hugged tightly and then walked inside to a warm house as Utenn was ordering his maid to prepare the table for his children.

"So how was the afternoon Athulenne? Was your brother attentive to you?" Utenn looked at Ulenn.

"Of course father. He is always very courteous and attentive to me when we go anywhere at all," she answered honestly.

"Good," Utenn kept his eye on Ulenn. He knew that as wonderful of a son and brother as he was, that there was more affection for his sister than there should be. As long as no lines were crossed then there would be no issue mentioned. Utenn knew that his daughter had no idea of it and did not want it mentioned to her. He was pleased that Ulenn was keeping it to himself and hopefully in time he would come to accept the bride he had chosen for him. For now, dinner was on the table and they were going to eat and discuss the day.

The Seyennes family tried to be as normal as they could with the mother of Utenn's children, Athalla, going mad over a year ago. There was no real reason for it except that it must have been an unwanted family trait that showed itself in her. She remained upstairs with a personal attendant to see to her needs. Utenn did not allow the children to visit for fear that she would influence them somehow. He did visit on occasion to make sure all was well. His love for her was real but he could not bear to see her now, not like this, for very long. Her mad ravings were hard to deal with for them all. Healers and clerics had tried to help the family but it was of no use. Nothing had seemed to work. Maybe one day his wife would return to herself and they would once again be happy.

In the kingdom of the Allerian elves emotions were running high. No one could sense any trace of Princess Ana. No one could use their magic effectively to determine anything at all. The clerics were of no use either. Agreus felt that he was going to have to do something he had been avoiding for years. Speaking to his father was the last thing he wanted to do since Hermes had plucked his brother Nomios out of the waters and left him instead to drown during the wars in India they had followed Bacchus into. He did not know whether Hermes knew he was still alive or if he figured him dead. It would be a most uncomfortable interaction. Agreus had preferred after all of his dealings with gods and demigods to stay to himself and do what he did best. He was the wisest of the pans and had thought it best to leave that existence behind. He had his forest friends and the elves among many other creatures he had discovered in time. Then came his own family and now his wife was in trouble. He would do anything for her so he was going to have to make the trip with his sons to the only temple of Hermes left standing that he knew of and do it the old fashioned way: offerings and prayer. Maybe he would answer him and maybe he would not. It depended on his curiosity about why Agreus had come to him. However, before he would leave he would freeze time so that the castle and village below would not continue to worry and fret while he was away. It was for their own good and they would never know. He would surround the entire kingdom with a blackout so no one could find it while he was gone. Only a few more things to do. He must inform his sons of what was going to happen because he needed their help.

In the morning, the pretend king ordered the women removed from his quarters so he could bathe and dress. He had an important decree to make. The entire council was being assembled and from there the decree would go out all over the kingdom. Ayyn had already placed an anti magic circle around the kingdom so that no spying eyes could see what was happening. His magic was so strong, now. He wanted it to be stronger, though. If only he could find a way to make that happen he would take it. It was never enough for him. He always wanted more. Perhaps, when he was changed and made fully immortal that greedy part of human nature had stayed with him.

Once the preparations had been made Ayyn entered the council chambers. He had a smile on his face this morning.

"All hail, King Cassen!" was called out by the chief of the guard. A hearty "All, hail!" followed it up from everyone else.

"Please, my council members, sit down. I have an important announcement to make. This may come as a shock to you all but I am going to be stepping down as king and my nephew will be assuming the throne. It would rightfully have been his if his father had not been cast out for his crimes. My nephew is Prince Ayyn Kelfinaar. He is a very trustworthy elf and has been preparing for this day all of his life.

I hid him away so that no one would want to harm my dearest nephew whom I love.

There were gasps and then silence.

The questions began: "Why did you not tell us of the Prince sooner? Where did he come from? Was your brother married before you banished him? Why did you hide all of this from the council? Did you think we would harm an innocent child for crimes he did not commit? I agree that we do not always have the same opinions but I think this point is something we all can agree on," Utenn, as chief council member, was displeased.

"Of course I worried for him. He is my family. Also, the answer is yes. My brother was just married when things took the course that they did but she died giving birth to Ayyn. It was all kept secret because our family did not approve of the match and he did not listen to reason but agreed to keep things quiet at least for a while until I could come to terms with her family but I was wrong to ask that of him. I see that now and I believe I am more responsible than I would like to think for what he did. I must step down. I feel I have made some grave mistakes in the past and now I am going to live to make things right for the young prince. I will remain in the castle and but for a few maids and my nephew I will be seen no more. I have made up my mind that it is time for someone with fresh blood and new ideas to take over so that I can live in my peaceful retirement. I am tired of ruling this throne and now it is his turn to take over that burden.

None of the council were sure of this political move but they would put the boy to some tests to determine if he was really the nephew of the king. They would welcome his rule if it were better than that of his uncle. They had grown tired of their lying king as much as he had apparently grown tired of them. None can sit the throne unless they are of royal blood. This would be determined before they allowed him to touch the crown.

"Now I will have the prince brought out for you to observe and test as I know you will," Ayyn walked into a waiting room with a back way out.

Ayyn quickly changed into his true form and walked out gracefully before the council. They were all amazed at the sight of him. He was remarkable. There was no doubt that he was royalty but the king's word was not enough since they had been kept in the dark about the younger elf," Utenn approached him.

"My young prince I will be needing a sample of your blood to determine your identity, please," Utenn was polite.

"Of course, Utenn," Ayyn answered, "Anything that the council needs will be at it's disposal."

The blood sample was quickly taken and it was very quickly determined that he was definitely a Kelfinaar. Of course a formal coronation would have to take place before he would become ruler but he was well on his way. As big as this castle was it would have been easy enough to hide him forever. A shout went throughout the kingdom of their soon to be new ruler and all of the women were talking of his charming good looks. The men spoke of his commanding presence and how the old king was better off in his retirement where no one could see him. They were disgusted with his lies and secrets.

A committee was being assembled to ready the coronation for a weeks time. After that Ayyn would have the throne. It was said he had a big announcement of his own to make at the coronation. No one was aware of Ana's presence but soon enough they would know because a wedding would be taking place peacefully or after a battle. Ayyn did not care which and he knew they would not care what the Allerian elves thought about his stealing their princess. Royalty must maintain the throne so heirs must be produced. The neighboring tribe to the north had failed to produce a princess for the purpose of marriage here so in their eyes other things had to be done to ensure the continuation of his line. All of this they would come to know but for now he needed to attend his "uncle".

After convincing everyone that he must be alone to see to the former king Ayyn went to the dusty room and entered the magical one he had created. The forgetfulness potion should be taking a strong effect now. He knew he must be very convincing.

"My dearest Ana," he called out to the princess.

She began to stir and rouse. "Where am I? I remember I was dining and then nothing before or after.

"I am your fiance Ana. We are to be married very soon. Do you not remember? It will come back to you. When you slipped and fell during a bath your head was bumped on the marble surrounding the pool of water. Your maids were severely chastised for allowing this to happen. Why, my dear you have been asleep for a week!" Ayyn lied so well.

Ana seemed very confused. Perhaps he was right. She could not remember anything about it.

"I am Ana and your name is?" she asked.

"Ayyn Kelfinaar, I am a prince and you are a beautiful princess called Kefshana or Ana which is what you prefer to be called. Oh my dear, I am so worried that you cannot remember! I have just the thing that will help. It is herbal medicine and it should begin to help you," Ayyn looked so concerned.

Still she was a little wary of this handsome "fiance". He gave her the potion which he had concocted so he could implant memories into her mind. She would "remember" anything he pleased.

Ayyn began to recount all of their good times together and how much in love they were. It was definitely becoming true for his part as time went on. This definitely helped in his appearance of honesty. Ayyn's heart might not be as black as he had once thought. He gave so much detail about everything. He must be telling the truth. Why would anyone go to such an elaborate amount of trouble? Ana listened to him intently. Something did not feel quite right about all of this but she began to soften some after a while. She could just have a feeling of paranoia due to the amnesia she was suffering. Ayyn was very caring and respectful towards her. He was not trying to force anything on her. It seemed he truly wanted to help her. Soon enough, she believed she was beginning to have memories of them together just like he had told her. They were jumbled together, though. She was beginning to believe that bump on the head had rattled her pretty well. He revealed that he was about to become king of this land and she would be his queen.

"We can wait to marry, that is if you are not sure of your thoughts right now. I was going to announce it at my coronation in a week, but." Ayyn was interrupted.

"Surely there is no need to recant anything. I have no doubt that by that time all will be right again," Ana said with some hesitation as she managed a smile.

Ayyn smiled at her, "Might I kiss your cheek, my dear. I have been here nearly the whole time you were asleep and I have missed you."

"Yes, of course," Ana allowed a small kiss on her left cheek.

"Now come with me and I will show you to your quarters my dear. I have maids waiting to attend your every need," Ayyn had thought of everything.

He took his princess by the hand and led her up the flight of stairs that would lead to the rooms that would be hers alone.

Ayyn had taken aside three maids and put them into confidence about Ana's presence. Under penalty of exile they agreed they would reveal her to no one and they would care for her privately. One of the young maids made the mistake of asking why his future bride must be a secret as it would please everyone to know a wedding would follow. He smiled and asked her to come with him so he could explain. She did not return that day and was replaced with another more prudent girl. The other two were definitely not going to cross him in any way. Ayyn smiled at how he had dispatched the nosy little thing. It was not a pretty sight in the end. He could not have some young simple minded girl accidentally mentioning something that might leak out now could he?

They were approaching Ana's wing which he had recently put back into use. It had been closed off for many years. These were the previous queen's quarters. King Cassen had never married so it had sat unused all of this time. No one ever came here and he would make sure they did not. Ayyn and Ana entered the newly refurbished rooms. It was beautiful here. She liked the look of it but she felt somber in her heart. She was not sure why. Deciding to make the best of things she thanked him for everything and greeted her three maids. They looked somewhat different than her but not much. She was paler than the others. The maids bowed in respect for their new lady. They were eager to serve and this was an important task they had agreed to. Perhaps if they did a proper job they would be elevated to a higher status of servant in the castle.

"So what do you think my dear? Can you stand it for a week not to leave these rooms? You are to be the crown jewel to surprise everyone at my coronation and I would not want to spoil all of the excitement for everyone," he gave her a charming smile.

"I believe that I can do that for you. After all, you have been so kind to me in this plight. I shall stay hidden here," she smiled at him.

She looked so lovely that he could not stand it anymore. He leaned forward and cupped her ivory face in his strong hands and very gently kissed her on her soft lips. She blushed at this gesture but it was not an unpleasant one. At least she could see no reason for it to be. They were to be married, after all, and he was so handsome to the eyes.

Ayyn read her thoughts and new at once that she was a little taken with him. That would definitely make it easier for his efforts to distort her memory not to be so painstaking a task. He decided to play innocent for a moment.

"I am sorry if I offended you, Ana" Ayyn feigned embarrassment.

"No, I was merely surprised is all, my lord," Ana did not want to upset her host especially after all of the nice things he had done for her.

She was trying to remember if she loved him or not. It was all a jumbled mess inside of her head. They must be in love. After all she was here and everything seemed to be done appropriately for such a wedding to take place.

"I am afraid I have a terrible headache. I must bathe and try to calm down, I think. Some tea perhaps would help," Ana was unsettled.

Ayyn could see he would have to use more of that potion if he were to properly set her memory to what he wanted so he ordered the tea be brought at once and bath to be drawn. A maid returned with an entire tea setting. Teska, the maid, reached for the tea to pour her lady a cup. Ayyn stayed her hand.

"I will attend to this Teska," Ayyn smiled.

"My lord," she bowed and allowed him to take over.

As he was pouring Ana's cup he slipped a larger dose of the memory potion into it. He then poured himself a regular cup and sat with Ana at the decorative table there in the room. He dismissed the maids to fetch everything she would need for a bath and the new attire that he had ordered was in the wardrobe to be taken out. While the maids busied themselves with the task at hand he talked with Ana for a while and then dismissed himself to go and take care of his royal duties. It was important with the throne vacated that he show he was worthy of it.

"I shall return later to check on you, my dear," Ayyn said as he closed the door. He was intending in their next talk to explain that her parents had sent her from the "northern" kingdom ahead of the wedding plans so she could witness his coronation and be part of the celebration. Ayyn would then make up some excuse as to what had happened to them on their way to see her married. He would assure her that they were pleased with the match and everything would be done according to the agreements that had been reached when he asked for her hand in marriage. He smiled as he walked slowly back to the courtyard to speak with some of the council members about his innovative ideas. He was using his knowledge of human political platforms to make his ideas seem wonderful when it was obvious to him that they would be a pipe dream. Is that not what humans did to amass followers to their causes?

Agreus' heart ached with sorrow for his wife. He new that his sons were suffering for the loss of their mother as well. Even though they said little unless spoken to he could sense the pain they endured. Until they were ready for rule they respected their elders enough to keep most of their thoughts to themselves but the time would come when they would have much more to say. Agreus began an incantation in his beautiful accent that Ana had always loved. The kingdom froze in time and was invisible to anyone else. They began the trip to the world of humans so they could transport to the temple to call Hermes for help or advice. Would he answer? Maybe he would come through for Agreus this time. Surely he owed him for the past misdeed of saving only one of his sons from the threat of death. Yes, this was Agreus' only option that was left at the moment.

Agreus, Agrieness, and Kashenn set off on a journey to the realm of humans to attend this temple and make an offering. Perhaps, by bringing his sons with him it would soften the heart of the god to see his grandchildren and how powerful they were. This may sway things in the favor of his helping them. They were off to Ephesus. Today the ancient Greek city with all of it's wonders would look much different than the last time Agreus laid his eyes upon it. It was now part of modern day Turkey. There were many temples and different religions that had made a mark on the lovely city. There had been many rulers over the ages and it was ancient according to a mortal's point of view. In this world all would decay and wither with time. Even though humans were very gifted at creating, they were also just as gifted at destroying things. Constant invasions and conquests over the years had left many wonder filled places in rubble and now they appeared more as a ghostly reminder of the past as new cities were built and old marble columns were tumbled to the ground. All of these were markers of a time long gone.

The three travelers stepped out of the realm of the elves and back into the human world. They were in the hidden glen that Ana loved so much. Agreus hung his head and walked towards his old cave. Agrieness and Kashenn followed him. The scrying stone was still inside and he had only just put the water from the magical little pool into the basin the day before. While they were away his duties would just have to wait. Agreus looked into the glassiness before him and began an incantation so they could view the temple in Ephesus. It would be dark there now and they would go unnoticed by humans who could no longer lay eyes on the magical beings. How things had changed over the ages! Humans were so much more agreeable to the demigod when they lived in a simpler time. They were just too greedy and self absorbed now.

Agreus finished his incantation and the temple appeared in the pool in front of them. It was empty and there was no telling how long it had been since anyone had been inside. It was in a state of some disrepair but not altogether awful. It would do for his purpose. They willed themselves through to this place. Father and sons climbed the stairs together and went inside. The elder lit a torch and placed it on the stone wall near the marble statue of Hermes, his father. They had brought with them coins of high value and olive oil for an offering. They placed these items on the altar and took a step back as Agreus began to call out for the god to answer him. Some time passed and nothing was happening.

"What now father?" Agrieness asked the weary Agreus.

"I do not know my son, I do not know," Agreus shook his head

"Father?" Kashenn placed his hand on Agreus shoulder. He was worried about his mother but equally concerned about his father's well being. Kashenn was very passionate and caring. He just wanted this god or grandfather to answer so they could find some peace and an answer to there cause.

Just as they were near to giving up they heard a voice. It came from behind the statue of Hermes.

"My son, I see you have been busy," Hermes stepped out into the light.

"Hermes, I was beginning to think you were too busy to answer your own son's prayers," Agreus answered back.

"I was watching the three of you for a little while. Come, tell me, are these your children?" Hermes asked Agreus who was watching him now.

"Yes," Agreus was short with his answer.

"Why have you not spoken to me in such a long time, Agreus? I am your father, after all. I thought you had died!" Hermes seemed agitated.

"You took my brother and left me to die in those rushing waters in India father and you ask why I have not said a word to you?" Agreus seemed pained.

"Agreus, I came back for you and you were not there! I tried to save you both. I am sorry you thought I did not care," Hermes began to calm himself.

"I am not here about me. It is about my elven wife. She is the Princess of the Allerians." Are you familiar with them? If you are then you know they do not reside here in this realm. Her name is Ana and I love her and our children more than anything. She has been taken from us by an awful culprit. Some how he is managing to block all attempts to find her which is odd since he is only a Dulerian elf. His magic should not be so powerful. I believe that he has always been underestimated and now he has done this awful thing by taking her. I shudder to think what he is planning given our history. Read my thoughts and you will see," Agreus closed his eyes as Hermes read his thoughts.

"Ah, I see your predicament. I am so sorry for your trials, my son. She is a beautiful creature, indeed, and you have some fine children of your own. I will try to help you," Hermes said as he attempted to locate Ayyn.

A few moments had passed when Hermes came to a startling revelation.

"That is not possible! How is it that a mere elf can block even a god's probing of his whereabouts?" Hermes was troubled by this.

Hermes was indeed familiar with all of the elves, especially the Dulerian colony.

"What can be done?" Agreus asked hopeful in his voice.

"I must return to Olympus and look into this matter. When I have an answer for you I shall come to you with it Agreus. I am sure the answer can be found. We will have him soon and your wife shall be returned to you. Until then wait for my arrival," Hermes vanished.

Agreus felt helpless for now. All they could do was wait on Hermes to return with any news that may be of use. They returned through the portal back into the glen.

"My sons I believe we must wait here in the glen. We can stay in my old cave. I have kept it in use during visits here. We must leave things frozen so that no one will grieve. I feel the queen cannot take much more of this. I will keep a watchful eye for Ana in case she were to some how return, though I doubt she can of her own accord. This is where she was abducted so here we shall stay and wait for Hermes," Agreus gave the orders to his sons.

They made ready for nightfall in the glen. At least they could attend to the forest while they waited. It was a sleepless night for the saddened family that Ana left behind her. It seemed Agreus stared at the stars through the opening in the top of the cave for what seemed like hours before falling into a troubled sleep.

A week had passed in the realm of the elves and the coronation was tomorrow for Ayyn.

He was in a very good mood. Who would not be in the case that they were being crowned king and seemed to be loved by all as well as accepted without much question. He was about to marry the beautiful princess that he was in possession of and now he could give that announcement to his public at the ceremony tomorrow. Ana could come out of her wing and be seen by everyone. Ayyn was basking in pleasure.

In the meantime he had kept himself busy with getting to know his people and discreetly doing things he should not for a prince about to become a king and a married one at that! All of this time he was still brain washing Ana to believe whatever he said and it was working. She obeyed his every command though she seemed somber at times. He believed she would perk up with the wedding announcement. Ayyn knew he could have any one of these young women here so she would feel lucky it was her that he had chosen. He supposed he could have overthrown the rule about marrying royalty but he would much rather keep the line as blue blood as possible.

Ayyn had been having a little fun with the chief council member's daughter, though. Athulenne was beautiful but not suitable for the wife of a king, in his opinion. He had read her thoughts and realized immediately that she had fallen for him quite hard. Having his way with her was probably not going to please her father, Utenn, but Ayyn intended to wipe her mind before the announcement was made that he had chosen another. The girl would undoubtedly tell what was going on if he did not and that would cause a whole other set of problems for him and he could not have that! She believed his lies that he was going to change the rules for her and make her queen. He had lied and made her believe he loved her. She was not a harlot to be put aside when no longer needed. It was more intricate than that. She was nobility but still beneath him. He did not want to make problems with the council for his folly.

Now it was time for him to check on Ana for the day and see that she was well attended to and ready for the next day's festivities.

Ayyn made his way to the wing of his newly beloved. He was all charm and smiles today and he hoped she would be too. He needed her to love him. It could not be a one sided thing for him anymore. Was he being impatient with her? Ayyn reached her quarters and entered to find one of the maids brushing out her beautiful silken hair. He watched for a moment and then announced himself. The maid was dismissed so he could speak privately to Ana. The little maid bowed and left the room.

"My dear, how are you feeling today?" Ayyn asked with questioning eyes.

"I am well, my lord. I felt I was beginning to miss your presence. How long have you been away?" Ana was surprised that she had missed him.

"Ah, so you missed me. I am pleased to hear this. I missed you as well. I have only been away from you to attend to the duties of the kingdom, my sweet," he found this conversation to his liking. All was going well.

"My parents, I cannot remember them but they must be coming to attend our wedding will they not?" Ana implored.

"Oh yes, once you lay eyes on them you will surely recall them. He began to describe them and tell her of the kingdom she was supposed to have come from. Ayyn told her all of the lies needed to squelch any suspicion on the matter.

"That is wonderful news!" Ana was elated.

"Now I must tell you, my dear princess, I love you without compare. Have you remembered your love for me now?" Ayyn had an intense look in his eyes.

"I believe that I have, my lord," Ana answered fairly certain that she was remembering a love between them.

"I am pleased to hear that. I was beginning to think you would not love me as I love you," he looked down for a moment.

"Oh no, my lord, no such thing should even be in your mind! I will love you fervently and with all of my heart! Please do not be sad, it is nearly your time to shine and I want to see your beautiful smile today," Ana felt badly that she could have saddened his mood.

Why would she refuse this handsome being? He was kind and loving. It was obvious that her parents had long ago approved of this match as was elven custom. She was sure from everything he had told her that she was happy about all of this.

Ayyn moved closer to his future bride and touched her soft hair. She smiled at him as he kissed her very innocently. His plan had worked. She was completely oblivious to anything but what she had "remembered." Ayyn called for a small celebration for the two of them. He had wine brought to her quarters and as they drank it they talked through the afternoon. Soon, he would have to return to the people though. Just one more day and everything would be out in the open. He needed to see Athulenne once more to wipe away all memory of their encounters. He would handle that tonight before she could speak out against him.

"Lu, I know you have been sneaking out at night. I have not told father because I do not wish you any trouble but you must tell me where you are going," Ulenn was insistent.

"Ulenn, all I have done is to be alone to think. I miss mother and our impending marriages will be soon so I am just in need of time to straighten out my thoughts," Athulenne lied to her brother.

She hated to lie to her most treasured one but it was necessary. Soon he would understand that she had to keep the secret that the prince had asked her to keep. He would then see the need to have hidden everything. He was going to change the rules for the king to marry whomsoever he wished. Ayyn was going to announce the wedding at his coronation tomorrow after speaking to her father. She was in an inexplicably good mood. She loved Prince Ayyn and he loved her. Lu felt like the luckiest elf in existence. On the nights that she had been sneaking out they were meeting for time alone together. She realized she probably should wait to be intimate with her future husband but somehow she could not resist him. Ulenn would be mad on that account alone. It was improper and unbecoming of a lady. They were planning to meet tonight so she would need to be extra cautious so she would not be followed by her nosy but well meaning brother.

"Fine, I will choose to believe the best of you and take your word," Ulenn was unable to stay mad at his lovely sister.

The marriages had him worried. He was still scheming of ways to get them out of it and away from here. It was not going to be easy but maybe the opportunity would present itself very soon. At least he was hoping and praying for it.

Agreus was walking in his glen when he noticed Ana walking towards him. The sun was shining and it was a beautiful day. He began to run toward her when suddenly she was grabbed from behind by the dark elf and held back from coming to her husband. The sky was darkened as she screamed his name.

"NO!" Agreus sat up on his bed covered in a cold sweat.

"Father, it is alright. You were dreaming," Kashenn was trying to comfort his disturbed father.

"I had a horrible nightmare about your mother," Agreus held his head as he got out of his bed to wash his face and regain control of his emotions.

Agrieness had gotten up early and was tending to the forest and all that lived in it. His father was in no condition to do these things so he decided it best to do these things himself and make it easier for the demigod. He returned when he was finished for the morning to check on the others and if there had been any news in his absence.

"Father, the duties of the morning have been done. Is there any news?" Agrieness asked as he entered the cave.

"Thank you my son. I am very pleased that you took it on yourself in this time to perform the duties of the forest. I am afraid that nothing has happened yet but I am going to look in on the kingdom to see that all is how we left it momentarily," Agreus walked to the basin.

Shortly, Agreus was scrying into the time frozen kingdom and all was quiet. No one was awake and nothing had changed. This was a good thing for the elven people that resided within the kingdom. He did not want everyone to be in a constant state of suffering as he and his children were. Agreus did expect Hermes to show up anytime knowing he traveled fast. Maybe he had something of use to say this time. They would continue to await his arrival.

Hermes had spoken to the gods and researched all that was known to them so that he might help the son that he owed. He could just let them resolve it on their own and let things play out without ever showing up again but he did want to make things up to Agreus. He had deeply loved Sose, the mother of Agreus, and he knew that she would want him to help.

He prepared to return to his son to bear the news that nothing could be done. He decided to peer into the kingdom of the Dulerian elves to see if there was something missed. There was some magic at work here that would allow no being to look inside the kingdom so it was obvious the princess must be there. What could be causing this strong barrier? The only thing that could do this was some power of another god or some token given by a god to the elf to cancel out prying eyes into the kingdom. Hermes himself had dealings with this tribe many ages ago during a war they were fighting on the sea with a rival tribe. They had discovered Hermes and began worshiping him and making the most lavish offerings to him. At that time, they were much simpler and sort of like the humans in nature so he had seen no harm in helping them have the advantage over their enemies. For a while, they continued to worship him and give offerings. Just like the humans, in time they stopped and the tie had been severed. Only their history would offer any memory now of the relationship they had with the god that made their ships faster. The king that ruled at the time had been given a token to signify Hermes' tie to the elves but he doubted anyone would even know where it was anymore. He was trying to remember what the amulet looked like and where it had even come from. Hermes knew he had stolen it from some Egyptian god as he was passing quickly by on a mission. The god had been sleeping and he liked the artifact so he took it. The item was very powerful and he was not even sure of everything it could do. If in fact the the abductor was in possession of it this could be giving him the extra boost in powers to do all that he was doing. It was beginning to make sense but in order to dispell the item they needed it back or at least a likeness of it so the right god could be found to assist in gaining full knowledge of it's powers and how to reverse it. This would mean that he would have to confess taking it and he hoped it would not start a war among deities. This was a twist he was not expecting to have to also confess to his son, but he must or all would be lost for him.

Ayyn had excused himself from Ana to do as he said. He went about his duties and made pleasantries with the important council members. After they had all left the castle that evening he made ready for one last meeting with Athulenne. Now was the time to erase her memory so no problems would come from their indiscretions. He met her in the usual place and secretly escorted her to a part of the castle that they used to meet. No one had seen her so they were quite safe from discovery.

"My dear, how are you this fine evening?" Ayyn asked Lu.

"I am well my prince. I could hardly wait to meet with you tonight. My brother is beginning to suspect something," The young girl seemed quite concerned.

"It is no matter. Soon there will be no more reason for him to be suspicious. I can assure you of that," Ayyn said with a flattering smile, "Come have a glass of wine to toast our coming happiness."

Without hesitation, the young Athulenne toasted and drank the goblet dry. She did not know there was a memory wipe potion in it designed to make her forget everything that had transpired between her and his royal highness. Ayyn began to speak to her of things that made no sense at all.

He was telling her that she had been quite the friend he had needed in this time of transition and that he was glad she was such a pure girl. Ayyn said she would make a fine wife for a noble elf some day. He then began to escort her out attempting to make her believe they were never lovers and nothing had ever happened between them. She was confused and did not say anything. She went along with what he was saying for now. This was not right! What was he doing? She smiled and waited for Ayyn to disappear into his quarters for the night. She then stole back into the castle room and grabbed the goblet from which she drank. Lu had a suspicion that he had attempted magic on her and wanted the glass tested. If that were true then he had planned this from their first encounter. She noticed that a small round orb on the bracelet she wore was glowing red. It had never done that before. Lu needed to find out the purpose of this, as well. She was hurt and she smelled a plot. Nevertheless, she hoped it was all just some sort of joke or teasing that Ayyn would soon tell her he did not mean. She did love him and was feeling quite jilted.

The sun was rising in the eastern sky over the kingdom. Today was Prince Ayyn's coronation. Quite early, chosen members of the council came to assist in dressing him in the appropriate elven attire as tradition suggested. The committee that was preparing the festivities were already setting up the great hall to accommodate the many who would be in attendance for this occasion. A great feast was to be held later in the day in honor of the new king after the crowning had taken place. Ayyn did find these robes a bit on the unfashionable side. He was used to his black leathers and crimson fabrics. Being in the human world for so long in the past had swayed his taste in everything. He loved his high black leather boots. He looked positively formidable and charming all at the same time when dressed in his usual attire. Ayyn felt a little on the silly side wearing this "thing" that was given him to wear but he would do as he was told for now. Everyone had been inquiring as to whether or not his uncle was attending. Ayyn had informed them that he intended to watch from a distance. He did not wish to interact with anyone at this time. Ayyn was glad that the kingdom had so readily accepted that the king had stepped down and gone into "seclusion." He nearly laughed at the thought of it all.

Soon, it was time for last preparations so he went to Ana's quarter's feigning a visit to his hermit of an uncle so the old elf could wish him blessings. It was early afternoon now. Ana was being dressed in the most lovely lavender dress and slippers. They matched her eyes so well. The maids were braiding certain strands of her hair for the formal occasion. They were nearly done when Ayyn arrived with jewels made of purple diamonds to match her outfit for the evening. He had used his magic to conjure up the amazing gems for her. She looked no older than when she first came to this world. She would always look this way and stay the same beautiful Ana she was now. This pleased Ayyn. He approached her with haste.

"You look so amazingly beautiful this evening, my lady," Ayyn nearly wept at the sight of her.

"You flatter me, my lord," Ana answered blushing.

"There was no flattery only pure honesty in that remark, love," he said looking deeply into her eyes searching for something.

"Thank you for that and how are you feeling about this day?" Ana inquired of her handsome suitor.

"I could not be a happier elf if I tried!" he laughed, "I will assume the throne and I have the woman I love. What more could I desire?"

"A wedding perhaps?" she said coyly.

"Ah, yes that would make everything even better. I agree wholeheartedly!" he was glad she had come around to the idea, finally.

"When do you think it should take place, my lord?" Ana wanted to know.

Ayyn grabbed her and pulled her suddenly to him. He was looking at her intently.

"You must stop being so formal with me Ana. I love you and I want you to feel comfortable with me at all times. There is nothing I would not do for you. Do you believe me, my sweet?" Ayyn was pleading with her now.

Ana looked up at him with trembling and touched his smooth face, "I am sorry for my formalities. I just do not want to do anything wrong. I want to make you happy with me. I fear I may say the wrong thing, my dearest prince."

"You will not do those things. Trust me when I say that you are a perfection in every way. Please just say that you love me and you want me. I need to hear it before I begin this evening. It will give me courage," Ayyn answered still with a pleading in his voice.

"I love you, Ayyn," the little princess answered him with what he wanted. She believed she did love him. She was a little afraid of all of this. Maybe timid is a more accurate assumption of her behavior.

Ana's confession brought tears to his blue eyes as he hugged and kissed her as if he would never see her again.

"Now, my sweet, I must return but your maids will lead you to where I will be with everyone at the proper time. I cannot wait for the kingdom to meet you. I know they will all love you!" Ayyn was smiling truthfully for the first time in a long time. True happiness was something he had never felt before. Usually, it was all hollow to him but with her it had become something he had never expected.

Hermes entered the glen where Agreus and his sons were waiting for him. They came out to meet him.

"What news do you bring us father," Agreus asked impatiently.

"I believe I know where your dark enemy is getting his power, Agreus," Hermes said with hesitation.

"Where?" Agreus implored.

His children stood by quietly and listened as they hoped for an answer.

"I gave their people an amulet ages ago before you were born, during a war. I helped them defeat their enemy at that time on the seas. They worshiped me then but no longer do they remember those ways. They were about the same in demeanor as humans were then, not this dark in nature. I saw no reason to refuse their request since they were good followers and provided all of the proper sacrifices," Hermes looked at Agreus with an expression of guilt.

"What are you saying?" Agreus was angered. "You helped them?"

"Agreus, it was a long time ago and I did not think that it mattered now. I could not have known they would even still have the item or be using it. I had nearly forgotten them altogether until all of this," Hermes defended himself.

"So then, if you gave it then take it back. Surely you must know how the thing works or can be undone!" Agreus was hopeful.

"Unfortunately, it was a stolen item I took from an Egyptian god on one of my missions. I caught him unaware as he slept and took it before he could notice. I know some of what the item does but not how to undo its powers. We will have to find him to get those answers," Hermes replied with resign.

"Alright, so which god did you take it from," Agreus asked.

"I do not know which one it was," Hermes answered.

"Are you serious? How shall we determine it then?" Agreus was so angry that his green eyes were glowing.

"Calm yourself my son. We must go to Egypt and search for him. I at least know what he looks like," Hermes offered his reply.

Still angry, Agreus and his sons were bound to go with Hermes to Egypt and look for this god who would no doubt be upset that something had been stolen and then have them ask for his help to rectify the trouble it was causing. They would need to go to Tjenu. It was an ancient place in Egypt that dated all the way back to the first dynasties. Hermes believed they would find the god with the four feathered headdress there. He asked them to all hold on and off they went as fast as Hermes could fly.

Utenn was preparing himself for this evening. He was glad that the kingdom would now be under the rule of someone who would take the advice of the council and be reasonable. Ulenn and Athulenne were dressing for the occasion as well. Their father was the head of the council so he was a major part of tonight. Athulenne was still hoping that Ayyn would announce what he had originally promised her and tell her the night before had been a prank or some such thing. She was going to wait and see before testing the goblet and inquiring about her bracelet her mother had given her as a child. She was still feeling hurt but hid it quite well. Ulenn was excited to have a young king sitting on the throne. He was sick of stupid rules and maybe this king would change things so the people could move forward and not stay stuck in traditions that no longer mattered. Maybe he could help with these rules of marriage that were forced on the young against their wills.

Ana waited anxiously to be sent for by her fiance. She was nervous and Teska could tell, "My lady, why are you so nervous? You will do fine and the people will love this change. Do not worry," she tried to be comforting to her mistress.

"I know everything will be fine. I just do not want to be disappointing to anyone. I do not want to embarrass my lord this evening," Ana fretted.

"I can tell from his demeanor that there is nothing you could ever do to displease his royal highness," Teska smiled at her.

Ana smiled and looked down at her tiny feet with the lavender slippers. She was happy to really feel like Ayyn was truthful about his feelings towards her. Suddenly, the door opened. His Highness Prince Ayyn will need the princess to begin making her way to the great hall.

"Well here we are, Teska," Ana said, "Please escort me to my destiny."

The two followed the sentry that had entered the room asking for Ana to come.

The coronation celebration was well under way and now it was time for the crowning of the new king. The chief cleric approached the prince with a platinum crown on a velvet pillow. He called everyone to attention and proceeded to place the crown on Ayyn's head.

"All hail King Ayyn of the Dulerian elves!" the cleric cried out with joy.

"All hail King Ayyn!" came from every spot in the enormous room.

Ayyn stood to receive the praise from his subjects. He smiled and made pleasing gestures to the crowd. As they began to quiet down he brought them to attention.

"My fellow elves, I have an announcement. I know that many of you have been awaiting this moment so without further delay I will make it.

Athulenne was paying very close attention now. She was expecting him to announce their love to the court but that is not what happened.

"My good people I shall take a queen now. She is already here and her parents have approved the match. We are very much in love and I wish you to meet her.

King Ayyn turned to the sentry standing near a doorway, "Now my friend. Open the door for my destiny to enter."

The sentry opened the door and Princess Ana was led inside by her now favorite maid, Teska.

There were gasps of astonishment in the crowd as they gazed on the beautiful princess. She was definitely an Allerian elf. Her parents must really respect the new king here to approve such a matching. It was unheard of for them to have much at all to do with the Dulerian elves.

"Please, let me introduce you to your soon to be new queen. This is the Princess Kefshana. She prefers to be called Princess Ana. Is she not a delightful creature?" Ayyn praised his future bride.

There was an eruption of approval and applause from those in attendance. Ayyn moved closer to Ana and embraced her.

"Come, sit with me. This place was made ready for you right next to me," he smiled his approval.

"Yes, my king, I shall join you," Ana smiled back at him.

Athulenne was seething with rage at the newly crowned king. She excused herself to freshen up but she hid in a small closet and cried herself into a fit. She fell asleep after awhile and was discovered by Ulenn who had been looking for his beloved sister.

"Lu, what is the matter?" Ulenn asked.

She got up and brushed herself off, "Come dear brother. I have much to tell you and I need your help while everyone is still occupied here."

"What is this about?" Ulenn was concerned.

"You shall know soon enough, come," Athulenne led him to the clerics chambers to use their magic potions.

"Lu, we will be discovered!" Ulenn protested.

"No, we will not!" Lu was determined to prove what she already new to be true.

"Let me see. Look for a potion that detects traces of magic," Lu was looking too.

"Alright," Ulenn was bewildered but did as he was asked.

"Ah, here it is," Lu pulled a cup from the folds of her long emerald blue dress.

"What is that for?" Ulenn was becoming impatient with her.

"That bastard used me, lied to me and has made a fool of me. I am going to prove it with this potion," Lu used just enough to swab the inside of the cup.

Sure enough, the cup glowed with magic residue.

"You see. He did try to wipe my memory!" Lu was furious.

"Who did this to you sister? Why was it done?" Ulenn was going to have vengeance on whomever had tried to harm his sister.

Lu recounted the tale of all that had happened between her and the king before now. She admitted to everything that had gone on in secret. She was embarrassed and upset that she was fool enough to believe he had loved her. Ulenn was enraged at this king. How could he do this to his sister? What would his soon to be bride and her family think of this? They both knew that no one would believe them so they decided to keep it secret.

"The one thing I cannot understand is why the memory wipe did not work," Lu was at a loss.

"Your bracelet, it is an anti-magic charm," Ulenn told her, "Mother gave it to you when you were a girl so no one could put a spell on you or use magic to harm you."

"That definitely explains it. He did not know that I was even wearing it and if he did notice then he thought nothing about it being of any consequence," Lu was angry.

"Sister, it is time you knew something that has been hidden from you for a long while now," Ulenn was nervous, "I love you more than I should and I am going to take you away from all of this. I am trying to find a way to do it so we will not be discovered and never be found."

"I do not know what to say, Ulenn. Why have you waited to tell me this?" Lu was curious.

"Fear of rejection, I suppose, so how about it dear sister? Will you have me? Run away with me. I will make it work. That I can promise you," Ulenn was waiting for her answer.

"You are a very handsome elf, my brother. We have always been very close. Yes, I can love you that way but no one will understand us. We will have to keep quiet until you find a place for our escape," Lu felt she could make herself happy with this situation. She would not be forced to marry someone she did not love at her father's orders. She was still angry and wanted to see Ayyn suffer for what he had done and soon she would get the chance to help make that happen.

Back in the banquet hall everyone was celebrating. It had just been announced that there would be a quick wedding between the two love birds. Tomorrow would be their wedding day. All of the kingdom was invited to attend. A scroll had been received announcing the arrival of her parents the next day due to the king already contacting them about the day it was to take place. All was right with Ayyn's world. *So this is what true happiness and love feels like.* He had never had it and now that he did he was not going to let it go for anything. He did not care what the Allerians thought. He did not care what her soon to be ex-family thought. They would make their own family. Ayyn intended to announce a delay in her parents arrival but go through with the wedding anyway. Then he would tell her that some horrible accident had happened on their journey and they had been killed. That would rid him of having to deal with any questions about them later.

Meanwhile, the group of travelers reached Egypt to search out the god who had originally possessed the amulet Ayyn was using to mask his plot. The city of Tjenu was different now but Hermes remembered what the god looked like. After some searching they found some hieroglyphs on ancient structures depicting who they were looking for. His name was Anhur-Shu, son of Ra. Anhur-Shu was a god of war and slayer of enemies. It was not looking promising that he was going to be very helpful. Hermes began to search for immortals in the area and he picked up on a sense of someone very close. Just over the hill was a grassy area and someone was sleeping on it.

"That is him just over there," Hermes was not sure about this at all, "I think that is how I last saw him. Strange."

Agreus and his sons, as well as Hermes approached the sleeping god and looked at him.

"I think he has been sleeping for a long time, father," Agreus said with a wrinkled brow.

"Yes, I think this is exactly where I left him sleeping the last time," Hermes answered.

"Is this what happens when people stop worshiping the gods? Do they just go to sleep?" Agreus asked.

"I think that is what he chose to do. Come, let us wake him," Hermes said warily.

Hermes called his name and touched his shoulder. Anhur-Shu began to stir. He sat up and looked around, "How long have I been slumbering?"

"I should think for thousands of years, my friend," Hermes answered.

"Why have you woken me son of Olympus?" the Egyptian god replied.

"I have some rather disturbing news concerning one of your artifacts. It has fallen into the wrong hands and is wreaking havoc in the dimension next to this one. There is an elf who controls it," Hermes responded.

"What does this artifact look like?" the sleepy god asked.

"It is red and in the shape of a whirlwind. It seems to be very powerful and causing this elf to keep prisoner my sons wife," Hermes explained.

"I see. So how did this "elf" get hold of my amulet? It is called Arim-thea. When in the wrong hands it can be very dangerous. Tell me how he got it," the god inquired.

"I took it from you a long time ago while you slept as the world passed by. For this, I am truly sorry. I just want to know how to stop this one who has it from using it if you will help us," Hermes waited to see what would happen now.

Anhur-Shu stood up and stretched his arms out and yawned, "So you stole it from me and allowed it to get into the wrong hands and now you need my help. Tell me Olympian, what will you do for me in return to pay this debt you owe?"

"What must I do?" Hermes knew this was coming.

"You must do favors for me when I require them and ask no questions about what I ask you to do in the future. That is my offer. If you want my help you will take it," Anhur-Shu sat down and watched them for a moment with a wicked smile on his tanned face.

"I will do whatever you ask just please give us instruction on how to undo the magic it has done in the elven realm," Hermes would deal with this "deal" later.

"Alright then. You will require water from the Nile, sand from the Sahara and the blood of an Egyptian god. Mine to be exact. I will allow you to have it once you gather the other materials. You will find me here when you return," with that he lay down again and stared at the sky.

Ayyn was now the king of his people and tomorrow he would be a husband. He would be a faithful one. He had decided he could not touch another woman now. It just did not seem right. He only wanted the attention of the one. Once they were married Ana would be proclaimed queen. He could tell she was nervous but she seemed happy. The night wore on and he thought it time for his princess to be attended to by her maids so she could get some sleep for tomorrow.

After she had bathed and dressed for bed Ana's fiance came to say goodnight before he retired for the evening. He bade the maids excuse them for a bit.

"You did well this evening, Ana," He smiled at her.

"I only hope I made you happy with me. That is my only wish," Ana answered bashfully.

"My dear, you have more than accomplished that. I have never been this happy in my life. I never thought that I would feel this way for anyone but you changed me. You have changed more about my nature than you will ever know," Ayyn was serious.

"I believe you, Ayyn, and I know we shall have a happy marriage together," she believed things would be perfect.

The unknowing princess smiled as she considered the ceremony that would take place tomorrow. She was without the knowledge that she was already married and had born two children. If only she had known she would have fought to return to them. Ayyn's magic had taken away the memories of her happy family.

Ulenn had been doing some research on a way out of this world and into another. He knew it was possible to do. He was aware just like all other elves in the Dulerian kingdom that Ayyn's father had been banished to the world of humans. Perhaps, this world of mortal beings was where he and Athulenne could go and be left alone. He just needed to find the right magic to open a portal for them. Soon, he came across mention in the archives of the exact portal that was used to banish the retired king's brother. All he needed now was to find it's location and figure out how to use it. This is where Athulenne would have to come in. She was pretty good with potions and magic whereas Ulenn fumbled a bit with those things. They were both still very young and had not grown fully into their elven powers.

Ulenn was pondering how a mortal world would be to their benefit. As all around them died and decayed with time they would live on and no one would question their inability to age. If it became a problem they could move around some or use magic as a way to disguise themselves. He was beginning to smile at the possibilities. Refugees on earth is what they would be. Ulenn's mind was made up now. It was time to show his findings to his sister so she begin working on a way to open the door he so desperately desired to open and then close for good. They would have to be especially careful not to let their father find out what they were up to. If he caught them the twins would forever be separated and forced into marriages or receive punishment according to the elven laws. *Now where is my sister?* Ulenn went out to look for Lu.

Athulenne was sitting at the little bridge watching the fish and wondering how in the world Ulenn proposed to get them out of this place forever. She hoped he would come through for them. He had never let her down before so everything should be fine. At least she was praying it would be. Lu could not help but feel that something was not right with Ayyn's surprise wedding announcement and how he just came to be found now. She was using her elven powers to feel around her for traces of thoughts and plots. Lu's powers were beginning to blossom so it was possible she could pick up on something if she tried really hard.

All that Lu was feeling was darkness in the surrounding land. She needed to get close to the princess to see if she too was under some spell. It was a possibility that he had done it to the both of them and if he had then she had the right to know about it. Lu began to plan a way to get near to her so she could try to read the princess' thoughts or sense some magic at work. She would need to disguise herself as a maid to do it. It could be a dangerous task and Lu knew if Ayyn caught her it would be her death.

Agreus, Agrieness, and Kashenn stood back as Hermes reached into the Nile to gather some of it's water. They wanted nothing to do with the strange looking crocodiles in the river. Hermes gathered the liquid into a small wooden vessel with a cork and they were off to the Sahara to gather the required sand. In a flash, they were standing on the dunes of the hot desert.

"This place is awful! How can anyone exist here and not die?" complained Kashenn.

"Many have died in this place," Agreus answered his elven son.

"Agrieness and I are going to be more accustomed to this sort of thing because we are pans and can remain part of this world. You, my son, are not meant to be in a desert but in the lush green lands of the elves," Agreus comforted the miserable Kashenn.

"Let us leave this place," Hermes said as he gathered the sand into a burlap pouch and tied it off with a leather strap.

They traveled back to Tjenu where the sleepy Anhur-Shu was waiting for them. They walked together over to the grassy area where was now sitting and watching wisps of clouds above him.

"Where have they all gone?" Anhur-Shu asked Hermes.

Knowing his meaning Hermes answered, "They stopped worshiping the gods long ago. Now they worship industry and social standing more than they should, my friend."

"So, they have all forgotten the ancient ways. Well, maybe it is for the best. I was tired of their feeble prayers so much that I went to sleep for such a long time. They are an ungrateful bunch are they not?" the sleepy one asked.

"Times have changed and they have moved on to other things and other gods," Hermes answered while noticing a little bit of anger in Anhur-Shu's booming voice. He was obviously a very old god; the oldest that Hermes had ever met. This had the Olympian god worried about the deal he made.

"Here it is," Anhur-Shu handed Hermes a vial of his own blood.

"How do we use these items to dispell the magic?" Hermes asked.

"Mix them altogether and rub them on the amulet and all that has been done by this elf will be undone," Anhur-Shu smiled wickedly at them.

"We cannot get near it. He is using it to keep us out of the Dulerian kingdom," Hermes was troubled.

"Well, that is another matter and it is for you to figure out how to get it back since you stole it away from me. Do not forget our deal Olympian. Return here once this is done. I have something for you to do," Anhur-Shu said as he cut his eyes at Hermes.

With that, the Egyptian god disappeared into the nether leaving the others standing there with an antidote and no way to get it to the infected.

"That went well," Agreus said sarcastically.

"We will figure something out. At least we have the ingredients to undo his evil. Come, Let us return to your glen and work on this problem," Hermes quickly whisked them all back to the hidden glen and into the cave they went.

"I must undo the magic I placed on the Allerian kingdom so I can tell the king that we have the antidote. Perhaps, from their vantage point the clerics can start looking for some way into getting past the barrier that stands in our way. That will give them some comfort at least," Agreus said with hope in his voice.

Agreus approached his little pool in the cave and peered into it while mumbling the words to bring the kingdom of his good friends into view. The castle appeared where everyone was frozen and unaware of anything happening at all. He unfroze time and it was as though they had just left. Speaking through the portal was what he was going to do for now. They needed to stay here for the moment.

"Your majesty," Agreus called to the king through the doorway.

"Agreus, tell us you have found something," the king implored.

"Yes, my friend, we have the concoction that will undo the evil magic that the dark one has used. He is possession of an ancient amulet given to his people long ago. It is more powerful than we could have ever known but we have spoken with the god who created this thing. He was helpful in gaining the materials we needed. Now we just need to find a way past the barrier. We can dispell his magic once we lay hands on this amulet. Some trickery will be needed to get it I imagine. We will work on it from here while the elven clerics work on it from there. It should not be long now," Agreus reassured the old king that all would soon be resolved.

"That is wonderful news, Agreus. Whatever we can do to help will be under your command. I will notify the clerics at once to begin looking for any tears in the boundary so we can get through," The king was definitely hopeful that they would find a weakness in the wall somewhere.

Ayyn, king of the Dulerians was wide awake at dawn. Today he would marry the one that he believed belonged to him all along. He was smiling at the thought of how lovely Ana would look in her wedding attire as stood waiting for her to approach down the isle where the wedding party would be waiting for the ceremony to begin. Already, Ayyn knew that his people were preparing the courtyard and the feasting hall for this momentous occasion. The royal wedding attire was made and being laid out for both Ayyn and Ana. Soon, permission would be asked to come in to begin assisting him to dress. He needed to make sure Ana was being prepared according to his wishes for her appearance to be what he had envisioned for this day.

Ana's dress was dark royal blue velvet with crimson woven into the fabric in places with actual platinum strands! Her slippers would match and her jewels would be diamond in the blue and crimson with platinum settings. Ana's hair would be woven into beautiful braids with platinum strands in them but most of her hair would be left loose and flowing in all it's shimmering glory. He smiled at his image of her. There was a knock at the door.

"Come," Ayyn insisted.

"Your majesty, it is time to begin," the chamberlain announced.

"Yes, let us start with my bathing so I can be dressed. Has everyone begun preparing according to my wishes?" Ayyn asked.

"Yes, my lord, they are busying themselves to meet your wishes as we speak," the chamberlain said proudly.

"Good. Then assist me with my ablutions," Ayyn was ready to start the day.

"As you wish, majesty," The chamberlain began to draw a bath and lay out the wedding clothes Ayyn had ordered made.

The king's outfit would match that of his bride. His tunic and slippers be of the same dark blue velvet as that her billowing gown. It was outlined in the crimson and platinum, as well. His hair was to be pulled back in a dark blue silken ribbon. He was going to look so handsome that he was sure the women in attendance would be jealous. Ayyn smiled at this notion. Against his chest he would wear his amulet to keep it safe during all of the proceedings. He could not let anyone stop him now. It was nearly finished.

"Send word to the maids in charge of my princess to begin her preparations, as well. I am anxious to get things going today. She is my destiny and I am ready to begin our lives together and start a family," Ayyn looked sternly at the chamberlain.

"Yes, my lord," the chamberlain gave him a smile and a knowing look of his meaning.

The chamberlain known as Eckbert left momentarily to send word to the those in charge of making her ladyship ready. He then returned to assist his master.

Ayyn was in full belief that today of all days would be nothing less than perfect and nothing was going to interfere with it or change his plans. That would be a big mistake for the one who decided to do any such thing. He was not worried, though. He had been extremely careful to cover his tracks so there should be no worries.

Athulenne had managed to get hold of a maids clothing and was secretly dressing herself so she could join in the wedding preparations. This would allow her to get close enough to the fair princess. She could at least try to determine if a spell had been put on that poor girl, as well. That would be a call to war with her family if it were true. She knew inside it must be true. Her feelings had not yet betrayed her when it came to her sensitivities.

Today the linens and such would have to be attended to by other maids due to the princess' assigned personal ones were getting her ready for this farce of a wedding. Lu was planning to slip in with them and enter the quarters of her highness. Here she could get a better idea of what was going on. She hoped her brother was being just as industrious as she was today.

Upon reaching the wing of the princess she knocked and entered with her head down to begin helping with the cleaning of rooms therein. The princess was being bathed at the moment and none of the others would even pay Lu attention. She was just another maid right now who was here to help. They would be grateful if nothing else for the extra assistance so everything would be done in the allotted time.

Lu was already getting a sense that magic had been used in these rooms. She needed to determine what had been done. She was still wearing her anti-magic bracelet so maybe it would glow when she came near to anything strong enough to set it off. Lu approached the ablutions area with her head still down to ask if any clothing or linens were in need of being taken away from there. Teska walked over quickly and handed her a pile of clothing that belonged to the princess. Teska hurried away to continue her business. Lu immediately got a tingling sensation from the clothing and noticed her bracelet glowing a hot reddish white. This meant that a strong magic was being used on the princess. Somehow she had to expose this and not meet her end.

Lu had found it odd that the Allerians would allow this union but Ayyn had been so persuasive to everyone else that his word was taken as gospel. She needed to find her brother and update him on her findings. Making her way down the stairs to the back entrance for servants she discarded the soiled clothing and her maids attire. Lu crept down to the bridge to see if her brother had come looking for her. There he was looking concerned at her absence. She ran up to him.

"I have much to tell you, my brother!" she shouted.

"I have just as much to tell you my sister," He was glad she was here.

They recounted all they knew of what they had discovered that day. The task was to now find a way to open the portal and try if possible to help that girl by alerting her Allerian parents. It was pretty obvious now that she was probably missing rather than having been sent by them.

"Let me see," Lu wrinkled her beautiful forehead.

"I can tell there is a force field around our kingdom and I need to weaken it to allow us to open the portal. I think we can send word to the Allerians without being caught. No one would suspect us of trying to do that," Lu was confident that all of this was coming together.

"While I am using my abilities to weaken the wall I need you to prepare a message for the royal family there to inquire of the situation and let them know that the princess is alright but is about to be married without knowledge of any of them anymore. Tell them who she is been betrothed to with magic erasing her memory and knew ones placed instead. That should help them and us," Lu was intent on destroying Ayyn's plans.

"Alright Lu, I am going to do it and see that it is delivered by a good friend that I know will not betray my confidence. He is a fast rider and will also return without being noticed," Ulenn was determined as ever to rid himself of this chaotic kingdom.

Lu set herself to the task of weakening the area she believed the portal would be while her brother carried out his instructions. All was going well with her plan.

Hermes had taken his leave to keep his promise to the Egyptian god while Agreus and his sons were awaiting word from the king on whether or not a weakness had been found. It would seem that something was changing in the formidable wall around the Dulerian kingdom. This was good news. Maybe, very soon they could break through. They would have to be clever once inside the kingdom so they would not be discovered.

Suddenly, Agreus noticed a strange glow on one side of the glen. It was like an opening was forming. This was not the portal that he used to enter the kingdom of the Allerians but a new opening that may be of use. He continued to watch to see if anyone would come through it. Soon, a couple of Dulerian young ones stepped through. This was definitely good. The question would be whether they would be helpful of their own free wills or if he would have to make them be. They were looking around and walking slowly. It was obvious that they meant no harm but all the same he needed to know why they were here.

While Agreus was watching the youngsters his son, Kashenn, came out of the cave and said their was a message from the king. Agreus told Kashenn to watch the two elves while he handled the message.

"Agreus, our clerics have discovered and opening in the wall and it is near your glen," the king said hopeful.

"Yes, and two young Dulerians have come through. I feel they have a part to play in all of this so I am going to question them and see if they will help us," Agreus said confidently.

"Yes, my good friend," the king was beginning to be happy with the turn of events.

While they were speaking, a messenger arrived from the Dulerian kingdom with a message for the king, himself. Agreus watched through his watery mirror into the kingdom to see what this was all about.

"My lord, I have a message from the Dulerian kingdom. My good friend Ulenn has sent this message along with his sister Athulenne who has discovered your princess held captive by our new king," The messenger asserted.

"What is your name, boy?" the king asked warily.

"Arthenis Nebayes is my name. I have been close friend of the twins I mentioned all of my life. I assure you I bring word of the truth so you may reclaim her. She is under a spell. She remembers only what he wants her to remember. He is going to marry her this very day if it has not happened already. Please help us to stop the mad king before he does this," Arthenis implored of the king.

"Who is this king?" Lord Kefna asked still wary.

"His name is Ayyn Kelfinaar, my lord," the young elf replied.

"Now, I believe you. We must act fast. This monster has been trying to get vengeance on our family for ages!" The king was enraged.

"Agreus, my friend, did you get all of that?" the king asked.

"Yes I did, your majesty. I am going to question the young Dulerians now!" Agreus went out to capture the two elves at once.

The young Dulerian messenger left immediately to return before he could be noticed by anyone with prying eyes in his own kingdom. He rode fast but unfortunately not fast enough. Now that the Allerian kingdom was showing back up on Ayyn's radar he had sent spies and assassins to deal with his enemies. Arthenis was shot through with a poisonous arrow. The group of assassins approached him with questions but he died before they could extract anything from him. He only smiled as he died knowing that he had done what was right in the end.

This did not bode well. The alliance of elves moved forward toward the innocent kingdom. They would slay the entire castle if need be to protect their new king. They believed in him and if this is what he wanted then they would do whatever he asked. They were as loyal as they could be to the dark king.

"Stop!" Agreus commanded, "Who are you and why are you in my glen?"

"Sir, we are but a pair of siblings trying to escape our world. The king is quite mad. We sent word to the parents of the stolen princess in his possession so they can stop his evil plans," Ulenn answered for the both of them.

"That princess is my wife and the mother of my children!" Agreus said with rage.

At this time, the twins stepped out from behind the trees to glare at the two younger elves.

"Please, do not hurt us. We had nothing to do with it. Please let my sister tell you a tale that will make things clear," Ulenn protested.

"There is not need. I am a demigod and I can read her thoughts. I will know if there are lies being told," Agreus gave a wicked smile.

Agreus took hold of Athulenne and began to read her mind whilst his sons held back Ulenn from approaching. Agreus saw everything that had transpired and knew this was the way to get them to help.

"So, he promised you things and did not hold up his end of it? I see. Well, I can offer you vengeance if you help me in return to get back my wife. Will you do it willingly or will I have to spend time making you want to help me?" Agreus said with authority.

The twins were afraid of them all but agreed to any terms he might name so long as he would help them escape into the human world to never have to be bothered with anything or anyone from the past ever again. These terms were acceptable so it began. They came up with such a plan as could not be any better!

In the land of the Dulerians a great and spectacular feast was being prepared. The wedding had gone off without any problems. Ana was concerned about her parents not showing up but Ayyn had an answer and promised to explain it all after the celebration had concluded and they were alone. She found this acceptable. After all, why in the world would they want her to stop her wedding because something had delayed them. The scroll received by Ayyn had said to have the wedding performed on that day. At least that is what she was told by him. He had also decided to put off the formal coronation to make her officially queen until after he knew that everything he had done in secret was taken care of.

"My dearest wife, are you alright?" Ayyn said as they sat at the table prepared for the king and his new bride.

"Oh yes, I am having a delightful time, indeed," Ana answered her new husband.

"Good, I want you to have the time of your life. I know I am having an excellent time myself," the dark king told Ana.

"That is happy news, sire. I would not have wanted it any other way for you today," Ana smiled as the king kissed her hand ever so gently.

"Tonight will be much more exquisite even than this," Ayyn gave her a little teasing smile.

She blushed at this but smiled, "Yes, I imagine it will be.

Ana believed she was untouched so she very nervous about tonight. It was her duty to do anything that her king wished of her, though. It would be alright. He was her husband, after all, was he not?

Ayyn sensed her nervousness and assured her that everything would be fine and he would not force anything on her. This seemed to calm her nerves a bit. Soon, the festivities would be coming to an end and they could finally be alone together without interruption. This had him nervous for some reason. Maybe it was because for the first time in his life being intimate with someone would actually mean something. He hoped he would not disappoint her. How odd it seemed for him to worry about such a thing.

"My dear, I believe it is time for us to be excused. It grows quite late and I want to spend time with you before sleep sets in," Ayyn looked at her lovingly.

"Yes, you are right dear, we should go now," Ana was growing nervous again.

Ayyn made the announcement that the two of them would be retiring for the night but they should continue to feast and party until they felt the urge to go home. Everyone bowed and gave cheers of joy for the newly married couple as they departed.

Ayyn decided it was best if he spent the night in Ana's wing with her. It was very comfortable there and no other women had tainted this place. They entered and excused the maids for the evening. Ayyn took a long moment to give his lovely wife a thorough looking over while smiling at her with all of his glamor and beauty. She was breathtaking to him.

In return, she was watching him with a nervous curiosity. She marveled at those blue eyes that looked like the sea on the clearest of days. His lightly colored silken hair hung loose over his shoulders and down his back now. His glistening skin was nearly glowing as he moved closer to Ana and took he r into his strong embrace. She let out a small gasp as he kissed her deeply and passionately. The rest of the night was spent doing what anyone does on the night they were wed. While Ana slept peacefully, he was holding her tightly and watching her. He could never let her go. Ayyn knew that his heart belonged to her forever, now. He would rather die than be separated from his beloved.

Agreus concluded his talk with the twin elves and thought it best to share everything with the king and queen as to what they were going to do to penetrate the kingdom and stop this madness. He only hoped he was not too late to save his wife from a fate worse than the most painful death. He approached the pool of water to call up the kingdom of the Allerians. As the throne room came into view his worst fear was before him. The king, queen, and anyone who had been in the throne room lay strewn about in death. It was obvious that the kingdom had been assaulted by assassins sent by the dark perpetrator.

"NO!" Agreus cried out in horror.

"What has happened father?" Agrieness was asking.

"They are all dead, my son, all dead!" Agreus was crying with glowing eyes.

"That whelp of an elf will pay with his soul!" Agreus was ready to go ahead with their plans immediately. Ana would be so upset by the loss of her parents. He could not think straight enough to focus on that matter at the moment. He just needed to get her back here to the glen safely.

"This I swear! I shall avenge my grandparents with my life if necessary!" Kashenn was inconsolable.

Agrieness was very quiet but obviously shaken and not himself. He did not know what to say or do about this tragic turn of events. All he knew was that he was hurt more deeply than he ever thought he could be.

"Alright young ones, here is the potion you will need. I am going to place a spell on you, Athulenne. I need you to get close enough to Ayyn to retrieve the amulet he wears. You must find it and rub this concoction on it. It will immediately dispell any magic he has used it for. Everyone will begin to return to normal and the magic circle around your kingdom will vanish. If he used the medallion on my wife she will remember everything. I am going to make you look like Ana so you can get close enough to him," Agreus chanted over the little elf.

Athulenne was the exact image of Ana. It hurt him to see her likeness.

"Now go. For your sakes I hope you do not get caught. Ulenn, follow your sister and keep watch in case she gets into trouble. You may have to rescue her if she is discovered," Agreus insisted.

"Of course, my sister goes no where that I do not," Ulenn said protectively.

"Good. Then you must go now while the portal is still open," Agreus urged them to be quick.

The twins went through the portal and entered back into the forest from whence they came. They crept up to the castle via an invisibility spell provided by the demigod. They entered quietly and located where the royals were inside the thick stone walls. This is where the brother and sister would need to part ways but he would follow invisibly when she became visible. His presence must go undetected so he could help if need be. Athulenne made her way into the king's quarters. She would wait for him here. He was in a meeting with the council at the moment and would no doubt return to his chambers to change and refresh himself before going to see his princess who would soon be queen here if they failed.

Soon enough, Ayyn did return to his quarters to do exactly as she suspected. What was this that she was picking up from him? True love? Could the monster really be in love with the wife of Agreus, after all. Marriage? It had already happened and they had already spent that night together. Athulenne was reading his open thoughts. Agreus would be so upset. Time moved differently here than it did in the human realm. It would seem time passed much more quickly here than it did there. That would explain how everything had been able to happen before they could return. This was not good but she had a job to do and this might make her getting close to him even easier.

"My love?" the pretend Ana said.

"Ah, my dear what are you doing hiding in here?" Ayyn smiled at who he thought was his beloved.

"I was waiting for you, darling. I could not bear to be without you a moment longer," Athulenne was thinking of how good an actress she was.

"Well, in that case, come to me my wife. I cannot have you missing me to the point of pain now can I?" He reached to embrace his wife.

"Let me lay with you here for a while, my beloved. The comfort of your embrace will make much happier than I have been all day!" Lu was doing a good job. He bought it.

The pretend Ana and Ayyn lay down on the king's bed together. Lu began to rub his chest as if to comfort herself. She could feel that something was under his shirt. It had a magical aura about it. This must be the amulet they were seeking. Getting her hands on it and away from him without notice was going to be difficult but she could manage.

"My love, are you alright?" Ayyn asked her.

"I am just so terribly worried about my parents. I have heard nothing of when they will arrive," she feigned worry.

"Is that all my love? Why, I have received communication that they are on the way as we speak so there is no reason to be concerned, my dear," Ayyn lied.

Athulenne already knew the fate of the little princess' parents and was disgusted by his deceit. She managed a smile and found his explanation acceptable. She began to run her hand underneath his shirt but staying below the amulet. He was becoming excited. She figured this would happen and she would have to do something she did not want to. Soon they were undressed and in the throws of passion. He believed he was with his princess so he was unhindered and had no care in the world. *Why could he not love me like that?* She managed to finish the deed and had slipped the amulet off of him during the undressing.

When all was done she tucked it into her skirt so it would not be noticed until it was too late.

"My love, I must return to the throne room. Will you join me shortly? I would like to announce the day of your coronation to the council with you by my side," Ayyn cooed to his lovely wife.

"Of course, I will just return to my wing and freshen up a bit. I will meet you very shortly, my love," Athulenne lied.

Ayyn was beaming with delight that Ana had taken such a bold step as she did. It was quite the turn on for him to have her come to seek him out like that. He was walking back to the throne room when he realized that he must have left his amulet in his chambers. He did not want to be without it for very long. It was the key to keeping all of this together. Ayyn returned to his chambers to look for it but it could not be found. He was worried now. Maybe it had gotten caught up in Ana's clothes when she left to freshen up. Ayyn hurried to her wing to check with her. He was sure it must be the case. It was just an accident that could quickly be fixed without a problem.

Ayyn announced himself at Ana's door. It was opened by Teska who bowed to the king.

"My lord, I am so happy to see you! Today must have been quite busy in the court. I have missed you terribly!" Ana threw her arms around Ayyn.

"Have you been here in your quarters all day? Teska, has she not left these rooms at all?" Ayyn asked confused.

"No my lord, she has been here all day waiting for your word to have her come to the throne room," Teska answered her master.

"Is there a problem, my love?" Ana was worried.

"Of course not, my dear. I was merely worried that you might need to get some fresh air and not be cooped up is all." Ayyn kissed her forehead.

"I shall send for you very soon, loveliness," Ayyn excused himself.

The king was in a near panic at the moment. He began to feel for the energy of the amulet. It was his for so long that he would recognize where it was located provided it was still in the castle. Someone was up to something and they would pay with their life. Not only had they taken his amulet but had caused him to be unfaithful by looking like his wife to seduce him! This was an outrage but who would do something like that? Ayyn began to feel the amulet located inside the clerics chambers. The clerics were not there at this time. They would be down in the court attending other things at the moment. So who was the perpetrator?

Ayyn walked into the clerics rooms to discover Athulenne with the amulet and something in her other hand.

"What are you doing Athulenne? I thought we were friends." Ayyn was impatient with her.

"I thought we were more than friends. That was what I thought until you announced your marriage to that poor girl whom you have fooled. You tried to wipe my memory but it failed you monster!" Athulenne accused him.

"Well, well. I see. If you give me the amulet I think we can solve this problem between us. You must give it over to me Athulenne. You cannot know what you are doing," Ayyn was pleading with her as Ulenn looked on unseen.

"Oh, but I do know what I am doing. I have met with the princess' true husband and her sons. They have given me everything I need to dispell your evil. You do not even know what this amulet is or all that it can do. It was a gift from a god long ago to this people and do you know who gave it? It was the father of Agreus, Hermes!" Athulenne's rage was growing.

Ayyn was enraged at the truth of all she said. He moved towards her to dispatch his problem and take back which was rightfully his. As he approached her he was stopped by a force surrounding the clever little elf.

"Your shield will not stop me Athulenne!" He broke it with a spell of his own.

"Your magic cannot harm me Ayyn. It did not effect me when you tried to wipe my memory and it cannot touch me now!" She finished rubbing the potion on the amulet and all was dispelled that Ayyn had used it for.

He felt the power go out of it and all of his magic done with it was gone.

"You foul wench! My magic may not effect you but my hands around your neck will certainly be effective!" Ayyn moved to grab Athulenne.

Suddenly, Ayyn was knocked to the floor by the unseen Ulenn. "Come my sister, we must return through the portal before the demigod and his sons arrive. We will go into the world of the humans and disappear."

The twins left quickly before anyone could see them. Through the portal they went as Agreus and his sons went through the watery mirror they liked to use. The portal closed in the forest behind the siblings as they ran for the cover of a nearby grouping of trees. Now that the force field was down around the Dulerian kingdom they could use the pool to see anything and anyone. They found Ayyn knocked out on the floor in the clerics quarters. He had not been able to prepare anything to escape this time and the medallion was being left in his cave by the twins so that it could safely be stored at a later time.

They made their way to Ana's room hoping the magic had been removed from her and she would know them now. They dragged the knocked out king with them to show Ana that they had caught her captor. She would be so pleased that they could all go home. They reached the wing that Ana was in and opened the door. Teska saw they had her king and nearly screamed. Agreus was able to freeze her before that happened.

"Oh my, sir why you taken my husband hostage?" Ana was crying at the sight of her king being dragged into the room.

"Please do not hurt him. I will do anything you ask just do not hurt him!" Ana fell to her knees near her king as he began to stir.

This was not right. Agreus realized Ayyn must have used his own magic and not the power of the amulet to do this to her. He did not have time to deal with this here. The guards would show up soon enough. He would just have to take her away and deal with it back in the glen.

"Ana, help me. These beasts have accosted me! They wish to take the kingdom and force you to go with them.

"Please do not take her from me! I love her. She loves me! She is my wife! Ana!" Ayyn screamed.

Ana was crying and pleading not to be separated from Ayyn. Agreus used his demigod magic to place Ayyn in one of the magic cells that he had no way of escaping this time. He would deal with him later, but he could not bear to see Ana cry over the monster any longer. Ana's sons grabbed her and they all went through the portal and into the glen. Agreus immediately put her under a sleeping spell with an incantation. He laid her on his bed. She had been through much and they must bring her memory back. The powerful amulet was sitting on a table in the cave as promised by Athulenne. They must have taken off to go make a place for themselves in this world. He really did not care where they were. It was not his concern. For the moment he would let her sleep while he and his sons went to sound the alarm in the Allerian kingdom. Just in case, he locked Ana up tightly so no one could penetrate the cave. Agreus decided to keep the amulet on him for now. It could be useful, perhaps.

Upon arriving in the kingdom they discovered the clerics had stumbled upon the gruesome scene in the throne room. Agreus explained what had happened and assured them that the criminal was in custody in the bowels of the castle. His sons were crying, but they must help him with preparing for the royal burial process.

It was a somber moment and a very unhappy day in the kingdom. The elven people here were in utter disbelief. The names of the assassins would be tortured out of the mastermind in the dungeon and they would be punished by death. Agreus and his sons watched the procession of the clerics and the people crying as the bodies were all prepared and moved into tombs.

A meeting was called afterward. Agreus assured the people that Ana was safe even though the foul creature called Ayyn had destroyed her memory. He told them he would restore it and the heir to the throne would take over as acting king until a proper time could be set for a coronation. This was not the time. The kingdom needed time to grieve first for all that it had lost. Kashenn had been trained for the day he would assume the throne but never did he imagine it would be like this.

Ayyn awoke in a cell. He had bars this time. He tried to touch them and was sent flying backwards. His magic would not work in here.

He would have to see what the beast was planning to do with him. All he could think of was Ana. He wanted her back and in his arms. How upset she had been when they took her from him. It was painful to think of it. An angry tear rolled down his cheek. Where were they keeping her? He could not sense her in the castle at all. Ayyn hoped they would not punish her for all of this. How cruel could they be? He had never liked them, especially that demigod who thought he had the right to mingle with elves. She should never have been the wife of an outsider. It was not even customary! Her parents were better off dead in his opinion.

Agreus left his sons in charge while he returned with the clerics to the glen so they could restore Ana's memory completely. Agreus felt it was important for her to now remember everything including her time as a mortal and everything that had happened. It would be a key component in her understanding that Ayyn was indeed a monster. He knew it would hurt her but she had to face it now to be able to move on with their lives together. Agreus was indeed upset that he had put her through a wedding with him and most likely a wedding night. It was not her fault but he would need time to get over it.

Ana still slept as they moved her out into the glen. They were going to leave her asleep for the ritual. It would be less painful for her that way. She would wake and then remember once it was done.

The clerics hung their heads in pain for what had happened to the princess and to her parents. They set up the circle of light and prepared for a full memory return. They did not want her to remember the things her parents had wanted her to forget but these circumstances were difficult so they let Agreus instruct them now. Soon, they were all chanting and moving in a circle around the princess. She began to stir and sat up once her memory had fully returned.

Ana was very confused. She had so many emotions as everything came rushing back to her. She remembered the humans and how they had treated her. She also remembered what Ayyn wanted to do to her then but she knew the person he had become really did love her. Ana remembered her husband Agreus, her sons, and her parents. While all of this was rolling around inside of her head she was crying softly. The princess new she had unwittingly been unfaithful to Agreus, but the strange thing was that even though the memory had returned she still had feelings for Ayyn, as well. Oddly, what he had told her about her role in changing him for the better was true. He did regret all he had done and loved her as much as her true husband. Ana was feeling as though her entire life had just been turned upside down when Agreus approached her.

"Ana?" Agreus spoke to her.

"Do not look upon me, husband," Ana whispered in shame.

"Ana, I know it was not your fault," Agreus answered.

"I am very confused right now. I need to be alone to clear my mind; however, I would like to know what you have done with Ayyn," Ana asked wearily.

"He is in a prison cell in the Allerian kingdom. Why do you wish to know this?" Agreus did not understand.

"What are you planning to do with him? I must know." Ana was insistent.

"I plan to have him executed in the public square for all that he has done. I was going to wait to tell you this but your parents have been assassinated and we are sure he was behind it." Agreus hung his head.

"My parents . . . . They are dead? Where are my children?" Ana's voice trembled with fear.

"Our children are fine. Kashenn is acting king at the moment and Agrieness is there to assist him. Both are in mourning for their grandparents." Agreus reassured her.

"I must see Ayyn before you carry out a sentence upon him, my husband. I will grieve for my parents but first there is something that must be done. I remember everything all at once. I know who I am and who I used to be. Likewise, I remember the rest. I love you, Agreus but I need to see Ayyn now." The princess would not be moved on the issue.

"My dearest wife, I would advise against it but I know you will only be unhappy if you do not have closure on this," Agreus was worried about the encounter.

"Come, let us return to the kingdom at once. I want to see my children and then I must handle this business of mine," Ana began to walk to the hollow tree.

Agreus and the clerics followed her and they all entered into the kingdom. As they passed, the villagers bowed low with somber faces.

They were happy the princess was returned but they new her pain would be hard to endure after all she had suffered.

The clerics returned to their stations, while Agreus and Ana entered the throne room. Both of her sons ran to embrace their mother. They all cried together for a few moments as Agreus watched over his grief-stricken family. She kissed her children on their beautiful faces and looked at them with love and pain in her face. Ana turned to Agreus and nodded.

"Boys, stay here. Your mother and I have something to attend to. We shall return shortly," Agreus instructed his sons.

They were obedient to their father and asked no questions for the moment. Now was not the right time to ask anything from either of them and they new that. They were still too freshly wounded in their own hearts to be bothered with anyone much at all themselves.

Agreus took Ana to the bowels of the castle where Ayyn sat in his prison cell awaiting fate to decide if he would live or die. Without Ana, it did not matter to him. He knew they had most likely restored her memories and she would think him still the monster that he no longer wanted to be. It was too late for him to be loved by her in his mind. Why would she in the remembrance of all that was done to her in the past at his hand? He was sure that he would remain forever unforgiven.

As husband and wife approached the dungeon where Ayyn was being held Agreus asked, "Are you sure you want to do this?"

"I must do this, Agreus and I must do it alone," Ana said with a look of stone.

"I shall wait outside the door. You have only to call out if you want me to come, my love," Agreus did not like this.

Princess Ana entered the door that led to a row of cells on each side of the musky dungeon. She very slowly began to walk down the middle never looking to either side. She could sense Ayyn in the cell at the end on the right. The guards bowed and moved aside for her to pass. Ana moved quietly down the isle until she reached the cell of the perpetrator. She looked at him as he lay there with his eyes closed. His face was reddened from crying. She was unsure what to do or say now that she stood in front of this one who had always made her existence hard for her and those around her. All of the loss that had been suffered was ultimately his fault but at the same time was he not trying to change? Ayyn did not understand what it meant to do something totally for another without something in return until he fell for her. She should hate him and she knew it. Somehow, she could not find it in herself to cast him aside for the cruel thing he had been. As she stood considering these things Ayyn woke up and looked at Ana without saying a word. He sat up on the stone bed and straightened himself up a bit. A piteous look was in his eye as well as one of sorrow. She could tell that he knew all that he had done was wrong and yet still he had done it.

Ana moved toward the cell bars and reached inside for him to approach. Ayyn climbed down to the floor and sat as close as he could to her as she sat down on the hard stone floor outside the cell. Without a word she placed her hands on either side of his head to read his thoughts. She needed to see the truth of his life. She needed to know how someone who could be so loving had turned into such a monster.

The princess was beginning to see the little half breed elf named Thomas that the good sister in the orphanage had taken such good care of. She saw that his parents had not loved or wanted him. His mother had cast him away to grow up as an orphan to prevent the embarrassment she felt at what had transpired. Ana saw how the other children and nuns had abused and neglected him because he was different. The only one who had cared for him had died and even then he was treated with such disdain at her funeral. Ana saw many of the hardships and traumas that he had suffered throughout his own life. It truly was tragic because he was so talented and could have chosen a different path. She saw how his father had been the one to tell him about the dark magic that would have involved her. It had been his father that had convinced him that it was his only way. She saw how all of these puzzle pieces fit together to lead him down the dark way that had caused him to make poor decisions. The real Thomas was not like this elf that Ayyn was now. He started off so sweet and innocent but was betrayed by those who were supposed to love him the most. This was something that Ana was quite familiar with while she was the mortal girl known as Claire. Instead of remaining himself he had chosen to harden his heart to gain vengeance for all that he been taken from him. She shook her head as she sat crying at his unfortunate life. He had become many things but the innocent Thomas was still inside of him.

The princess slowly reached for his hands to place them on each side of her head so that he could witness how she had been treated by the mortal parents and how Agreus had been the one to protect her from their wrath. Ayyn was softly crying as he saw all of the abuses she had suffered because of him. He was beginning to understand why she loved Agreus so much. Unlike him, she had someone to step in while she was still young to at least offer comfort and love as she endured the horrors at what had once been her home. Ayyn did not hate him so much anymore. He was glad that she had a protector all of the years that it would seem she was in need of one and it was all his fault.

Ayyn could no longer bear the silence.

"I am so sorry, my love. I should never have done any of those horrible things. To know as I do now that I have been completely responsible for all of your suffering pains me beyond imagine. I understand if you hate me because I surely would deserve it," Ayyn pulled closer to her as the bars remained between them. They sat with their heads touching and with arms embracing one another.

"Yes, I should hate you but I do not. My parents are dead and my kingdom is ravished. Even as a mortal I suffered due to your plotting but I cannot make myself hate you because I know that the time we spent together was real. I know you love me and I cannot get my love for you out of my head right now. The potions you gave me only erased my memory but the new ones created were as real as the rain. Now, I stand in a conundrum. I have a husband and children that I dearly love and they want to see you dead. However, I carry this new burden of love for you and do not want to see you die. Once again, no matter what the end brings, I will suffer. I will be made to suffer because I will still love you whether you die or not and I will never be able to be with you. I have a husband that has loved me for ages and I him. I am confused that I can love more than one man, nevertheless, I do but I can never have you both. I have a duty to my family and to this kingdom. Unfortunately, I have no final say in your fate but I will try to save your life," Ana was very emotional.

"There is no use in saving me, Ana. Look what I have become. I know you saw me in my youth as an innocent but now I am a monster. You were saving me from myself. Without you I would have no purpose in continuing to live," Ayyn said with a shaky voice as he brushed against her belly with his hand.

"Ana, you are pregnant!" Ayyn was astonished.

"I have only been with you so it must be your child. Agreus will be furious. What shall I do now? This changes many things. Yet still I am not the one who has final say in what will be done with me, either," Ana was scared.

"Come away with me, Ana. Let us raise our child together where no one can find us! You must not let them kill the child! It is not his fault," Ayyn begged her.

"I will not let them harm my own child but I cannot leave here. I have a duty to those I already serve. As much as it hurts me to have to let you go I must find a way to do it for both of our sakes. There must be someone out there for you love besides me. If only I can convince them to let you go back to the mortal realm you can still find it," Ana tried to reason.

"No! I will never love another but you. Please! I do not want to be separated from you and my child. I want to raise him!" Ayyn said with a tear-stained face.

Ayyn pulled Ana to face him between the bars and kissed her gently on the lips. He could see the pain in her eyes and the love she still felt for him. She quickly stood up and ran out of the dungeon sobbing uncontrollably. Ayyn called after her.

"Ana, do not leave me. I love you," he whispered through his misery and anguish.

Agreus was waiting patiently outside the door. He had given them their privacy as she had requested.

"Is this thing done?" Agreus asked her.

"It has to be but I have discovered that I am pregnant and it is his child. I beg of you do not kill him. Banish him to the mortal world but do not kill him! I cannot bear the thought of it," She continued to sob.

Agreus embraced her now. He was sorry because he knew this would be very difficult road for her. He would raise the child as his own but she would always know his real father was out there somewhere. However, if letting him live would keep her from dying of heart break then he would discuss it with Kashenn. After all, this was not her fault. The child should never need to be told the truth of any of it. This was the only way to keep peace in the family.

"My dear, I will take care of this. The child will not be harmed and I will raise him. As for Ayyn I will speak with Kashenn about banishment with the condition that he be made mortal before going back there. Does this seem a fair deal to you?" Agreus asked.

"Yes, it would be a much better way. I know it would be a fitting punishment in the eyes of the villagers for him to become completely mortal. Maybe this will end our tribulations," Ana said wearily.

"You need to rest," Agreus told her, "I will take you to our room and then I will take care of the arrangements for the prisoner with our sons.

Princess Ana was so tired from this entire ordeal that she did not protest. Instead, she followed Agreus to their quarters and lay down on the bed there to rest. She fell asleep but it was a troubled one.

Agreus called Kashenn and Agrieness into a private meeting concerning all that she had said to him. They were upset that the dark one had done this to their mother but there was no one to blame, except Ayyn. The innocent would not be made to suffer for the deeds of the wicked. The three of them decided together that they would welcome this new brother and keep quiet about who his father really was. If it would make things easier on their mother to raise the child by leaving the monster alive in mortal form then they would do it. He would eventually die any way. What harm could it possibly cause. What were human years to the immortals? They made all of the preparations to make him mortal and send him through the portal to earth. Ayyn would have to endure pain and human trials like never before. He was at least half elf before all of this was started so long ago.

"Now, at least the monster will face death in his mortality," Kashenn spoke to his father.

"I would personally like to remove his head for touching my wife and impregnating her but perhaps, she is right to want to spare him that gruesome fate. Perhaps, he will have learned something of mercy and kindness when he returns to the world of humans," Agreus was trying to see the brighter side.

"I do not like this, father. What if he gets back here somehow and continues to torture our family? How can we live in peace while he is still alive?" Agrieness had a bad feeling about the whole thing.

"Son, he will die a mortal death and will not be able to return here since I have the amulet that he was using to open doors in the first place. There is nothing to fear from him anymore," Agreus reassured Agrieness.

The meeting between father and sons had now concluded. They trudged down to the dungeon to inform Ayyn of his fate. Upon arrival, they noticed the sound of quiet sobbing coming from Ayyn's cell.

"Ana?" Ayyn called out.

"I am afraid not, monster. It is her husband and her sons.

"I have come to tell you of the judgment which shall be handed down to you. I must say that you have Ana to thank for the part where your life is spared. If it were up to me I would see you dead for what you have done to my family!" Agreus was angry.

"For what it is worth, I am sorry for Ana's sake that I have done any of this," Ayyn said softly.

"Now, the good part for us is that I am going to make you mortal before I send you through to the human world so that you cannot find your way here again. It would seem that my wife cannot bear the thought of me killing you so you will die a mortal death as the fates see fit," Agreus announced with his arms folded over his muscular chest.

"Are you aware that she is carrying my child?" Ayyn asked solemnly.

"Your child? You mean my child!" Agreus replied.

"He is my son and you know it!" Ayyn was full of rage now.

"In flesh only, however, he will never know of you. It is what is best for him and the rest of my family," Agreus said with a wicked grin.

"How does our little wife feel about your plan to claim my son?" Ayyn said with malice.

"She will do as I ask and she is my wife alone! Do you understand me you evil thing?" Agreus turned his back on Ayyn.

Agreus ordered his sons to prepare the portal while he prepared to make the prisoner mortal.

"Please do not do this to me, Agreus. I deserve to know my son. I love Ana as much as you do and I swear I will leave you be if you just let me know my son. Why can I not at least have part in my son's life? I am willing to push my love for Ana down if you will have mercy on me. I am willing to endure whatever punishment you would have me suffer here in this realm if you can but see past my wrongdoings. Ana knows that I am not as evil as you would make me out to be. She has seen inside my thoughts and knows my past. If she is willing to move past that and still care what happens to me then why can you not show a bit of kindness to me in this way?" Ayyn's words fell on deaf ears.

"Agrieness, help me with this concoction given to me by the clerics. It will turn him human and we must do it before he goes through," Agreus ignored Ayyn.

"Kashenn, prepare the amulet to open a portal to this creature's original homeland back in the human world where he may find something familiar to base the rest of his existence upon," Agreus ordered.

Ayyn knew there was no escaping this trap that destiny had set for him. Some how he must find a way to break it's hold on him. Right now, all he could do was watch as the potion poured on him changed him into a mortal. He saw the portal open with the use of what was once his amulet. Ayyn was truly afraid for the first time in his life. The guards that stood by were at attention in case he tried anything.

"My sons, push this "human" through into his own realm. Now!" Agreus shouted with authority.

Ayyn was sent through to his old stomping grounds in England. He was furious with what had been done to him and once more something of great importance had been stolen from him. He could not bear eternity without knowing his son or ever seeing Ana's sweet face again. No matter how long it took or what he had to do he would find a way to get it all back. He would have his vengeance on those who had no mercy on him. They would be sorry and they would pay!

Ayyn began to walk towards what used to be his property. The Lord of Black Thorn Manor had returned home once again.

Soul Shift: Earthbound

The now mortal Ayyn walked slowly toward his old castle. Black Thorn Manor still stood and seemed in good repair. He wondered at this since he assumed that no one was living there. When he had come to the new world he had not sold it to anyone. Thomas, as he was known then, had kept it in case he needed to return here. It was his property. Could someone have gained control over it? He needed to find out so that he could begin his mission of removing this wretched magic that would age him more quickly. The most he could hope for was to regain his half elf status since he was born into this realm in that form. At least that would give him time to try and figure a way to gain access to those whom he loved and take them away. He would need to plan some way to cover his tracks so they would never be found again. This was his plan now.

Ayyn would have been true to his word if Agreus had let him remain but now all bets were off. It was as if he could feel horns of his own growing even though there were none. Now, he wanted nothing more than to take his wife and child never to be seen again by the lot of them. In Ayyn's mind she was still his wife and she was going to bear him a son. He could have a family of his own. What wretch was it that decided that his fate should always be to have nothing and be alone? Why should he be the one to suffer and have no family? Had he transgressed in some other life and was now being punished in this one?

Reaching the front gate of the manor Ayyn noticed some men in brown robes walking around the property and pruning bushes or just strolling about.

"Monks! What the devil?" Ayyn was not amused.

"How on earth did they get their hands on my property?" Ayyn said aloud.

"Hello there my friend," an older monk approached Ayyn.

"Well hello. How long has there been an order of monks at this estate?" Ayyn asked.

"It sat vacant for a long time. It would seem the previous owner left and never came back so the family that sold it to him donated it for God's purposes. Also, there was rumor that it had been gained through a ruse and the family decided not to honor the selling of the deed to the man it was supposedly sold to. All of that has been long ago I'm afraid. Would you like to come in and refresh yourself? You look travel weary and perhaps some supper would help you on your journey," The old monk was very kind.

"Yes, I graciously accept your hospitality. I have traveled a long way and am tired and hungry," Ayyn was amused.

"What is your name and where are you headed, my friend?" the monk asked.

"I am Thomas and I am on my way home from far away," Ayyn said.

"Well follow me and I will assist you in any way I can," The monk led the way.

The monk known as "Brother Simon" was providing Ayyn with some clothing so that he could bathe and join them for supper. Ayyn sat in the steaming tub of water and looked at his reflection in the water. He still looked young and fit. His eyes remained the same blue that his mother had possessed and his hair was still blonde. His ears were not pointed anymore and his skin seemed more of a tanned color than the beautiful caramel color it had always been. Ayyn had felt the immortality leave his body when he had initially returned. He felt all of the aches and pains of a normal human who had been walking for miles. Also, he was dirty. This was unusual to him since filth really had never clung to him before now. It was a bothersome thing. Bathing was always enjoyable but now it was absolutely necessary since humans apparently had an odor if they did not.

Ayyn was plotting against the passive monks. There were not that many of them and surely he could find a way to dispatch them without any trouble. This castle was so remote that no one would notice and if anyone came nosing around he would put on one of the brown robes and deny them entrance due to some prayer time or something that he made up was going on at the time. Now, how could he kill them without to much of a mess? He still had to live here, after all. The less he had to clean up afterward the better. He longed for Ana to be here with him now. Her comforting embrace could make the darkest of days melt into a dream. Ayyn shed a tear for their unfortunate separation.

"Soon, my love," Ayyn hoped.

"Thomas, the brothers are preparing to meet in the dining hall for supper. Are you going to join us?" Brother Simon called out.

"Yes brother, I am on my way," Ayyn dressed quickly.

"Would you mind helping the young brother in the kitchen serve the bowls of soup?" Brother Simon asked.

"I would be delighted to do it, Brother Simon!" Ayyn saw an opportunity.

Ayyn made his way to the kitchen area to assist Brother Francis who seemed to have his young hands full. He took stock of everything in the area and noticed rat poison on a shelf near the sink.

"Hello, Brother Francis, I am here to help you serve supper. My name is Thomas," Ayyn lied.

"Oh thank goodness! I need to go and see about the rolls before they burn in the oven," The brother left the room.

Ayyn grabbed the box of poison and dumped it into the huge pot of soup cooking over the stove and stirred it in. He smiled to himself. He was figuring that ought to do the trick. Then he would just burn their bodies once they died and he could tear down the walls that were over his private quarters. Surely, some of his things should still be where he had hidden them. Ayyn was all too happy to begin putting soup into bowls while the young brother returned with rolls to pass out in the dining area. They carried everything out and set it on the long wooden table for the consumption of the monks. Ayyn sat a bowl for himself down last at the end of the row. Brother Simon said a prayer in Latin and then bade everyone to eat, quietly.

Ayyn watched the brothers with disdain as they ate the poisoned meal. He pretended to sip it from his spoon until they all began to grab their abdomens and scream with pain. They profusely vomited and writhed around on the floor as they cried out in death. Ayyn was not counting on having to clean up vomit. What a nuisance! Oh well, at least they were dying and he could have his castle back.

Agreus and Ana were in the process of welcoming a new son into the kingdom. The little elf was a boy as expected and he was given the name Julienn. He was adorable and even though his coloring was a little different than Ana's it was nearly impossible to spot the difference. The one thing that he did have in common with his biological father were those blue eyes that glistened like the glassy sea on the sunniest day. Little Julienn's hair was as white as the clouds and he was a splendor to behold. The Allerian people saw his birth as a blessing after all that had been taken from them. Their hearts had been brought out of despair by the little miracle.

Of course, the immediate family new the truth behind the babe's coming to be. Kashenn was especially worried that he would have his father's traits and one day try to usurp the throne from him. Once again, the kingdom would be plunged into darkness if that happened. He would watch his half-brother very carefully over the years to make sure he had none of the evil his father.

Kashenn had his coronation during the time his mother was pregnant with the little one. He was now King Kashenn of the Allerian elves. He was a good and noble king. He was always fair, though there was rarely a need for any judgments to come down on anyone. Mostly, he dealt with political things and helping the people. Kashenn enjoyed the throne and was the rightful heir as named by his departed grandfather. He would never allow the son of the dark one to take his place. It would, in his mind, dishonor the memory of his beloved grandparents who had fallen to the assassins sent by Ayyn.

For now, the child was small and of no consequence in that way. Kashenn never thought about how as the only son of the recent king of the Dulerians, Julienn should have a right to rule that kingdom, but even so he would never know his true identity. If Kashenn had his way they would send the little elf away. He understood why they could not and did not but he was not very forgiving on the matter. As king, he would try to get along with his half-brother for the sake of his parents and act as if nothing were wrong. Perhaps, that would be enough.

Agrieness had taken over full time back in the glen and the surrounding woods. He felt his time was best spent taking care of the growing things and all of the inhabitants of the forest. As a pan, he could be part of the human realm without it effecting him because pans originated in this realm. Agrieness had decided after watching silently by at all of the traumatic events of his mother's realm that he did not believe romantic love was something that he wanted to experience. It brought sheer happiness at first and then could be just as easily ripped away or tainted by someone or something. He had decided that in time he would tell his parents that he was going to remain here in his father's home to avoid anything that might lead to love. He would just as soon tear out his own heart and hand it over before allowing anyone to put him through what he had witnessed happen to his mother. He felt sorry for his father, Agreus. Agreus was having to live with the knowledge that he would raise the son of the enemy. He wondered if his father could do it. Agrieness was gentle and kind. He would be good to his half-brother but he was not so sure that Kashenn could do the same. For now he needed to refortify the barrier around the glen to assure that no one ever found it. Not even if it was something like what happened to his mother. Agrieness just wanted solitude for now. He needed time to heal and put the past behind him. He walked into the forest to begin his incantations and repairs of anything out of place. Maybe he would add some new foliage this spring.

The Dulerians were at a loss. Their king had been missing for years without a trace. The only witness to anything was Teska who was made stark raving mad by the freeze of time that Agreus had placed on her and never removed. By the time they discovered her in the princess' wing she was already out of her mind. They discovered her madness once the clerics had found a way to bring her back. Teska was talking out of her head and not making much sense. The princess was also missing. This was altogether a dark time for the Dulerians. To make it worse, Utenn, leader of the council had lost his twins around the same time. They had all disappeared without a trace. These were bad omens. *What was to come next?* The people wondered. Utenn was devastated at the thought of his missing children. He had been asked to be temporary caretaker of the throne until all of this could be rectified or a new king could be crowned. There was still an investigation going on into the disappearances and the elven clerics were probing the maid's mind for any clues while she remained placed in a sleep for her own protection. Time in the elven realm had really flown by as the time in the human realm had barely past at all.

They were all very saddened by the losses. The council sent riders in every direction with messages to find out if anyone had seen the missing ones or heard tale of what happened. So far nothing had been sent back with a promising lead. The council would have to wrap things up soon so they could move on from this tragedy. The old king seemed to have disappeared as well. He was no where in the castle to be found. Was it possible that he had anything to do with these events? Cassen was a crazy and unstable elf. He would be punished severely if that were found to be the case. Unfortunately, that would lead no where for the elves since the old king was long dead at the hands of his nephew.

Meanwhile word had reached the Dulerians of the tragedy that had befallen the Allerian king and queen. Utenn felt that all of these bad tidings were related somehow. He must get to the bottom of it once and for all. He decided to go himself to speak with the court in the Allerian kingdom. Perhaps, they could shed light on something for him, at least for the sake of his beloved children if nothing else.

His men carried the white flag so they would not be arrested on sight. They traveled through the dark and beautiful forest all day and into the late evening as Utenn wondered, *"Will I ever seen my little girl and my handsome son again?"*

What had happened to the twins? After they had escaped into the glen and left the amulet for Agreus to punish the evil doer they had made their way to New York City with the help of Agreus who had pointed them in the right direction. Until they could figure out where to be he had told them about Ayyn's penthouse which was fully stocked and comfortable. In this world it had not been vacant that long and was already paid in full by him before he left this world. They would need to get food but there was plenty of money in a drawer in the wardrobe. Athulenne could buy appropriate clothes and so could Ulenn. They could probably live it up on Ayyn's money for a little while at least until they could purchase somewhere truly private and away from the nosiness of others. This world was indeed strange to them but they were willing to make the adjustments needed to blend in here.

Ulenn had a thought. What if his sister's growing abilities could change his appearance into that of Ayyn and he could take over his accounts as they were called. It was were money and such were kept. They could gain access to all of it. No one had seen Ayyn in a long time and would not recollect much other than his appearance and his social standing. In this world it would seem he had only been away for about twenty years. It had been centuries in the realm of the elves. They could take over his life here and become "socialites" themselves. This would make it easier for his sister to love him. She would see Ayyn and he would have the love he wanted from her. Now, he just needed to convince her that this was a good plan even though it strayed from the original one. Maybe, this would finally solve his problem with getting her to look at him the way she had that monster.

Ayyn was elated that his castle was rid of all of those horrid monks. He threw the last body on the blazing fire in the field out back. He watched until the fire died down. Tomorrow, he would put what remained in a mass grave at the very back of the Black Thorn property. Now, he was ready to rip down the walls that covered his old quarters. There was a secret door that he doubted had been discovered in all this time. He would find all of the potions and herbs he would need as well as the book his father had given him. Ayyn needed to find a spell quickly to remove the magic Agreus used to make him mortal. This meant that he would go back to being only half elf but that would give him a much longer life and more time to figure out how to get Ana and his son out of their realm so he could keep them. *Agreus and his sons must die!* Ayyn thought. He new they would never let them be in peace as long as they continued to live. Agreus was only a demigod so he could definitely be killed but how? Kashenn would be the easiest because he was elf kind and Agrieness would go the way of his father once Ayyn had figured out how to kill the pans. He could then remove the princess' memories once more so that she would remember nothing painful. After all, he did not want his beloved to suffer with bad memories. As for their son, his plan was to do the same to him so that all he remembered would be him. The loving husband and father that Ayyn wanted to be would come to pass if he could help it.

"Soon, my loves, very soon," Ayyn whispered.

Kashenn sat on the throne while his mother and father were in the glen with his brother Agrieness. Apparently, his beloved brother had decided it best for him to make his presence minimal in the Allerian kingdom for now. That was fine if it was what he needed. Kashenn could always call to him through the watery pool in the throne room. There was still one located in the cave so they could communicate if they wanted to. The truth was that Kashenn believed all of the things that had happened were too much for Agrieness to face. He was the sensitive one and he looked older in his eyes than he actually was. He would speak to his brother soon to make sure this was what he really wanted but for now Julienn had come into the throne room. He was about eighteen years old. Full of vinegar and attitude, he was always disobeying and doing things he was told not to not only by his parents but also by the king.

"What are you up to today, Julienn?" Kashenn sniped.

"Most likely making your day unpleasant I imagine as I seem to always get under your skin for some reason brother. Why is that? Do you hate me so much? Is it because mother favors me over you?" Julienn said cruelly.

"Julienn, I will not be drawn into this with you again. Mother loves us all the same even if you wish it were not so. Please, go and find something to do to entertain your troubled thoughts and leave me in peace. I may be your brother but I am also your king. For mother's sake do not force me to punish you!" Kashenn smiled sarcastically.

"For mother's sake then," Julienn left the room.

Julienn was so much more like Ayyn than they even knew. They figured he was just going through a rebellious phase or something. He was still in the dark about his true father but he had always felt different than the others. Feeling alone and different was a bad combination in Julienn's case. No one else besides the immediate family knew that he was Ayyn's child. This meant that the historians did not know to hide certain things in the archives better than they had. The clerics magic had failed to make him a more even tempered child and they did not know why. The truth was that they used the wrong mixtures. They would have needed a stronger dosage and an added ingredient to calm him because he was not pure Allerian. This had all escaped the knowledge of his family. Mostly, they overlooked his behavior as just being childish. Princess Ana assumed he would grow out of it, but Agreus was not so sure. He cared deeply for the child. He had raised him as his own, but he was not like the other children. They had been such good and respectful children but Julienn was more like Ayyn than even Agreus knew. He could see his real father in him, though.

He hoped it would not cause any harm. Looking at Julienn was like looking at a photograph of Ayyn. They did not look exactly alike but it was a pretty close match. If that boy ever discovered the truth there was no telling what trouble he might cause.

"Well, if I am to entertain myself I suppose I shall study a bit on this illustrious boring kingdom!" Julienn was never content.

It troubled him that he could not find happiness in anything. He did not know the truth of his birth. If he had, then maybe it would have struck him that anything born in grief is bound to bring about unhappiness. That had been true for Ayyn and now Julienn was feeling the effects even though everyone had gone to so much trouble to hide it from him. At his young age he had already been fooling around with the girls from the village. He could not find contentment in their comfort, either. There had to be something more to his life than this.

Julienn sat in the archives appearing studious to the historians. He was reading about the ways and customs of his people. He read about his ancestral line and those who came before until he was exhausted by the stiff nature of the history here. Suddenly, a wooden box caught his eye in the very back of the archival library. It was very high up on a shelf and all of his people were of a shorter nature. Julienn brought it to the chief historian to question him about it.

"What is inside this locked box?" Julienn asked.

"Secrets, I imagine my young prince," Tannas answered him.

Tannas had become chief of the historians a long time ago. He was proud to assist the young Julienn who reminded him of when he was that age.

"May I see inside, Tannas?" Julienn looked at him with those big blue eyes.

"Well, I suppose it cannot hurt for you to know of what happened to your grandparents. In fact, I think you should know the story so you can keep a wary eye out for any sign of the evil one who perpetrated their deaths," Tannas figured he was doing the right thing.

Tannas could not have known what else had been placed inside that of that box in secret by none other than Agreus himself. He was the one who had placed it so far up as to be forgotten in the dust.

"Thank you Tannas. I never knew them but perhaps this will help me feel as though I have some connection with them," He smiled at the well meaning historian as he walked back to the table where he had been reading scrolls.

Julienn did not care about his grandparents. He cared about secrets and if this box had to be kept sealed then something must be in there that he needed to see. Maybe he would find the answers he was seeking. What in all of the realms could be so important that they had felt the need to lock this box? Julienn slowly opened the dusty lid and slid it back. He coughed a little as dust flew in his face. The six foot and five inch young elf peered over into the box and saw a stack of parchment. His height had always been useful. He could reach things that others could not such as this box!

Julienn began to read through the information contained here. There was an entire explanation of what had befallen the kingdom on that awful day when the old king and queen were slaughtered along with any servants in the throne room. There were likenesses of them drawn on parchment. The names of the assassins were listed as well as their punishments. Everything you might expect was in this box that would help the people to remember what happened if ever they needed to consult the records. Why was it locked, though? Julienn had reached the bottom of the box and made quite a discovery. There was a secret chamber in the bottom that slid open when pressed down and over. He removed the small lid from the opening in the box to discover more parchment and some sort of amulet or medallion.

"What is this?" Julienn whispered to himself.

He unfurled the rolled up parchment and what he discovered nearly caused him to faint with horror. Julienn read the story of all that had happened with his mother and he found the likeness of an elf that stood accused of it. The elf looked just like him! Could this really be happening? It was obvious now why he had been treated differently by his brothers and Agreus who was supposed to be his father. Agreus had never treated him wrongly. It was just obvious that there was something not right between them. The only one who had been genuine in his family was his mother. She truly loved Julienn.

Julienn had always heard that the victor wrote history how he wanted it remembered. He smelled more secrets to be discovered. If this was all true then Julienn felt he had more right as heir than Kashenn because he was a child of two kingdoms. His father had been a Dulerian king and not that demigod from the realm of humans! The only way to know what happened was to memory shift with his mother. Her true feelings about this "Ayyn" would be known. He would know whatever she knew about him. If he still lived, Julienn would find a way to get to him. He must know the truth of who he was and if he had cause to do the things he had done or if he was the devil incarnate as these papers would have him believe.

Julienn turned his attention to the amulet that he found inside the compartment. He could feel the power from within it. Perhaps, he could use it to find his father. He needed one of the most trustworthy cleric friends he had to help him uncover it's secrets. For the moment, he needed to sneak all of this material out of here and not get caught. Julienn slid the compartment back in place and took the box back to Tannas who would use magic to once again lock it away.

"Did you find everything you wanted to know, my prince?" Tannas asked.

"Oh yes, and it has helped me so much. Thank you for allowing me to look inside," Julienn smiled as he left the archives slowly.

Yes Tannas, you fool! I have discovered much, much more than I ever thought I would! Julienn returned to the castle to find his friend. The young cleric called Relenus was the same age as Julienn and eager to practice his art. This amulet would give him a reason to serve the prince and improve his own magical skills. He would definitely be secretive about it for Julienn.

Julienn approached the young cleric and called him aside.

"Relenus, I have something for you. It is for us, actually and it must be kept a secret." Julienn began.

"Julienn, what have you got? I want to see it!" Relenus was on board already.

"Shh. No one can know. Come with me to a secret chamber so I can take out what I have," Julienn insisted.

The two youths went to Relenus' private room. There it was safe to talk and they would not be discovered.

"Here it is," Julienn brought the medallion out for Relenus to inspect.

"There is strong magic in this item, Julienn. Where did you get it?" Relenus asked curiously.

"That is a private matter but what I need from you is a determination of what it does," Julienn would not reveal more than necessary.

"I can say without a doubt that it does many things but what they are exactly I cannot say for sure. I will get to work on it immediately, highness," Relenus replied.

"Oh and Relenus, no one can no about this. It could be my death if it were discovered that I had it. No one knows that is not where it supposed to be and they will not know unless someone says something," Julienn warned.

"You can count on me, Julienn. I will keep your secrets. I swear it! I will consult you when I know more about this amulet or whatever it is," Relenus needed to get back before the other clerics began to wonder where he had gone.

Julienn went to his chamber and lay on his bed to think of all this new found information. Tonight, he would invite his mother for tea and conversation and then force a memory shift on her. That would alleviate some of his questions for now.

"Agrieness, my son, I am so proud of you for taking up my mantle and doing such a wonderful job. You are now the protector of this forest and all who reside there in. You do not have to stay here all of the time, though. Are you certain this is what you want to do? We are not used to being away from you like this," Agreus smiled at his responsible son.

"Father, I assure you it is what I most desire. I love it here as I am sure you have for such a long time now. I will miss being with my family all of the time but I am grown and I need to learn to do things alone. I will always love you all no matter where we are," Agrieness reassured his father.

"My son, let me kiss you," Princess Ana reached for her tall, masculine son to lean down to meet her embrace.

"Do not worry, mother. I know you and father will be here quite often anyway. I will get to see your beautiful face all of the time!" Agrieness smiled at her.

"We must return home, my son but we shall soon see you again," Ana teared up that her son was not returning with them.

"Do not cry, my sweet mother! I am here and will always be here," Agrieness teared up, too.

Agreus gave his son a smile and then escorted his lovely wife back through the hollow tree that led into the Allerian kingdom.

"Kashenn, how do things go in the kingdom today?" Agreus asked his son who sat on the throne.

"Fine if you consider that little rat skulking about as though he is always up to something," Kashenn said of Julienn.

"Come now, Kashenn, your little brother cannot be all that bad. He is just young and immature. I am sure he will grow out of it in time. I love him as I do you and your other brother," Ana was hurt that Kashenn had never quite been able to accept Julienn.

"Mother, I know that and I am sorry if I hurt you with my words, but I cannot help feeling that he is always up to no good. He is so unsettled all of the time and has found pleasure in nothing. Quite honestly, it worries me that he could . . ." Kashenn was interrupted by a stern look from Agreus.

"I am sorry mother. I should be kinder to the boy. I will try," Kashenn took his mother's hands and kissed them as he smiled at her.

This seemed to make her happy again. Agreus could not help feeling that Kashenn may be right, but it would do no good to upset Ana. They would need to just keep a closer eye on Julienn.

It had been long enough that Ana was able to think of all that had transpired and not cry. She never fell out of love with Ayyn but she managed to push it out of her mind for the sake of her family. Agreus must never know that she was still not over it. She loved Agreus without question and would never leave him of her own will, but she struggled to forget the one who made her love him while looking upon the face of their only son each day. She saw him in her son's eyes every time and it sent a dagger through her heart to know what his fate had become.

Ayyn was looking through his collection in the secret room and gathering all that he would need to remove this curse of mortality placed on him by Agreus. He took all of the items into a room downstairs so he would have more space to operate. He was not even sure that it would work but he had to try. He did not want to die as a mortal. Ayyn wanted to look upon his son and Ana again. The winter solstice was tonight and he could use it's power to help fuel his ritual. Ayyn set up the candles and lit them. One for each color of the seasons and one for the color of blood and a black one for the removal of the curse. He found a spell for the removal of magical curses that was particularly strong in the book he had been given by his father. As a human he was unsure how good he would be at performing the rituals but he had a feeling that the mortality had only effected his appearance and his lifespan. He did not believe that all of his abilities were completely gone. Ayyn would have to use the book again instead of his memory because the curse on him had made it impossible to recall these things at will. It was a good thing he had made a copy of the book itself. Those rats in the elven kingdom took what they thought was the book but it was just its covering filled with copied spells. He had the original pages here in the castle all along.

The winter moon was high in the sky now. It was time to begin the rite to remove the curse. Ayyn began to chant the spell over and over. The flames on the candles were burning high and brighter than ever. Soon, misty strands were leaving his body and being consumed into the candles. At the end of the ceremony the candles burned completely out. There was a mirror in this room and luckily for him the monks had installed some lighting as was the custom now. In the dark room Ayyn found a switch that operated the lights. He had these when he had been in the new world. He enjoyed them for the convenience of it. The switch flickered on the dim light in the room and he stood before the mirror. In this mirror he saw himself fully returned to half elf status. The removal of the magic placed on him had worked!

"Silly demigod! How did he think he would stop such a determined one as me?" Ayyn said out loud.

Ayyn laughed heartily and wickedly, "Soon I shall have my princess and my little prince back. There is nothing to stop me now. It should not be too difficult to find a way back to take them."

Ayyn turned to once again look himself over in the mirror. His lustrous complexion had returned. His ears were right again and his eyes were blue green and glistening more than ever. He stood tall and strong and realized he was still wearing those ridiculous clothes given him by the monks. He went back to his secret room and opened a closet. It had been a long time since he was here but he still had a couple of the outfits and great coat here. He put on one of the dark suits and the great coat, along with a pair of knee high black boots that he had left behind in case he needed them. It was a good thing that no one ever discovered his secret room. The magic had worked to prevent it. Now he was back at square one in this world but he had an important decision to make. Should he start over and live alone rebuilding his fortune or should he risk everything for love? The answer was obvious. Ayyn needed to do some research on how to open dimensional doors if anything was even written about it. Without his medallion he would have to do things the old fashioned way.

"Athulenne, I have a wonderful plan for you to consider," Ulenn was sure she would like it.

He told her of all that he had imagined for them.

"Well, what do you think?" Ulenn asked.

Athulenne was unsure what to say, but she considered it for a moment. Perhaps, if he looked like the one she had wanted so badly she could love him the way he wanted. It strayed from the plan they had made to keep to themselves, but did Ayyn not owe her something for the pain he had caused her to suffer? Using his wealth and status in this world could gain for them everything they could desire. She would need to think on it for a couple of days. Should she cross the threshold with Ulenn? Even if he had the appearance and voice of Ayyn he would still be consciously her twin. Maybe.

"My brother, give me a couple of days to consider it with all diligence and I will have an answer for you," Athulenne smiled at him.

She did not say no so that was at least a start on his road to getting what he wanted.

"Princess Ana, your son Julienn requests your presence at a private tea party in his quarters for the two of you. He says he wants to spend time with his lovely mother if you would join him," the maid sent by Julienn presented his message.

"Yes, of course, I will go at once. I love to spend time with any of my children!" Ana was excited that Julienn seemed to be doing something mature for once.

She loved the boy with all of her heart. Ana was well aware that the others did not necessarily feel the way she did and she knew why. All she ever asked is that they not let Julienn be aware of it. She came to his quarters and announced her presence.

"Ah, my beautiful mother, you are a sight to behold!" Julienn flattered her.

"Julienn, you always know what to say to me, my dear boy," she was thinking of the things Ayyn used to say to her.

"Come in and sit with me. I have prepared some tea for us so we can sit and talk for awhile," Julienn made her feel at ease.

"Alright. Let us have a little tea party then! Just the two of us!" She was enjoying the pretend formalities with her youngest son.

Without her knowing it, Julienn had slipped a sleeping potion into her tea that he had gotten from Relenus before hand. He did not want to consciously make his mother memory shift with him. He doubted she would agree and forcing it on her would bring down the wrath of Agreus and sons. This was the easiest way to get inside of her mind. When she nodded off he would freely be able to see anything he wanted to know.

Agreus was still in the throne room with Kashenn discussing matters that Julienn did not care about and he knew he would be undiscovered for awhile. Julienn and Ana sat and laughed and talked until she finally dozed off in her chair. Julienn smiled with excitement at this moment. Finally, some light would be shed on whatever they were hiding from him. He began the process of reading her thoughts. He was in shock and awe at the long history they all had with Ayyn. He could see that some terrible things were done by him but he was able to see everything she had seen when she read Ayyn's thoughts. Julienn understood why his father was the way he had become. He felt the darkness in himself, as well. He also realized his mother and father's true feelings for one another as he witnessed memories from the past. This angered him. It would seem that his father had been ripped away from him even though Ayyn had agreed to leave Ana alone. He would have born the burden of unrequited love and left them in peace if he could only have stayed to see his son grow.

Julienn did not care what his father had done in the past. The memories he saw showed change and it was due to his mother. He knew he was not liked by his brothers and Agreus so he had no problem with what he was about to do. He must find a way to get to his father before it was too late to save him from a mortal death. Julienn only hoped Ayyn had done this already, after all, he was very clever and had natural abilities that could serve him even in his human state. He did not want his father to live as a human and he was going to find a way to help him. After all, who did not deserve redemption when they were truly sorry? No one here, except his mother, had felt any compassion or mercy for him. She had suffered more from Ayyn than the others and yet still loved him after finding out the truth. There had to still be good in him or she would not have felt that way. Had she not also married his elven father? With that being the case it was time he got his wife and son back!

Julienn needed to speak with Relenus to see what he had divined from the amulet. He had a feeling it would come into play in all of this.

"Mother, mother? You dozed off in your chair." Julienn woke Ana.

"Oh, I am sorry, my son. I suppose I was tired from being in the glen all afternoon. I think I need to go and lay down for awhile. I love you very much!" Ana left Julienn's room and headed for her own. She was in her old quarters now that they all resided back in the main castle. As she lay down on the bed she fell into a troubling sleep. Ana could see Ayyn's face as he cried out for her from behind the prison bars. She cried out in her sleep at the pain it caused her. No one was there to here her cries in the night this time.

Agreus had been informed that Ana went to bed so he went back to the glen to speak with Agrieness before he retired for the night. He was not concentrating on Ana so he was unable to notice her nightmares. Julienn sensed his mother's anguish based on the memories he had gained from her so he went to check on her.

"Mother, why are crying?" Julienn said softly.

Ana woke with a start, "Julienn? I suppose I was having a bad dream."

"What was it about?" Her son asked.

"Oh, my dear, it is nothing I should be telling you but only a burdensome thing that wears on me from time to time," Ana lied knowing it was more than just once in a while.

"I see. Well, if you should need me then send for me, mother," Julienn knew the dream had to be about Ayyn.

"Relenus? Are you in there?" Julienn asked in a hushed tone.

"Yes, highness. Come inside quickly," The young cleric answered him.

"What have you to tell me about this amulet I have given you?" Julienn demanded.

"I must say that I am impressed by it. From what I can tell it would seem it holds the power of a god. It matches the description of an item used to open doorways into other realms. I think it was used to send those who were cast out into the realm of humans. There is mention of it in some of our tomes in the royal collection held by the clerical order. It is very old and I still do not know all that it can do," Relenus was proud.

"My friend, can I trust you with a very dangerous secret?" Julienn asked him.

"Of course you can, Julienn. What is it?" Relenus asked.

"I am not the son of Agreus but of the elf who this once belonged to. It was hidden from me and my mother forced to keep it secret. I need to go and see him. Will you help me use this to open a door to where he is?" Julienn begged of him.

"Sire, are you sure?" The cleric was afraid.

Julienn pulled out all of the stolen information from the archives including the likeness of Ayyn and where he was sent. He showed it to his friend and waited for a response. The cleric looked everything over and agreed that it must be so. Relenus agreed to help but they needed to be outside in the forest where they would not be discovered.

The two young ones set off into the forest under cover of darkness and found the location where they could use this amulet without being noticed. Agreus was no where to be found so he would not notice it either. Relenus showed Julienn how to use it to open a gateway between the two realms.

"Please be careful and return safely, my friend," Relenus was worried for the young prince but understood why he felt the need to do this.

"I shall. Do not worry for me. I know my father will be happy to see me. Now get back to the castle before you are discovered!" Julienn went through and was now standing on the front lawn of Black Thorn Manor.

Slowly, the young prince began to walk toward the front gate. He was looking around at everything in the moonlight. Things looked different here but not so much that it was an awful sight. Julienn approached the door and knocked on it.

Ayyn heard the knocking and became wary. He crept down the stairs to get the drop on whomever it might be. He went outside a back door and came around behind Julienn. He seized him and spun him around quickly. Ayyn's mouth was slightly ajar. He could not believe his eyes! Before him stood a near image of him. This must be his son! But how?

"Father!" Julienn shouted.

"My son! Oh my god, my son. How is it that you have come to be here? What does your mother call you?" Ayyn was beaming with pride.

"Julienn," the younger elf said as he held up the amulet.

"Julienn! I am so sorry that I was not there to raise you. I wanted . . ." Ayyn was cut off.

"I know everything, father. I only just discovered the secrets that were kept from me all of these years. I am angry at them. Mother is the only one who has truly loved me and she still dreams of you. I know that she does. No matter how she has tried to put you out of her mind it cannot be done," Julienn told him.

"Can this be true? Did she tell you?" Ayyn asked.

"No. I used a sleeping potion to read her mind after I discovered all of this," He handed his father all of the parchments he had taken from the archives.

"I knew that they made her keep you from me. She has felt a duty to the kingdom and suffers for it. I know she loves Agreus for all that he has done for her but she loves you as well. She has mourned the loss of you for eighteen years. I know time passes slower here so it seems much shorter for you but to her it has been such a long time to miss you. Every time she looks at me she sees an image of you there. How could she not?" Julienn wanted his parents together.

"Julienn, I have done some really bad things and I do understand why your mother stayed behind to her duties, but I love her all the same and I am glad you are here, my boy! Come inside. We have much to discuss!" Ayyn led his pride and joy into a comfortable room so they could speak for as long as they needed.

"Father, tell me about this amulet? What all can it do?" Julienn asked.

"I will tell you anything you want to know as well as how to get back at precisely the same time you left so that you will not be discovered," Ayyn replied.

"I do not wish to go back and leave you here! I have only just found you after all of this time. Do you not love me, father?" Julienn cried.

"Of course, my son. I love you more than I can express, but you must come back and forth for a while until we figure out what to do about all of this. I still want your mother with me, too. Do you think she will come willingly or will I have to take her?" Ayyn implored.

"I think we must take her. She is a creature of duty and would prefer to suffer rather than hurt the others. She believes you still a mortal. It causes her pain to think you will die," Julienn confessed.

"The only way to change that is for you to help me get her back. I have magic that can hide us from that beast she calls husband and his sons. You know they will never let us be unless we kill them. I wish it could be another way but they do not understand they should let her go," Ayyn said.

"From here I can use potions to remove her memories of them and if you wish I can change it so that you only remember being with us. I will leave that choice up to you, my son," Ayyn sat by his son and held him tightly.

For the first time in his life Julienn felt complete. He needed his father's affection. Now he understood what had been missing for all of those years and nothing could have filled the void but his own blood. After much visiting and tears Julienn went back through the portal and promised to return as soon as possible.

Utenn and his riders arrived in the kingdom of the Allerians waving a white flag. They were met by the captain of the guard. The message written inside of the scroll was carried inside to King Kashenn. He was taken aback. This was not something he wanted to have to deal with at the moment. He had them taken into a meeting room while his mother and father were summoned on the matter.

With a heavy heart they went to meet Utenn. Ana remembered him from the Dulerian kingdom. She was sorry that his children were missing. She was unaware that Agreus helped them to escape. The plan was to let Utenn read Ana's mind so he would understand what happened with the Dulerian king and herself. They approached the meeting room with their son, the king.

Utenn stood up in amazement, "Princess?"

"Yes, Utenn it is me. You must be confused about seeing me here. I am going to let you read my mind so that you can see the truth for yourself," Ana stood in front of Utenn.

He placed his hands on her head and began to search her thoughts. He was horrified at the trials this little princess had been through. He saw everything and realized they had all been duped. Utenn promised to carry this news to the people so the matter could be put to rest.

"My children, I would also like to inquire if you have heard anything about them. They have been missing for nearly as long and I miss them," Utenn shed a tear for his loss.

"I am so sorry but I have had no news of them, Utenn," Ana replied.

"What were their names again?" Agreus asked.

"Athulenne and Ulenn, they are my twins," Utenn looked at him suspiciously.

"I know what happened with them. They are alright but they are not in this realm." Agreus told him.

"What? Where are my children?" Utenn was getting upset.

"They chose to go into the realm of humans to escape the turmoil they felt they were being put through in return for the vengeance your daughter wanted on Ayyn for making her impure and then not marrying her. Without her, he could not have been stopped. A debt of gratitude is owed to your children for this. I did not know they were your children, though." Agreus explained.

"Agreus, you let his children leave the realm without his permission. Why?" Ana looked hurt and surprised that he had not told her of this.

"They were grown. I did not know they were "missing" as it were," Agreus did not like to be questioned.

"What can be done to bring them back?" Utenn asked angrily.

"I can use the mirrors to go back and forth between realms. I will go there and try to get them back. Is this a suitable agreement?" Agreus asked.

"Yes, I agree to it," Utenn answered flatly.

When they were returned they would be punished for running away and he would separate them for good. It was the only way to keep them to their responsibilities as nobles.

"I will leave momentarily," Agreus left the room.

Utenn approached Ana, "I am so sorry that we did not know to help you before it went so far and now you suffer. Your mind was wiped and you fell in love with him and you have born his son."

"That is true but my son is wonderful and handsome. He knows nothing of his father. He believes it is Agreus. We felt it best he not know the truth and yes I will always love him. It is my burden to bear. I love my family and my husband but I will never be able to rid my heart of what Ayyn and I shared together," Ana answered with teary eyes.

Utenn hung his head in shame at his people. They should have known something was wrong.

"Utenn, it is not your fault. I will be alright and I know Agreus will get your twins back for you. Please stay in the kingdom until he returns," Ana insisted.

"Yes, my lady. We will wait here until he returns with them," Utenn was filled with anticipation.

"I would like for you to meet Julienn in case you see him elsewhere. You will know it is him and not anyone else," Ana said.

"I would be delighted to meet him," Utenn replied.

King Kashenn bowed to his mother and excused himself. He would hear no more of this talk today. Julienn was sent for and he came to meet the chief council member of his father's people.

"Utenn, please meet Julienn," Ana introduced him.

"Pleased to make your aquaintance, sir," Julienn bowed to Utenn.

"The pleasure is mine, young prince. Your mother speaks very highly of you." Utenn told the boy.

"Oh, my dear mother flatters me constantly, sir," Julienn gave a familiar smile.

Utenn noticed just how much he looked like Ayyn. Julienn could see it in his eyes. He knew Ayyn and he knows I look just like him. He continued to smile and make pleasantries while dinner arrangements for he and his men were made.

"Will the king dine with us?" Utenn asked.

"I doubt it. He never dines with anyone. I think he is jealous of me! Mother is always bragging on me even though she loves him just as much." Julienn kidded with Utenn.

"I insist that you and your men be my guests at a banquet tonight. Mother will come and we shall make the best of it until her husband returns with news from the human realm," Julienn would take care of the details for the evening.

He was curious about the Dulerians. They were his people too. Julienn was truly a child of two kingdoms. This was a way for him to get to know something of his father's people. It was also a way to annoy his brother to no end. Kashenn did not like Dulerians in his kingdom or in his castle after what happened to his grandparents.

"Athulenne have you considered what you wish to do," Ulenn asked

They were still in Ayyn's penthouse. They had gotten new clothes and were beginning to look the part.

"I have considered it and I am willing to go through with it, Ulenn," Athulenne did not think she really had a choice if she were to find any happiness in life.

He would not be the one she truly wanted but she could make him look and sound the part for her own self. Maybe some form of hollow happiness could be found in the abominable thing she was about to do.

Just when she was about to prepare the magical herbs that would accomplish the deed Agreus stepped out of portal that was opened.

"Agreus, why are you here?" Lu asked.

"To stop a war from starting," Agreus said as he froze the twins in place. He whispered in their ears an incantation to send them back to the castle. They would remain asleep until their father wanted them awakened to take them home.

"I have returned your children. They are asleep in one of the upper rooms. They have done nothing inappropriate with one another. I know that was your biggest concern," Agreus told Utenn as he stepped into the dining hall.

"Thank goodness," Utenn breathed a sigh of relief, "When will they wake?"

"I can have them awakened whenever you are ready to return home," Agreus answered.

"May we continue to dine for awhile before you leave? I have many questions and I would love to meet your children, too," Julienn asked ever so politely of Utenn.

"Well, I suppose it could not hurt to continue for a little longer if is alright with your mother, that is," Utenn and his men looked to Ana for confirmation.

"Yes, please stay as late as you like and Agreus can arrange for the children to wake at your command. That will make it easier," Ana looked at Agreus. This was his doing, after all.

"Then ask away my young friend!" They talked late into the night while Julienn used this opportunity to gather information.

The group of elves carried on with dining and talking late into the night. Eventually, Utenn woke the children as he was instructed by Agreus and he took them back with him to their own kingdom. Julienn had met the twins, Athulenne and Ulenn. They were very unhappy at the turn of events but the girl had given Julienn a certain look. He knew that look very well. She was taken with the young prince. Maybe he could pay her a visit at a later time. Julienn did not like that she had helped capture his father but he suspected she was a beguiled lover. He was sure he could help her forget her pain. He laughed to himself as her brother tried to appear over protective out of jealousy when it was obvious that he wanted more from his sister than a bridesmaid for his upcoming wedding.

Agreus and Ana had long ago excused themselves to bed. They were both weary with troubled thoughts and hearts. That night they lay there wide awake as he held her and tried to comfort her. He knew she had felt troubled for a long time but he did not realize to what extent. Agreus had always assumed that it was the look of the boy reminding her all of the time of the dark one. He knew she did not hate Ayyn the way he did. She was entirely too forgiving, in his opinion. He could not fault her in her goodness, though. He loved that she was so good.

Ana was shielding her thoughts so that Agreus could not entirely read them. He probably new she was not feeling like herself but he did not know that she was curious about what had happened to Ayyn when he was sent back to the world of humans. She had hoped he had regained his half blood status even though she felt a little guilty for being in direct conflict with her husband's wishes. She just did not want him to die. That was all. She did not want to abandon Agreus for Ayyn no matter how she felt. She was a happy wife with him. It just may take a lot longer than she thought to truly get over her second "husband."

She found it hard to be intimate with Agreus while she felt this way because she could not totally devote herself to him while another was in her thoughts. She hoped that one day all of that would change and go back to how it was before anything happened. Ana continued to lay there and let Agreus embrace her while she tried to find sleep.

Agrieness walked through the glen on this sunny day and enjoyed the breeze as it carried the sent of fresh flowers. He was free of the burdens of elf and man here. The pan was glad that he could be removed from all of their troubles and just be free to do the one thing he enjoyed and that was taking care of his own responsibilities. Love was something that he would make a willing sacrifice to avoid the problems of the worlds he had been a part of. He was glad his parents had loved enough to create him and his brother and now he would share love with nature instead of selfishly keeping it for another.

"My brother, are you awake?" Kashenn called to Agrieness through the watery pools they used to communicate.

Agrieness had come in from his day of toiling and fell into a deep sleep, but he woke to the sound of Kashenn's voice calling out for him.

"Yes, my brother? I am here. What is the problem?" Agrieness asked sleepily.

"Julienn is entertaining a group of Dulerians that came looking for answers about everything. Apparently, they were deceived as we were and their chief council member's children were missing but Agreus brought them back. You know, the young elves that helped us catch the dark one? They had run away from home so Agreus got them back to avoid any political trouble with the Dulerians. Julienn is making me crazy with this. They have what they came for so why not leave?" Kashenn was obviously upset.

"What did mother and father say?" Agrieness asked.

"They are allowing him to finish his feast with them before bidding farewell," Kashenn answered.

"Then why are you so worried about it? Cut the young elf some slack. He is just not used to visitors and he is curious," Agrieness reasoned.

"Brother, I feel like the little rat is up to no good. Why should he care about those people? Their assassins killed our grandparents!" Kashenn retorted.

"Kashenn, it was Ayyn's assassins and not those people's. They had no knowledge of it and besides, they have all been punished properly by the cold grip of death," Agrieness said wearily.

"What shall I do, my brother? I want to believe the best but I have never been able to. He looks so much like his father!" Kashenn said with resignation.

"My dearest Kashenn, I know you have a lot to deal with as king. I know that you are wary of Julienn, but do not hurt mother with your misgivings. She has been through enough. Perhaps, he can be put in charge of something to keep him busy but make him feel important. That may help him grow up some. Think of it? What responsibilities does he have? No wonder he bothers you so much," Agrieness said wisely.

"Ah, brother you are right. I will speak to our parents about it tomorrow. Surely they can find something for him to do of use. That may calm him down. You always know what to say, Agrieness. I am glad you are my twin. Sleep well dear brother," Kashenn ended the communication.

Agrieness rolled over on his soft bed and lay their thinking about the advice he had given. He hoped his suggestion was going to be enough to satisfy his brother. He shuddered to think of what would happen if he and Julienn really got into a squabble. Mother could not handle it. He tried to sleep while his mind remained troubled. "Mother . . ." Agrieness mumbled.

Ayyn was waiting for Julienn to return so they could mastermind a plan together. This time he was going to be certain that he got everything and everyone he desired. Ayyn had always thought to himself, *Why can the phantom not win in the end just once?*" He had loved The Phantom of the Opera written by Andrew Lloyd Weber since it was first released. Ayyn had been to the theater on numerous occasions to see it performed. He marveled at the phantom and Christine. He had always wanted to strangle the character of Raul. Ayyn sympathized with his plight and considered the character of the phantom to be a kindred spirit. If he considered himself a type of the phantom then that made

Agreus a type of the character Raul. So it would seem that his beloved Ana was Christine. *"I can be the phantom that finally gets the love of the girl and the happy ending!"*

"Father, I have returned!" Julienn stepped into the drawing room where Ayyn was reclining on a soft chair.

"Julienn, I am so glad you are here! So tell me what has been happening back home?" Ayyn asked.

"It was the oddest coincidence. An elven group of riders came from the Dulerian kingdom looking for any word of you and mother. Also, they were looking for a couple of younger elves that had helped capture you and apparently had run away here into the human realm!" Julienn answered.

"Who was the leader of this group, my son?" Ayyn hissed.

"The leader was called Utenn. He said he was the chief of the council and his twins had been missing for long time. Agreus admitted to getting them to help him catch you in exchange for asylum here on Earth. They did not want to be married to people they did not love as per the arrangements of marriage Utenn had made for them. Agreus brought them back to Utenn so a political engagement would not get started between the two kingdoms. Utenn learned the truth about, well, everything father. He knows what happened with you and mother. What they do not know is that I know everything, as well. Their looks betray them. I can see in their eyes that mother has revealed it to them, even knowledge that Agreus is not my true father," Julienn gave an account of all that he had learned.

"So that little wench, Athulenne was in this world? I wish I had known it. I would have taken the opportunity to track her down and kill her with my bare hands! She was jealous of my love of your mother. I tried to make her forget everything before hand. How was I to know that she was protected from magic by her stupid charm bracelet? All because of that little slip up they were able to find a weakness to exploit. They used her anger at me to take away my wife and child! Does that sound noble to you, my son? Agreus and his ilk are no better than I am. For all their righteous indignation they are just as bad!" Ayyn felt justified in his anger.

"Father, Agreus had the twins hiding out in your properties in New York," Julienn shuddered with fear.

"My son, do not fear my wrath. It is not directed at you. I am not surprised that Agreus sent them there. No one would have noticed them for a while. I do feel taken advantage of a bit and in doing it he has made a fool of me. They have probably stolen money from me and used it for their own purposes while they were staying in my home. At least, they were sent back to be married against their wills. It serves them right for having done this to us!" Ayyn said indignantly.

Julienn changed the subject to that of his mother.

"Father, I am planning to take a walk with mother in the forest when I return home. I have a potion that will cause her to become drowsy and go to sleep so I will catch her when she falls and bring her through the portal that the amulet will open. Agreus always goes to the glen at a certain time of the morning so I can ask her to stay behind with me this time. I am sure she will do it. She favors me best out of all her children even though she would never admit it to the others. Once we are here we can talk to her and see what she wants to do. Maybe she will come willingly and see our way of things. If not, I will still have to bring her back to the castle, but we will continue to plan in secret our revenge. She will not divulge that I have brought her here because she will not want me harmed or we can make her forget she was ever here until all is done and Agreus is dead," Julienn was happy to be planning with his father.

"I think we will need to wipe her memory of coming here so Agreus cannot read her mind and find out anything. You do know she is going to be angry with you for taking her? I expect she will calm down once we explain it will not be but for a little while and you will take her home. She will plan to punish you I imagine but I will slip her the memory wipe potion before you leave so she will wake up believing she was in bed all along. If she chooses to stay here with me then I will have to be fast with my magic to conceal our whereabouts. I am not going to force her to do anything until we have at least given her the opportunity to make the right decision," Ayyn said to his beloved son.

"Yes, you are absolutely right, father. Giving her the opportunity to choose it first is very respectful of you. I believe it is the right decision," Julienn was ready to go through with the nefarious deed.

Princess Ana was walking in the garden and thinking about her life and her choices. Was she an inconstant wife? She loved her husband very much so why could she not remove that which tortured her soul both night and day? She and Ayyn had not been together nearly as long as she was with Agreus when the former decided to take her away. How could she have been so smitten in a short amount of time? Perhaps, it was his smile and his gentle touch. He was an elf and so was she. They had many things in common as far as that sort of things goes. Ayyn was from a different tribe but they were not so different in the end. Ana remembered hearing a tale a long time ago about how the two tribes used to be ruled under one banner. They were one people until the sons of the king had a dispute and the tribes had split into two. Ana did not know whether this was true or myth, but it was an ancient story that one would hear spoken of from time to time. Why did things have to be so difficult? She knew she must choose whether to remain constant or stray from her duty to her husband. Even if she did, would she be able to save Ayyn in time? Ana's head was hurting from the thoughts that traveled through her mind.

How could she even consider doing anything like that after all that Agreus had been through with her. His life was dedicated to hers and their children. Julienn was going to be the one to suffer in the end without knowing the truth of his father. She could see it in his eyes. He was already suffering with the same feelings of being alone that Ayyn had when she read his mind in the prison that day so long ago. *"Damn them for putting her in this position!"* she thought to herself. She knew that this contest between Agreus and Ayyn would eventually be the death of her if it was not finished and somehow deep down, she knew things were not over yet.

"Mother, will you take a walk with me in the forest? I would like to gather some lilies for you," Julienn ran up behind Ana.

"Oh, you startled me son. Yes, I will go with you into the forest but let me tell Agreus that I will not be joining him in the glen today, first," Ana walked back into the castle.

Soon Ana was coming out to meet Julienn for their trip into the wood. Agreus understood and went on alone to the glen. He would enjoy his time alone with Agrieness today. Julienn and Ana made their way deep into the forest where the purple lilies were blooming this time in the season.

"Here mother, I brought some water for us to drink in case we grew thirsty," Julienn handed her the water with the sleeping potion.

"How thoughtful of you! You are such a good son, Julienn. You know that I love you more than anything do you not?" Ana did favor him over the others.

"Remember mother, no matter what happens that I love you and I only want what I think is best for you, alright?" Julienn hid his meaning.

"Of course, but why would you . . ." Ana began to stumble and fall.

Julienn caught her and carried her in his arms. He opened the portal that led back to Black Thorn Manor and walked through to greet his father.

"You have done it, Julienn! Lay her on my bed just in the next room. We shall let her sleep for a bit before waking her. I am nervous and unsure as to what I should say first. I do not want her to fear me on sight!" Ayyn exclaimed.

"Father, calm down. I will go in and prepare her first so that she will not be in shock or afraid, alright?" Julienn comforted him.

"Alright, you will make her understand before she sees me then? That may help some. I hope you are right about this," Ayyn was shaken.

The two of them sat and talked about what the future might hold for them and how happy they could be as a family while Ana slept. Julienn heard her as she began to move around so he excused himself to go and ready her for the shock of seeing his father once again.

"Where am I, Julienn? We were walking and then I cannot remember what happened next," Ana looked worried.

"My beautiful mother, I have a surprise for you and I do not want you to fret. Everything is alright and no one is going to harm you, I promise," Julienn comforted her.

"What do you mean . . ." Ana saw a figure standing in the doorway.

Could it be? After all of this time was it him? She was beginning to breath hard and become a little anxious. The last time she saw Ayyn she had run out of the room leaving him crying after her. It had made her feel so guilty. What would she say to him now?

"Ana," Ayyn called her name.

It was him. How did she get here? What was happening? It was all a blur. The little princess hid her face in her hands because she did not know what else to do.

"It is alright, my sweet. I am not going to do anything to you that you do not wish. I am sorry we had to bring you to visit like this but I could not risk anyone finding out. I am sure you understand. I have missed you so much and our son is the picture of perfection," Ayyn bragged on Julienn.

"Yes he is, but I wonder how he has come to know all of this," Ana looked confused at Julienn.

"All will be explained, but first, would you like anything at all? Something warm to drink, perhaps?" Ana looked warily at him.

"There is nothing in the tea, I swear it," Ayyn told the truth.

"Yes, thank you. I would really like some. I am cold here," Ana was shivering.

"Mother, I am sorry for tricking you," Julienn hung his head.

"We will talk later, my son but for now I need to be alone with Ayyn," Ana said sternly.

"Ana, please do not be mad at our son. He will bring you home shortly. The boy wanted us to have a chance to talk and clear the air about a few things," Ayyn said earnestly.

"I am glad he did if you want to know the truth. I have wondered after you all of this time hoping you were alright. I never wanted you to die and I see you have rid yourself of the curse placed upon you by Agreus. That was my wish for you. I knew you were clever enough to figure it out.

I want you to understand that I was really hurt when I discovered what you wanted to do with me all of those ages ago. I know that it was your father who convinced you in your vulnerable state to do it. It was hard for me to reconcile you as that person and the one I had grown to love. I am still confused by the idea that you could have even looked at me with love in your eyes after all of our history," Ana said to Ayyn with a look of question.

"I am so sorry for all of that. I never expected that you would effect me the way you did. I was a monster, Ana. You and you alone changed all of that. It is ironic how it has become considering how it all started.

I do not want to harm you any more than I would want to harm our son. You gave me the one thing that no one else ever could and that is happiness and love in there truest forms," Ayyn was now sitting on the edge of the bed and looking at her with those bluest of blue eyes.

The princess was captured by his gaze, not by magic but by the love she still felt for him. Ana was struggling within to remain faithful in her heart to Agreus but it was a terrible thing to try and master. Ayyn saw the struggle inside of her and moved closer to her. Julienn left the room realizing that it was best he leave them be for awhile.

"Ana, I want to hold you again. It is my desire to be close to you and feel the warmth you carry with you, my sweet. I will not hurt you. I love you too much to ever hurt you again," Ayyn moved ever so slowly as close as he could to her and placed his arms around her as she shook.

"Why are you shaking, my love?" Ayyn implored of her.

"I am afraid . . . I am afraid of myself and what I might do," She looked at him with love and anguish.

"I still love you, Ayyn. I was your wife, too. I do not know what I should do now that I am here in this place with you. This time it would be by my own choice and not by magic that I allow myself to fall," Ana said with a trembling voice.

Ayyn was smiling as he held her to him. He knew she could not resist him for long. This is the moment that he had been waiting for since they had parted. He placed his hands on her shoulders and with one finger he slowly moved her face upward to look into his. Their eyes locked and she felt her heart skip a beat. He moved with all gentleness towards her and kissed her deeply as she shuddered from the sudden warmth of his mouth on hers. She had not felt passion like this in such a long time. Agreus had never truly been able to return to the way things were before her accidental infidelity. Ana had not allowed herself to think on it for too long for the fear of the pain it would cause her. Now, here with Ayyn it was like everything had melted away. She kissed him back without thought or care of the consequences. They spent quite some time together in his room as they made the most of their time together. They lay in each other's arms as she was thinking of how she never wanted it to end.

"It does not have to, my love," Ayyn said suddenly, "You and Julienn could stay with me.

"Ayyn, the others would never let me go and this time I am afraid that they will kill you. I do not want you to die!" Ana cried.

"I would die a thousand deaths to be with you and our son, Ana. It is a risk I am willing to take," Ayyn was never more sure of anything.

"I am not sure that I want to risk it, my love. I know that Agreus has done some things to you that I am not happy about but he has for the most part been good to us. I fear he does not love Julienn like he should, though. This has always made me unhappy and that is why I suppose I shelter him more," Ana replied.

"He is my son and I will not let the other's continue to treat him as though he does not belong. You know that I am aware of what that can do to someone and you know it, as well," Ayyn was angered at the injustice.

"You are right to feel this way. I do not wish for Julienn to suffer the feeling of being different as we have. I am so confused! I do not understand why things have ended up in such a way that we must all endure the suffering that love and vengeance has brought to us. It seems that things should have been so much simpler and yet what have I done to have to make the decisions I am faced with?" Ana cried as she lay on Ayyn's chest.

The truth was that she had done nothing at all to deserve any of this. She never had been the one responsible for any of the tragic things that happened over the years. Ana was just the innocent victim in it all. This would not stop her from being the one to suffer the most. After a while, Ayyn and Ana made their way into the drawing room where Julienn was laying on a sofa and staring into nothing. He was thinking of all that lay before them. The hardships that had befallen them all were nearly too much to bear without going quite mad! He sat up when his parents entered the room to hear anything they might tell him. Had there been a decision made?

"Julienn, your mother and I need to talk to you, my son," Ayyn looked at Julienn with a heavy heart.

"Your mother has not come to a decision as of yet so you must take her back but she does not want to forget this day. We will put a thought halo in her mind so that no one can read what has happened here. I am glad she wants to keep her memories of us together. I do understand that she needs time to consider all things. Your mother is going to speak to the others about how they treat you differently. We are not happy with the difference in nurture you have received from them," Ayyn comforted Julienn.

"That is right, Julienn. I am not at all pleased with the behavior of Kashenn and Agreus toward you over the years. They always knew about who you really are and they promised they would treat you the same as they would any other brother and a son. I have seen the cruelty that Kashenn shows to you and even though Agreus is not mean to you he has kept you at arms length because you remind him of your father. If we are to stay together then he will have to change. I do not know what I wish to do. I cannot keep both Agreus and Ayyn, that is obvious. I do need to make a decision about what is best and right now I am too emotional to do that. I need time alone to think about all things. I will say this for Agrieness, he has never been unkind to you and he stays mostly to himself so I am not at all unhappy with him. I hope you are not unhappy with him either," Ana looked tearfully at Julienn.

"My sweet mother, I am not unhappy with Agrieness. As you say, he has never been unkind to me and he is happiest doing what he does best. His first love is the forest and all that is in it. I do not believe he has much care about the decisions we make for ourselves as long as he is free to make his own," Julienn replied.

"You are wise to see that. It is in his nature to be drawn away by all that grows and lives in the forest. He is a caretaker of the such things and is more like the pan he is supposed to be than Agreus. He feels freest when he is alone to shepherd the world," Ana was glad that Agrieness did not suffer the ill effects of love the way his parents had.

"Father, I will return soon. I will see mother home and come as soon as I can. I love you both and am glad I have been granted this one day to be alone with the both of you," Julienn shed a single tear for his parents.

Ayyn and Ana embraced their son and they were emotional as well. This was hard on everyone.

"Ana, I love you my darling," Ayyn looked at Ana with longing.

"and I you, Ayyn," Ana said as she and Julienn stepped through the portal.

Agreus was in the glen with Agrieness admiring all of his talents. His son was a more devoted pan than he had been. He had allowed himself to be drawn away by the young Claire who had eventually become his wife, Ana. If he had it to do all over again he was not sure that he would have done anything more than inform the elves of her plight so they could get her back. Perhaps he should have stepped out of the way and allowed her to marry one of her own kind. However, he did not regret his children, especially this one. He loved them both but he was closest to Agrieness. Agreus did love his princess but he saw how the love he had shared with her had inadvertently caused so much suffering. He was confused about whether or not he should have told her the truth when she had questioned him that night about his feelings. Maybe if he had kept it to himself then most of this could have been avoided for her and her family. The only thing that held him back from thinking it was all folly was his children and Ana's beautiful soul.

"Promise me something, Agrieness. Promise that your duty to the wild will come before anything else that may cross your path, my son," Agreus said with a bittersweet tone.

"I promise father. What has made you ask this of me? Is something wrong?" Agrieness was worried.

"I just feel that I have been a big part of the loss suffered by the elven realm. Maybe if I had not . . ." Agreus was interrupted.

"Do not say it, father. Nothing that has happened can be changed. The only thing to do is to move forward from this point. You must not regret anything or it will forever dominate your thoughts," Agrieness pleaded.

"You are a wise pan, Agrieness. That is part of the reason I love you so much! I will try to move on from it. I have not been the same with your mother since certain "things" happened. It was not her fault and yet I cannot seem to shake the feeling that I was betrayed by her. It hurts when the one you have given your life to is with another, even if it was not her doing," Agreus said with pain in his voice.

"Father, if you do not find a way to get over this you will continue to push her away. Julienn is not your son but you took the responsibility of him as your son upon yourself willingly. Even though you chose it freely you have not given him the love you gave to Kashenn and me. If you are not careful this could send him down a dark path that his real father once chose. He is still my half brother and I do not want to see mother hurt anymore. I am tired of all of this pain that everyone is living in all of the time. It is time to bring an end to all of it," Agrieness was exasperated.

"You are right. All you say is true. I will try to fix things before it is too late," Agreus kissed his son before bidding him farewell for the evening.

Agreus entered the hollow tree and returned to the Allerian kingdom to find Ana sitting in the kitchen at the servants table. She had been doing some thinking and dozed off in the middle of it. He picked her up carefully and carried her to bed to sleep. She had been so tired lately. He hoped she was not becoming ill.

Agreus entered the throne room afterward to check on his son, the king of these lands. Kashenn sat on his throne. He was quiet these days and it seemed as though a bitterness had set in on him.

"Kashenn, what is troubling you my son? You seem to no longer find joy in your days." Agreus asked.

"I am merely concerned for my kingdom as any good king would be. I fear that Julienn will cause some sort of trouble without any responsibility so I want to know how you think mother would feel if I gave him some. It would keep him busy and perhaps out of trouble," Kashenn looked off blankly.

"I agree that some responsibility would be in his best interest. Let me know what you have in mind and we shall set it all up. You are right to say that it should keep him busy and out of trouble. Idle hands do tend to find it, after all," Agreus left the room to ponder what they could find for Julienn to do when suddenly they came face to face with each other.

Agreus and Julienn rounded a corner in the long hall that led to the courtyard nearly running into one another. Julienn had been outside and Agreus was going out. He thought this would be a good time to talk to the boy about Kashenn's plans for him.

"Julienn, I would like to speak to you about something," Agreus spoke up.

"Yes?" Julienn asked.

"Kashenn feels that you may need some responsibility. How would you feel about that?" Agreus asked.

"Well, I feel alright about having responsibility. How do you feel about having it?" Julienn retorted.

"I do not follow, Julienn. What is this about?" Agreus was agitated.

"I was doing some thinking of my own and just so you know I am aware of my mother's human past and the part you played in it all of the years she lived with them. How is it that you allowed her to continue on with those people knowing that she was in a bad situation all of that time?" Julienn asked.

"I was always listening for her to call for me to protect her!" Agreus said angrily.

"Yes, I know you were. You became her knight in shining armor did you not? She came to depend on you and no one else because you made it so that she had no one else to depend on. Tell me, how is that you felt you had the right to keep the Allerians in the dark about her for so long? She could have been easily removed and protected from the humans until her soul shift and you know it! The truth is that you did not want to be alone and she amused you and made you feel important. She made you feel needed because you were all alone, too! You are a pan! Your kind is known for trickery. How is that when you were just about to tell the king about her you decided to get her pregnant with your offspring? She could never be married to an elven prince then could she? They would gladly give her to you and see it all as one big blessing and answer to prayer. You may have fooled them but you do not fool me! I know you are not my father and you know it so let us not play these games. I will not suffer your indignation anymore!" Julienn shouted.

"How clever of you, Julienn. Yes, she did peak my interest. She was a very good dancer and I was her teacher. I could not let her leave me for that school she wanted to attend for those humans. I had to interfere with the response to keep her from going. I did not want her taken away from me! She was mine. I saw her that day in the glen and she became my ward. As she grew into an innocent young woman I knew the time was coming to save her soul. I had no choice but to take her for myself before I returned her to her people. I had to ensure that we would be married. I would never have been able to let her marry some elf. Do you not understand that I loved your mother and I would have done anything to keep her?" Agreus told the truth.

"So, all of this suffering is partly your fault is it not? That is how I see it! You should have let her own people decide what to do with her, but you have been controlling her since she was a child. She never really had a choice but to love you. Yes, my father did some bad things but you are no better than he. At least, he admitted his faults and apologized. He tried to make some sort of right out of the bad and you turned your back on him and cast him out! Why would you do that to me? I was just a child. I did not deserve to have my father snatched away from me. He was willing to agree to any terms as long as you let him see me grow up. Did you know that mother has been unhappy with your decisions concerning that issue all of this time?" Julienn smiled.

"So, you know about Ayyn. That is fine, Julienn but do not make trouble for me and your mother or I will . . ." Agreus was cut off.

"Agreus? Is what you say true? Could you have saved me sooner? Did you control me and make me love you so that I would be given to you by my father?" Ana was standing behind him in tears.

"Ana!" Agreus called after her as she ran.

Julienn smiled callously as Agreus tried to catch up to his mother and reason with her.

He had always thought it strange that he did not consult with the elves sooner. She could have at least been kept safe until the day came for her to change. The truth was that Agreus had kept her as long as he could to himself. Even if Ayyn had never been with his mother and Julienn had not been born he still felt justified in bringing this to his mother's attention. She should see the darker side of her Agreus instead of so naively believing and trusting that he had always had "her" best intentions in his mind. To Julienn, he was just as selfish as they claimed his father had been.

"Has it all been for naught, my love? How could you think only of yourself? I was blinded by you for all of my childhood. Why?" Ana said in pain.

"I love you, Ana. I could not have you married to some elven prince but I could not keep you safely in the realm of humans, either. I knew it was not customary for an elven princess to marry someone like me, but if you had already given yourself to me then your parents would allow a marriage between us believing that I had not known you were their daughter at the time. They were happy with all of it, Ana or have you forgotten?" Agreus said angrily.

"Could you not have told me all of that instead of letting me believe it all just happened? Why did you lie to me? You have made a fool of me, Agreus!" Ana replied.

"You will listen to me. You are my wife and that boy of yours is causing trouble for us. He should be sent away! I should have had it done when he was born!" Agreus said in anger.

"How can you say that about Julienn? He is my flesh and blood. I am his mother. It hurts me to the deepest part of me to hear you say these things." Ana sat down on the grass and cried.

"I am sorry, Ana. I should not have said those things to you. Can you forgive me for all of the things I have done?" Agreus asked regretfully.

"I do not know but I shall try. I need to be alone to think for a while," Ana began walking down the hall out of the courtyard. She was going to her room to be alone.

Was nothing sacred? She was in shock from all that she had learned a few moments ago. Agreus and Ayyn had both been selfish. She never expected that from Agreus. She understood why Ayyn had acted the way he had back then but Agreus? The last thing Ana ever thought was that she was lured into depending only on him as part of a plan. She knew that they both truly loved her but they had done things all wrong. If someone loved you were they not supposed to tell you the truth? There would have been no need to lie to her because she loved him so much. This complicated matters even further. She had just been to see Ayyn and she had wondered if she was wrong for still loving him and keeping it from Agreus when she found out Agreus had hidden things from her all of her life. Technically, she was married to both of them so morally anything that happened was not against the law. However, she knew that was the main reason that Agreus had banished Ayyn now. He did not want anything to persist between them. Ana's head hurt from all of this nonsense. No rest would be found for her tonight.

Agreus was the one who had told her so long ago that elves did not divorce and that it was a crime. Even though the marriage to Ayyn was surrounded with bad circumstances it did not change that she had taken an oath to him and had meant it. Ana had unwittingly gained two husbands and Agreus would not have it. She finally realized that he had not had him banished for crimes against her kingdom and her parents; it was so he would keep his hands off of her which had become his right no matter how he had gone about getting that right. Agreus knew that the Dulerian tribe of elves would honor her marriage to Ayyn before they would her marriage to Agreus because he was not elf kind. Had they been of the mind to they could have taken her back to their kingdom as their princess since a legal marriage to their king of the time had happened. It most likely would have caused a war but they still could have claimed the right if Utenn had not been of good character. How clever he had been to rid himself of having to deal with that. Ana did not know who she could trust anymore.

Utenn's children did not know how lucky they were to have a father like him. He was planning out their lives to be the best they could be even though they were ungrateful children. By this time, they were married to their intendeds and they would learn to like it or at least learn their duties. Ana hoped they would find true happiness with the ones they had been betrothed to. She had hoped that Kashenn would speak of finding a wife for himself but he was not at all pleasant of late. Agrieness had made it quite clear where he stood on love. He was probably better off for the sake of his responsibilities to not seek it. As for Julienn, he was not ready to be a husband. He still had some growing up to do before he would make a good husband.

Julienn had watched as his mother slowly and silently walked in the direction of her quarters. Agreus had taken a walk out into the garden where there was an exquisite maze. They were both clearly upset and needed time alone to think on the things that had been happening for so long. Julienn decided now was a good time to sneak away and inform his father of all that had transpired and see if he was ready to act upon their plans. Out into the forest he ran as he took out the amulet and readied it for use. Through the portal Julienn went and into Black Thorn Manor where Ayyn sat looking out of a giant picture window thinking on his sins.

"Father, I have much to tell you. Mother has seen Agreus for the controlling trickster that he is and she is upset with him. Shall we go through with our plans now?" Julienn could hardly stay in his skin.

"Tell me Julienn, do you think she could truly be happy here with me? I feel badly about having to take away any part of her memories because I love her and it feels wrong. I know I would never have said this in the past but as time goes on I change more and more for the better and it is your mother who has made this change in me." Ayyn considered what he must do.

"Do not speak like that father. We must do this for her. She is more a prisoner than you would imagine. With us, she will find solace and happiness," Julienn pleaded with Ayyn.

"Am I not responsible for helping to shackle her to that personal prison inside of her mind? Much of what she suffers is my fault, Julienn," Ayyn turned to look out of the window again.

"You are better than that now, my dearest father. You just want to make things good for my mother do you not? As you say, she has caused change in you. There is a good person inside of you no matter what you have had to do. Have you not also suffered?" Julienn cried.

"Do this for us father. I beg you, do not allow me to go through eternity suffering with the rift that exists in my own family. I want us to all be together. Ultimately, I believe that this is what is best for her," Julienn fell at his father's feet as he sobbed.

Ayyn looked down at his grown son who sat sobbing like a child kneeling before him. He leaned forward to embrace him, "Then I will do it for all of us, my son. I will do it for you."

He could not bear to see his son in this manner. Julienn was his pride and joy. Perhaps, he was right in believing that it would all be for the best. Deep down he knew that she loved him so how could this harm her? Ayyn decided that it was best that they go ahead with it before he changed his mind and gave her the option of the butterflies.

"Come Julienn, we will go now and do what we have planned. I have the poison on the table in that little bottle. I will disguise myself as a servant in the kitchen and plant the poison in the king's meal and that of Agreus. After that we will grab your mother and leave that awful place. Once we are back here I will perform the memory wipe and begin transplantation of new ones," Ayyn focused once more on the task before them.

"Once we are inside the castle walls I will need you to go and distract your mother while I handle the details in the kitchen. Then I will come to you both when it has been done. Wait for me in her quarters, Julienn. Do you understand?" Ayyn asked.

"Yes, father I will follow your instructions. I promise you," Julienn was once again happy.

Ayyn and Julienn walked into the middle of the drawing room to open the portal. They opened it into a small storage room near the kitchen. Julienn looked out of a crack in the door and saw an empty hallway.

"Alright, I will head for mother's room while you make your way down the hall to the kitchen. Change to match what a servant would look like and we will see you soon, father," Julienn hugged Ayyn tightly and kissed his cheek as he ran out of the closet to find Ana.

Ayyn drank a potion that made him appear as a servant in the royal kitchen. He walked quickly toward the area where plates of food were being prepared so he could slip the poisonous mixture into the proper meals. He arrived in the kitchen and began to search for the right settings. As he was doing this none other than Agreus himself entered the kitchen to request his food be sent to his quarters. He was not feeling up to dining in the great hall tonight. Ayyn did not want to be discovered so he slowly turned and walked out of the area and back down the hall. He would have to wait until the meal was being delivered. Perhaps, he could be the one who brought it up and put the poison in on the way. For now he was hiding in the shadows of the closet.

Agreus had sensed something earlier when he was in the maze that felt familiar. A type of magic was being used that could only come from one item that he knew of. Somehow, Julienn must have gotten his hands on the amulet and that meant he truly knew everything and had most likely been conspiring with the dark one. Just now, in the kitchen he felt something unusual from one of the servants. He must not be what he appeared to be so Agreus was going to seek him out. It must be Julienn or Ayyn. It could even be another conspirator. Agreus was not sure but he was going to stamp out the problem before anyone else could notice.

Ayyn had left the closet and was making his way down the hall to ascend the stairs to Ana's quarters. Perhaps, he should take her first and then come back to finish this. Agreus thought it best to warn Ana that something was going on and not to leave her quarters until he came for her. So, Agreus began to make his way towards the stairs that led up to her rooms when he noticed a kitchen servant out of place. This person should not be in this part of the castle at all. Even if a meal or tea was to be brought up to anyone it would not be this type of servant. Something was off about the way he walked, as well. Agreus caught up to the "servant" and spun him around. As soon as he touched him, the potion was dispelled and before him stood Ayyn, his age old enemy.

Meanwhile, Julienn had gone to his mother's rooms and found her sitting there at her tea table. She was sad and deep in thought.

"Mother, I have come to check on how you are feeling. Dinner will be soon. Are you hungry?" Julienn asked.

"No, I am not hungry after the events of the afternoon, my son. I think I would like to go and speak to Agreus. We should not be at odds with one another no matter what has happened," She rose to leave the room.

"Wait mother, I agree that talking to him is a good thing and should be done, but he has not yet returned and I thought we could speak for a moment," Julienn was stalling.

"We can speak after a bit, Julienn. I need to see that he is alright and I know he is in the castle. I am always informed when he has returned," Ana moved to go around Julienn.

"Mother!" Julienn tried to stop her.

"Get out of my way, Julienn. I know you are trying to stop me from talking to Agreus. I understand that the two of you have problems but I love you both and I must ensure that what is best for the kingdom is done. I need to talk to him now," Ana pushed past her son and left the rooms.

Ana had decided that her presence in the kingdom had caused too much pain and anguish for the elven people. She felt that by leaving it some peace could return. She knew that the people loved her but in time they would come to understand that the personal issues that one elf suffered were not greater than that of the entire kingdom's well being. She believed her son would remain a good king and in time he would marry and produce heirs. She would go back to the human realm in a self imposed exile. At least, then she could be free of the burdens she had been saddled with in this kingdom. Ana loved her family but she believed that it was in their best interest to let her go and return to where she came from. Ayyn would take care of her no matter what she decided their relationship would become. She did not know how she felt about it but she knew he understood her despite everything and

Julienn would be happy to at least have his parents near one another. Agreus would never forgive her but she knew that if she made the decision of her own free will he would not stop her. This decision was not made lightly. It would forever change all that she had known but it was time for change to happen before her kingdom crumbled into dust. She would mourn the happiness that she would always remember with Agreus but she had forever been disillusioned to the truth. Ana carried a letter in her left hand that explained everything in great detail. She must do this before she lost the nerve to take a stand.

Julienn chased after his mother to stop her from going down the stairs. His father had said to wait here and that is what they must do. Ana reached the bottom of the stairs and walked swiftly to one of the parlors where she felt Agreus. Something was not right. He was in a rage and not at her. She must hurry to see what was happening.

Princess Ana in all her royal beauty slowly entered the room and to her horror she saw Agreus and Ayyn locked in a battle of swords. She understood why Julienn had tried to stop her, now. Just as she was about to order them to stop she saw that Agreus' blade was going to pierce Ayyn and she must not let them destroy one another. Ana could not live with the knowledge of one killing the other. The lovely little princess made a last minute decision to thrust herself in front of Ayyn as the shining blade reached out for him. The blade found a mark. Agreus' sword pierced the chest of his beloved. Ana had a look of shock in her eyes as though she could not believe this was happening to her. As the blood began to spill onto her milky glowing skin and run down the lavender dress that matched lovely eyes so well Julienn had caught up to her and saw that Agreus had pierced his mother with his sword.

"No! Mother!" Julienn flew into a blind rage and came at Agreus from behind as the demigod stood in disbelief and at what he had done. Two swords entered Agreus from the back as Julienn drove them home.

As the little princess began to crumble to the stone floor, Ayyn swiftly reached out to catch her in his arms. He was in inexplicable pain at the sight of his love dying before him. She was whispering for him to draw closer so she could say something for only him to hear. He sat with her in his embrace with tears streaming down his face while leaning in to kiss her and hear her final words.

King Kashenn had been alerted that trouble was happening in the parlor as servants fled in every direction. He entered to see Julienn delivering the killing blow to Agreus. He watched in horror as his father fell to his knees and landed at the feet of his dying mother.

"Father!" Kashenn rushed forward at Julienn with his own sword drawn and sliced his throat before the younger elf could turn aside. Julienn's blood spilled out onto the floor as the light left his eyes for good. There was no life left in his body.

"I have been waiting to do that for a long time," Kashenn growled through his teeth when suddenly, a look of surprise came over his marble face.

Ayyn had run him through for killing his beloved son. Kashenn fell forward and landed face down at his half brother's feet. The crown fell from his head and rolled away. Ayyn saw that Julienn was already gone. He returned to Ana's side as she was still suffering in death's grip.

"Ayyn," she handed him the blood spattered letter that had been meant for Agreus.

Ayyn quickly read it and realized she had been going to leave this place and return with him. If only he had known her decision this travesty could have been prevented.

"No, my dearest love. Do not leave me now!" Ayyn cried as he held her. There was no time to try and save her and he was sorrowful at this matter of truth.

"I will join you in death. Without you I have no reason to be. I love you, Ana," Ayyn spilled his warm tears of love and regret upon her soft face as he drank the deadly poison he had intended for Agreus and Kashenn. He lay with his beautiful face to hers as they breathed their last and died in each other's embrace. The letter slipped from his hand and landed on the floor next to them. Surely, the fates had cut the strings that held their lives that day.

Soon, the gruesome scene was discovered by Agrieness who had come looking for his family. He had not been able to call them through the watery mirrors and his father had not shown up as he normally did. He saw the letter and read what it had to say. Agrieness was glad that his father had not been able to read it before he died. He would have been devastated. As for his mother, she had planned to do what she felt was necessary and he could respect that. Agrieness had word sent to the Dulerian kingdom of the events and soon Utenn and his riders arrived as requested. He was now the king of the Dulerians and Agrieness in all of his wisdom suggested he take this kingdom and join it to his own since they had originally been one people. That should bring a new era of peace to this world. The king and the young prince were buried with their grandparents as well they should be. The one thing Agrieness requested was to take the anointed bodies of his mother, father, and Ayyn back to glen to be burnt on funeral pyres as was his custom. It seemed fitting to him that they should burn together. This request was granted to him and he took them and the amulet away from here so no more damage could be done.

After the fires had gone out on the pyres Agrieness took the amulet and tossed it to the bottom of the deep lake nearby. No one would ever be able to use its powers again. All respect was paid to the dead and now he was going to return to all that he knew he must do. As the sun set behind the trees that his parents had loved so much he returned to the forest and to his responsibility as guardian. Agrieness never returned to the realm of elves. He was born with a duty and in his immortality he would continue to forever uphold them as the wise pan that he had become.

About the Author

My name is Candace Beck Moesta. I have been a writer all of my life. When I was younger a wrote poetry, lyrics, and short stories. I had some of my poetry published as a teen and have been asked multiple times to write children's books. One day I may do that but for now I prefer to write about more adult themes. I studied at SMCC and USM under an English Major. I took some time off to raise my family and attended nursing school. I worked as a nurse for over a decade to ensure that my family was properly supported and now I am going to return to finish what I started and one day achieve my goal of obtaining the PhD in English I so richly desire. I love classical literature as well as some of our more recent writing legends. E. A. Poe, Emily Bronte, Nathaniel Hawthorne, and George Gordon Lord Byron are some of the writers I enjoy as well as Ann Rice and the late Tom Clancy. I live in the south. The name of the town I reside in is McComb, MS. I am not originally from here, though. I was born in Hollandale, MS and raised in Louisiana. I am a wife and a mother of two wonderful sons. My family is a wonderful blessing and also a constant source of inspiration!